COME FORTH AS GOLD

a novel

Erica Dansereau

Identifiers: Library of Congress Control Number: 2022903463 | ISBN 979-8-9858237-3-8 (paperback) | ISBN 979-8-9858237-2-1 (hardcover) | ISBN 979-8-9858237-0-7 (ebook)

This is a work of historical fiction. Any references to historical events, real people, real publications, or real places are used fictitiously. Other names, dialogue, characters, and events are products of the author's imagination. Any resemblance to actual persons, living or dead, is purely coincidental.

Cover design by Brittany Howard
Interior design by Patrik Martinet
Author photo by Walkyria Whitlock
Cover images: Canva

www.ericadansereau.com

Everyone called you Boots,
but I had the honor of calling you Granddad.
This is for you.

"But he knoweth the way that I take: *when* he hath tried me, I shall come forth as gold."
Job 23:10

COME FORTH AS GOLD

PART ONE

1

1945
Goldfield, Nevada

THE SOUND OF Kitty's front door slamming shut jolted my attention away from the vulture enjoying his jackrabbit feast up the road. I turned to see Kitty hop down her steps in a huff. A voice inside hollered out her name, but she didn't bother answering the call. I straddled my bike in front of her house, which was next door to mine. She fetched her bike, a rusty hand-me-down from my brother, but as she pulled up next to me, I noticed a raspberry-sized gash just above her temple.

Smoothing her hair to cover the wound, she said, "So, are we going or what?"

"Soon as you tell me what happened."

She rolled her eyes and pressed her lips together. "It was an accident. Come on."

The mid-morning sun shone brilliantly upon us. I lowered the bill of my cap and glowered toward her home, wondering what Jeb was doing inside and how he was responsible for

Kitty's injury. I knew he'd be to blame somehow. "Do I need to go in and ask your dad? Or will you just tell me yourself?"

"He stumbled into me, and the bookshelf caught my face. Happy?"

"He's already drunk?"

She shrugged. "Just super hungover, I think."

I searched her whiskey-colored eyes and soft features, golden from a summer in the sun, praying she spoke the truth. She blinked but did not falter under my scrutiny. "Alright," I muttered. "Do you want a bandage or something? My mom's home. She could help."

"I'm fine, Claude. Really. Now, are you gonna take me on an adventure like you promised or what?"

We took off, pedaling through our small town. My troubled thoughts about Kitty's drunken father were whisked away with the delightful breeze that pushed against us as the desert opened before us. September had just lumbered in and broken our kick-bucket desert town away from a week-long heatwave. The cooler temperature left me with a sense of exhilaration I hadn't felt in a long time. It wasn't just the weather that had me feeling hopeful. The war was finally over. Our troops could finally come home. We'd all heard it on the radio a few days ago. Everyone had run out of their houses, whooping and hollering. The fact that my brothers hadn't quite been old enough to serve had comforted me the past few years. But finally, I was now able to release the fear of my dad being drafted and sent into combat. He'd been involved in the war effort by servicing and repairing anything the base in Tonopah needed. As I pumped my legs and sped toward the outskirts of town with Kitty by my side, I breathed easier knowing that my family would remain safe. *Together.*

We passed by the burnt remains of an old cabin, destroyed by county officials years ago on account of tuberculosis. We gave it a wide berth and continued, the miles growing between us and all other traces of human life.

"What exactly are we fixin' to do, Claude?" Kitty asked, out of breath.

"Figured we could explore someplace Cliff and Vern claim is haunted. I want to prove them wrong," I said. "Unless you're too afraid."

She gave a wry smile and pedaled faster. "I'm not afraid."

The old miner's cabin, long abandoned and falling apart, was right where my brothers described it would be. The closer we rode, the funnier I felt deep in my gut. We came to a stop out front. I adjusted my cap to give my sweaty head a chance to breathe and hopped off my bike, expecting Kitty to do the same.

But she sat still as a mouse, a frown on her face. "Here? You sure we can go in there?"

"Thought you weren't afraid."

She crossed her arms over her chest. "I'm not. I just don't want to get into trouble, that's all. See the sign? No trespassing."

I gestured at the still, open desert around us. "And who's gonna see us? We're all alone out here. Besides, that sign is ancient."

She chewed on that a moment and slowly got off her bike. "You'll protect me?"

"Of course, I will." My parents would tan my hide if we got hurt out here. Though that whooping wouldn't compare to how badly I'd punish myself should anything ever happen to Kitty May Ralph, my lifelong neighbor and truest friend.

"And you'll get rid of any ghosts that follow us out of there?"

"No such thing as ghosts," I replied confidently.

She let her bike clatter to the ground and joined me. "For

your sake, you'd better hope not, Fly."

Everyone called me *Fly*. I never really knew where the nickname came from, but always guessed one of my friends made it up on account of my last name, *Fisher*. *Claude "Fly" Fisher*.

The rotten wood steps leading up to the cabin gasped out a warning beneath our weight. *Turn around.* I hoped they wouldn't snap. As a testament to the rugged determination of anything that managed to survive out here, this abandoned home, wilted and lonely, stood in defiance to the raging fires and heavy floods that had ravaged half the town decades ago. Not to mention the harsh, dusty breath of desert air that still choked it daily.

"This place gives me the creeps," Kitty whispered.

"Let's get out of here then," I offered, admittedly because it gave me the creeps too.

"Not until we get you your ghost," she said, suddenly bold. She grabbed me by the arm to stop me from turning around. "Unless *you're* chicken?"

I laughed. That was the thing about Kitty. Her spunk always surprised me.

"You hear me squawking like one?" I kicked the door open. We stood there at the threshold and squinted into the cabin as daylight revealed the extent of ruin inside. Who knew how long it had been since the sun touched these walls, these floorboards?

"You go first." Her voice came as a tiny whisper next to me.

"Bawk! Bawk!" I whispered back. I nudged her in the ribs and stepped inside.

Dust danced in the air, and I pulled the collar of my white T-shirt over my mouth and nose. Worn shreds of canvas dangled from the underbelly of the roof. Faded newspaper and old, rusty cans littered the floor. I kicked one aside, and it rattled to the corner of the room and came to rest beside a rodent nest.

Kitty crept in. "How long do you 'spose this place has been empty?"

I shrugged. "Since the big flood or since the ore ran out, whichever came first."

She took a few brave steps farther into the room. "You ever wish you were a miner?"

"No. My granddad was a miner. Such a hard, dirty job that swallowed him up whole."

Kitty's eyes went wide. "Swallowed him whole?"

"Cave-in." I shook my head for dramatic effect. "Worst accident they'd ever seen." This part wasn't true, or at least I didn't know if it were. But Kitty ate up every word, hungry for a good story, so I wasn't about to fail her. "My dad was barely old enough to write his own name when he lost his pop." I clicked my tongue and gave her a long, sad stare.

"Wow," Kitty murmured. "I never knew that. Your poor dad. Your poor grandma . . ." She stepped bravely across the cabin, the floorboards creaking as she did, and ran her hand along the far stone wall. "How old was she when she became a widow?"

"I don't know. But I know she lost my dad's younger sister too. Diphtheria."

"Your dad had a sister?"

"He doesn't remember much about her or his dad."

"That's awful." She frowned and looked around. "Who do you think lived here? Someone your granddad knew?"

"Here? In this cabin? Who knows? You know much about a boomtown?"

She shook her head, her sandy blonde hair tickling the tops of her shoulders. "Just what they taught us in school."

"Dad used to tell us bedtime stories about Goldfield—things he saw firsthand growing up here in the middle of the boom, things that were told to him by the miners that my grandmother rented their spare bedroom out to. He described it like this—men, they caught drift of the promise of gold, a whisper from the greedy devil that wealth and prosperity were just across the torrid desert, and all those suckers came a'runnin. My granddad included. It was insanity the way they responded to the call. And like a stampede, they came by the dozens, setting up tents and shacks and sleeping in barrels, right here in our town. A bonanza."

"There was gold by the millions, right?"

"Millions and millions." I flung my arms wide. "This place was a riot in its heyday. Jam-packed with people up and down the streets, piled into the saloons like ants on a crumb!" I whistled loudly and Kitty's eyes sparkled. "They were pioneers, rushers, and they made this town roar with life. Even the gunslinging Earp brothers were here!"

"I remember learning about them!"

"Yup. Wyatt, taken with the gold rush, strutting between here and Tonopah. Virgil, with his crippled left arm, patrolling our streets as sheriff . . ."

I pretended to draw a pistol from my belt and aimed at Kitty. But she was quick to the draw as well and pretended to fire at me first. I clutched my chest, my mouth agape. "Yer a ruthless one, Ralph," I wheezed out as I staggered around.

"Yer kind ain't welcome in these parts, Fisher. This is my frontier," she growled, but immediately fell into a fit of laughter, breaking character. "I'm so glad I wasn't born in those days!"

"Ah, come on! It wasn't all bullets and blood. Especially here. Boy, that old hotel in town was one of the best in the west. Would you believe that? People traveled miles and miles to stay there. Can you imagine spending a night in that place now?"

"Heck no. Not even for all the gold in the world. It's spookier than this place."

"Spooky, but not haunted. Just like this place. See?" I spun in a circle and peered around the cabin. "No ghosts."

"And what're you gonna do if one pops out? Can't exactly fight something you can't see." Kitty pretended to throw a punch at the invisible. She kicked a can at random, then suddenly scrambled backward and ran smack into me.

"What's wrong?" I said, clutching her arm.

She pointed to the rotted floor, shaking her head. There, having been hidden within the rusted can, was a glass syringe with a needle fitted on its end. She flipped around to look at me, horror painted on her face.

"Maybe we shouldn't be here," I murmured. I'd heard a thing or two about drifters coming through with their dope. The wind picked up outside, and I glanced over my shoulder, half expecting to see a ragged junkie stumble through the door at us. "Come on," I said.

We hightailed it out of there, but as we ran down the steps, Kitty's shoelace caught an exposed nail on the rotting porch. She tripped, her chin skidding against the ragged wood, and yelped in pain.

"Are you okay?" My gut sank. I pulled her up by the elbow. A drop of her blood splattered on the back of my hand.

Her chin quivered. "How bad is it?"

I cupped her face in my palms and tilted it skyward to better inspect the damage. "Your lip is split, and your chin's pretty torn up. Looks like there are some nasty splinters stuck in there. Want me to try and pull them out?"

She shook her head and three beads of blood rained from her chin. I took the bottom of my T-shirt in my mouth and tore off a shred of fabric to hold against her wound. She flinched, and the porch boards moaned with the threat of collapse.

17

"I'm so sorry, Kit. You think you're alright to bike home?"

"I think so," she said with a tremble. She moved my hand away from her chin and with it the piece of my white T-shirt, now mottled crimson with her blood. "Let's go, please. It actually hurts pretty bad."

The miles stretched far longer on our journey home than our journey there. Slow and quiet, we biked back to town. All the while I berated myself for bringing Kitty to such a decrepit place at all. I glanced at her when we finally turned onto our street. Her tears had dried and crusted with the wind. So had most of the blood.

We bypassed Kitty's house—her father wouldn't have a lick of sense as to what to do and was probably passed out anyhow—so we went straight to my house next door. We barreled through the back door, into the kitchen. Mom took one look at Kitty's busted chin, wiped her flour-dusted hands on her apron, and called Dr. Jensen in an instant.

Dr. Jensen came in a hurry, and I squirmed more than Kitty did as he stitched her chin back together. He cleaned and bandaged the gash above her temple too. Mom paid him five dollars when he was through and walked Kitty next door to tell Jeb what had happened.

I paced the kitchen and stewed in my shame while I waited for her to return.

When the back door opened again, Vern and Cliff came inside, fresh in from playing ball with their friends. They were seventeen and sixteen. Irish twins.

"Missed you out there today, Fly," Vern said. "We could've used a batboy."

"Thought that's why you invited Cliff," I muttered.

"What happened to you? Get in a fight?" Cliff pointed at my shredded shirt with his baseball mitt still on his hand. He took a seat at the table and tossed his mitt onto the floor.

Vern, suddenly interested, grabbed a kitchen chair. He spun it around backward and sat down too. "You went to that cabin, didn't you?"

"Yeah, and it's not haunted. Just dangerous. Kitty split her lip and chin open. Had to get stitches." I took a seat with them and dropped my head into my hands.

"Are you serious?" Vern said.

"Dang," Cliff mumbled. "Is she alright?"

"She'll be fine." The recovery of my self-respect, however, was doubtful. "Thanks for the idea, by the way," I grumbled.

"Come on, Fly. That was no place to bring a girl. Especially not your *girlfriend*," Cliff crooned. He reached over, tousled my hair, and made kissing noises.

I shoved his hand away. "Stop. She's not my girlfriend."

"Yeah, Cliff," Vern said, giving me the brief illusion of his defense. "She's not his girlfriend. She's his wife!"

They snickered. I gave them a dirty look and opened my mouth to retaliate, but Mom walked through the door.

"You two"—she pointed to my brothers—"give me a minute with Claude, would you?"

They stood, and Cliff muttered, "Nice knowin' ya."

Vern lightly hit my shoulder and grinned his big, lopsided smile—the one that, in spite of everything, made me feel included, like I actually belonged in their brotherhood. "Good luck," he said and followed Cliff out of the kitchen.

I looked at my mom and moaned. "You don't have to say anything. I'm an idiot, I know. I'm so sorry."

"What were you thinking, Claude? You know better. You're lucky something worse didn't happen."

"I know. Trust me. Is Kitty okay? How'd Jeb react?"

"Kitty's okay. But Jeb . . . Let's just say we had a few words, most of which didn't involve you, but rather that cut on her head." Mom stared through the wall, past the shelves of spices and the apricot wallpaper, toward the Ralph's house and scowled.

"You knew he caused that?"

"It wasn't as fresh as the one on her chin. I asked Kitty, and she told me what happened."

"Do you believe her?"

She shrugged and thought a moment. "I think I do. I have a hard time picturing Jeb hurting her like that on purpose. He may be a drunk, but I've never seen him violent. Maybe we'll start keepin' an extra eye on her though, huh?"

I nodded, already intending to.

"I wish he cared enough about her to change," Mom whispered under her breath.

How the very people who gave Kitty life didn't care for her never ceased to trouble me. "Can I go check on her?"

"You can see her tomorrow, because for the rest of the night you won't be seeing anything other than the four walls in your bedroom. You're grounded."

The punishment was less severe than I'd expected, more mercy than I deserved. I brought myself to my feet and glanced out the kitchen window at Kitty's opposing one, hoping she'd appear so I could lamely wave and offer another apology from here. But she didn't, so I went down the hallway to the bedroom I shared with my brothers. There I stayed and counted the hours until nightfall when sleep would allow them to pass more quickly.

I'd only been asleep maybe twenty minutes when tapping on the window next to my bed woke me. Another tap came, and I shook myself awake. I peered out. At the sight of Kitty waiting in the dark, I looked over my shoulder toward my brothers to make sure they were asleep in their bunks on the other side of the room. When I saw that they were, I slowly cracked the window open and hoped its whine wouldn't wake them.

"What are you doing here?" I whispered. "You'll be in trouble if your dad catches you gone."

"Couldn't sleep. And don't worry. He polished a bottle of something off a while ago. He's passed out cold," she whispered back. "Plus, after your mama's scolding this afternoon, I don't think he has the guts to punish me right now." Kitty glanced over her shoulder, then back at me. "So, how much trouble did you get in?"

"Surprisingly not much. Just grounded for the night. You alright?"

She shrugged and hugged herself against the night chill. I sensed she didn't want to talk about it.

"How's your chin?" I pressed.

"Fine. See?" She turned her head and jutted out her jaw to show off her set of stitches in the moonlight.

"I'm real sorry you got hurt. And sorry for taking you to that shack. That was an incredibly stupid thing to do."

She waved me off. "It's alright. Honestly, it was kind of fun."

"Fun how?"

"The adventure. And hearing you talk about the stories your dad used to tell you."

"Well, I only told you the romanticized version."

"As opposed to?"

"You saw that syringe. Dope fiends . . . they're around now just like they were back then. Alcohol flowed like a never-ending river. Drugs made their rounds. It wasn't all riches and happiness."

"Was it really that bad?" She tucked a strand of hair behind her ear and shivered.

"Life here was different back then. Diseases floated around like nobody's business; grown-ups and kids died young. Just like my granddad and aunt. It was a hard time, and soon everything was gone."

"Oh, it wasn't all gone!"

"Sh!"

She clapped her hand across her mouth.

I continued on, whispering, "Goldfield, as anyone knew it back then, was. The people depleted the mines and moved on. Then the flood and fires happened, wiping out half the town. This"—I pointed to the quiet land behind her—"is all that's left."

"You say that like it's not enough."

"You know, Cliff said something to me the other day about getting out of here someday, joining the military, moving on, seeing what else is out there. He called this place a wasteland. Dried up and hollow. Here, hand me a rock." I held out my hand.

She bent down and found a small stone in the dirt and handed it over.

I dared to slide the window higher in order to prove my next point by mimicking the same illustration my brother had shown me. I chucked the rock. "See? That's our future right there if we don't get out of here one day. We'll speed through time and end up facedown in the dirt. Just like all the people who came here before us."

Kitty glared at me. The moon highlighted the tears that began snaking down her pink cheeks. "All these people who choose to live here are facedown in the dirt? Is that how you see it?"

"What? No . . . I'm just teasing." I couldn't believe I'd made her cry twice in one day. I reached for her, but she pulled away.

"If it's really that bad, then my mama's the only one who had sense enough to leave, huh?"

Kitty never talked about her mother. That's how I knew I'd

really messed up.

"Aw, Kit. Forget I said anything. It was all Cliff's stupid talk. You know he's been itching to get out of here and see the world since the minute he was born."

Kitty blinked back another set of tears. Before I could figure out why she was crying, she dashed away from my window, around the corner of the house, and out of sight.

Without thinking about the noise, I slid my squealing window all the way up. Just as I swung one leg over the sill to hop out and go after her, my bedroom door opened. There stood my dad, as disappointed as I'd ever seen him.

2

I STUDIED JEB, wondering how Kitty, such a beautiful and friendly girl, came from the mold of a man so cold and broken. He didn't know I watched him through the slats of our back patio railing. He sat on his back porch and whittled away at something with a pocketknife, mumbling to himself all the while and occasionally stopping to take a swig of liquor.

Engrossed, I waited and hoped he wouldn't slice another of his fingers clear off. How many times had God extended His grace and protected Jeb's hands, I wondered, considering how taken to the bottle he always seemed to be? After all, that's why Dad had to fire him from the auto shop years ago.

But to a man like Jeb, maybe fingers mattered as much as God's grace. It took believing in something first for it to matter, right? Jeb didn't believe in God, and from what I could tell after years of living next to him—our interactions as sparse as rain— he never would either.

When Jeb came home one day years ago and found Kitty and me on my porch, curled in on either side of Mom as she read us Scripture, he laughed and laughed.

Fairytales, he had called them. "You're filling their heads with make-believe, Virginia. Bunch of nonsense fairytales."

Mom had only smiled and said, "One day God might just slap you right awake, Jeb."

That had only made him laugh some more.

But later I wondered if I was the only one who had caught sight of the pain etched in his eyes and the flash of fear that had disappeared as quickly as it had come. Jeb let us be after that, didn't question my mother reading to us anymore, didn't interfere with a lot of things. He mostly kept to himself, to his bottle, to the guys down at the saloon, and to whatever job he was lucky enough to land for the time being.

And quite frankly, I liked it that way.

But now I felt the urge to walk over. To tap him on the shoulder, ask when—if he cared enough to know—Kitty would be coming home. We'd never discussed her tears outside my window. In fact, she'd spent most of the week keeping to herself until she caught up to me after school today in a huff of excitement. She told me that our friend Julia had invited her to go with her on a family weekend trip to Reno. Kitty said they were leaving straight away . . . as soon as they stopped by her house to check with her dad and then to Dr. Jensen's to have her stitches removed. She was off shopping, exploring a new city, staying in a hotel.

But as happy as I was for Kitty, the degree to which I missed her troubled me more. Not that I could've hung out with her if she were in town anyhow. When Dad caught me sneaking out of my bedroom window, he'd grounded me for a week.

I left my patio perch and slipped through the back door, into the kitchen. Down the hall, I found my brothers in the living room. Cliff sat on the couch and Vern sat in the armchair. Both of them were dressed in freshly pressed trousers and collared shirts. A game of Chinese Checkers was on the table between them.

"I call next game," I declared, sitting down on the rug.

"Sorry, Fly. We're only playing best two out of three," Cliff said without looking at me.

"Okay. Then I play the winner of that."

"Can't," Vern said. "We're leaving after."

I waited a beat, giving either of them a chance to elaborate, but they were too focused on their game. "Well, where ya going? Maybe I can come?"

Vern chuckled under his breath, finally shooting me a glance. "There's a dance at the school tonight." He jumped one of his marbles over two of Cliff's. "Aren't you grounded anyway?"

"I haven't heard of a dance happening."

"Upperclassmen only," Cliff said. "Sorry, man."

I sighed and fell backward dramatically, sprawling out across the floor.

"What's the matter with you?" Vern asked.

But the answer wasn't simple. I wished I understood my sunken mood myself.

"Where's Kitty? You fighting with the wife?"

"Oh, shut up." I kicked Cliff with my foot.

"Seems like you poked a sore spot," Vern muttered. I lifted my head enough to see his mouth curve into a teasing grin.

"Will you two ever knock it off with that baloney?"

"Will you ever just admit that you're smitten with her?"

I kicked my foot toward the table on impulse before I could grab hold of my emotions and sent their entire game of Chinese Checkers flying across the room. Marbles rained across the floor in a heavy dance.

"What did you do that for?" Cliff chucked the single marble he held at my forehead.

I grabbed a nearby marble and launched it back, but I

missed. It pinged off the clock hanging above the couch instead. So, I grabbed another and hurled that one too.

Vern raised his hands in disgust. "Sure are in a rotten mood, huh? Lighten up, man. We were just teasing around." He stood and touched Cliff on the shoulder. "Come on. Let's get out of here."

Being the obstinate little brother that I was, I lay on my back and stared at the ceiling, pretending to ignore them as they left the house. To be honest, I didn't know why I'd reacted with such strong annoyance. They'd been teasing me about Kitty forever. It hadn't bothered me until recently. I'd always been able to joke along with them. But I couldn't anymore. Perhaps this was because it no longer felt like a joke, but something palpable, something evolving, something real.

I lay moping. Moody and alone on the living room floor, I considered all the ways I could humiliate my brothers at their dance in front of whichever girls they were trying to impress. Most likely they had gone with Maisy Thomas and Belinda Benny. For longer than I cared to admit, I lay there, plotting diabolical plans that included Mom's Jell-O salad in the fridge and their perfectly pomaded hair.

A repetitive rapping on the door interrupted my ideas.

"Hey, Fly! You in there?"

"Claude!"

If I were quiet enough, my friends would go away. Then I could keep wallowing in the misery they had no idea I was in. But a series of knocks and a chorus of calls ensued, and I picked myself up to answer the door.

Three of my friends stood on the front porch. "We're playing kick-the-can. You in?" Pete asked.

"Can't." I wore my sour attitude like a heavy coat.

"What's the matter with you?" Richie asked. "You look, well, like garbage."

I grimaced. I felt like garbage. "Thanks. I'm grounded."

"That all?" Pete asked. "You actually do look sick or something, Fly."

Franco backed away from the door. "If you're sick, I don't want whatever bug you've got."

"If he's sick, the whole town's gonna catch it within two days anyway," Richie said.

Little did they know, this kind of bug wasn't contagious. I sent them away, wishing I could chase after them, if only to take my mind off things. But instead, I found myself alone again. Kitty off in Reno, my brothers at their dance, Mom and Dad playing cards at a friend's house.

I gathered up all the marbles and fiddled with the radio a long while, searching for a signal, but it only came through scratchy and intermittent at best. And when I gave up, I was alone with my thoughts. *What was the matter with me?* My friends had asked. But the problem at hand couldn't be put into proper words. The more I dug to uncover my feelings and the further I moved into unfamiliar territory, the clearer the truth became.

3

ALL OF OUR mouths moved in unison, speaking to the stars and stripes with our right hands pressed against our chests. I chanced a glance around the room. Of course, Mickey Johnson robustly said each and every word with the seriousness of a soldier, his body swelling with patriotism and pride. He came from a long line of military men, the latest being his older brother, who had just returned from overseas, and his uncle, who never made it home. Mickey told us that he was buried somewhere in the countryside of France.

I continued scanning. Karen O'Betty's face looked as cross as ever, and Franco Ramirez towered tall behind her. Freddy Sue stood in the next row, then Pete Tobin, my good friend of many years, and beside him, Julia Garrish.

And next to her stood Kitty, directly across the classroom from me. She caught my eye as soon as I looked at her, so I stuck out my tongue and made a face. The one she made back at me was an ugly one, and I couldn't help but crack up.

"Mr. Fisher!"

I jumped, turning to see Mrs. Newton staring me down

from behind her desk, arms crossed, brows raised. "You all may be seated," she said to the class. Pointing at me, she added, "Except for you, Claude."

Singled out, I stood alone. My stomach sank. "I'm sorry for the disruption, Mrs. Newton."

"Pray tell, what's so funny? Is there something distracting you, Claude?" She came around from behind her desk and leveled me with a scrutinizing gaze. "It seems to me that you've had a bit of trouble paying attention to matters in the classroom lately. Would you agree?"

I squirmed. "No."

"No? Then you wouldn't mind a little pop quiz, just for you, would you?"

Of course, I minded. "Sure."

"Yesterday you seemed awfully distracted during our history lesson, so let's start there. We discussed the United States' decision to enter World War I. Can you recall one of the early catalysts that prompted our eventual entry?"

No, I couldn't. I gulped. "I don't know."

"Lusitania?" she offered.

"Oh," I said. "Uh, the Lusitania sunk?"

"Indeed, Mr. Fisher," she said. "And what exactly caused the impressive British vessel to sink?"

Acutely aware that this exchange would result in me getting paddled all the way back to first grade, I decided I might as well make my answer good. "The crew had one too many crumpets."

A few brave souls chuckled at my joke as Mrs. Newton's face fell. "The Lusitania was attacked by a German U-boat. Nearly 1,200 innocent lives were lost in the horrendous event. I hardly see how this is a joking matter. Mr. Fisher, you're thirteen years old, is that correct?"

"Yes ma'am," I said. "Fourteen in a few weeks."

"You know, growing up is a privilege, a privilege that comes with many rewards. I'm sure you're looking forward to these upcoming years as you grow from a boy to a man?"

She was going somewhere with this; I could feel it. Begrudgingly, I nodded in agreement.

Mrs. Newton continued, "But with age comes many responsibilities. You may think of age as a number, as something concrete by which to measure oneself, when, in fact, it's the most abstract thing of all. Would you rather be wise beyond your years or forever foolish as a child? Just because the number of your age gets larger and more consequential, doesn't mean you automatically do too."

I eyed the paddle that hung from a nail behind her desk and shifted uncomfortably as all my peers stared at me.

"I'd like for you to write an essay about the matter and turn it in first thing tomorrow morning."

"An essay? With all due respect, Mrs. Newton, I'd rather have the paddle."

More chuckles came from my classmates, and to my surprise, a smile formed at the corners of Mrs. Newton's lips too. "On second thought, this essay is for the entire class. You may be seated, Claude." She addressed everyone now. "Your assignment is to write a two-page reflection on what you believe your responsibilities are: as eighth graders, as friends, as people. I'll leave it ambiguous; feel free to interpret it how you feel. But I'd like you all to consider this next period of life that you are entering. What does it mean to you, to grow up? Think about who you are now and who you're on track to becoming, versus who you'd like to be. Do the two match up?"

"Way to go, Fly," Richie Garrison muttered from his desk behind me.

I'd have apologized, but I didn't want to get into further trouble for talking in class. And to be frank, I was thankful I wasn't the only one stuck with this cruddy assignment. Besides, it might do Richie some good, I figured. He was always getting into trouble, and when he wasn't, he should've been.

—

"My dad said he'd have my bike tire fixed by the time I got home today," I said. "Wanna ride up and penny the tracks? I keep hearing rumors about the railroad shutting down for good. Could be one of our last chances."

"You have pennies to waste?" Kitty scowled, disgruntled about something. I couldn't imagine it being over some smashed coins. Something clipped came through in her tone, an edge usually not present in Kitty's demeanor at all.

"Alright, so what do you say?" I pressed. "Wanna go?"

"We have an essay to write tonight, thanks to your shenanigans, Claude. Or did you forget?"

"Hey now, you're just lucky you didn't get caught making faces too! What's the big deal anyway? Why're you acting so angry with me?"

She stopped and turned to face me. "I'm not mad. It's just given me a lot to think about. That's all."

"About what a knucklehead I am, or what?"

She crossed her arms. "No."

"Then what?"

A flash of hesitation crossed her face, but she sighed and said, "The fact that some people age but don't grow up."

Her parents, I realized. Of course.

"Is that what you're going to write about?"

"Guess so." She shrugged, and in a swift moment of vulnerability, she continued. "I don't want to turn into them, Claude. I don't think I've ever feared that until today."

"You won't," I promised her. "So, what do you think of what else Mrs. Newton said? About who you are versus who you wanna be?"

Kitty picked up her pace, purposely creating distance between us. I'd asked the wrong thing. Should've changed the subject when I had the chance. I jogged a few steps to catch up and fell into pace alongside her once again. "Ah, Kit! What's wrong? What'd I do now?"

The muscles in her jaw strained like she was fighting a good cry. She turned her hardened face away from me. Seeing her all choked up nearly sent me into a crying spell of my own.

"I'm sorry. Let's talk about something else. Did you see George at recess? He mooned the postman as he was walking by! It's probably a good thing if you didn't see that, actually. Big old freckled white butt, just as anyone would suspect."

I figured this would elicit a giggle or two from her, maybe shake loose a gasp, or at the very least, a smile. Instead, I was left with the unpleasant image of George McLaren's buttocks in my mind and Kitty as quiet and brooding as I'd ever seen her.

We turned the corner onto our street, and her pace slowed to a crawl. My gaze followed hers, and together we watched her father assist a strange man with loading Kitty's heavy antique dresser—given to Kitty as a baby from her maternal grandmother—into the back of a pickup.

"Hey!" Kitty cried, bursting into a sprint. "Hey! That's mine!"

I ran with her. By the time we reached her house, the man was already in the driver's seat, prepared to leave. She hopped onto the back bumper of the truck, determined. As she was lifting one of her legs over the tailgate, Jeb yanked her back down, dumping her onto the dirt.

She scrambled to her feet. "What're you doing? That's mine!" she screamed.

The man inside the truck looked out his window, waiting and confused, but Jeb waved him off.

Kitty's chest heaved as she watched him drive away. "What

right do you have—"

"Are you gonna pay the friggin' bills? Do you like to eat? Then I've gotta do what I gotta do." Jeb's rage-filled face quickly wilted. "I took all of your stuff out of it. It's in your room," he muttered as though this act would fix the damage done. With that, he turned and walked away, going inside their house.

Kitty thumped down in the dirt, a puff of it engulfing her legs. She pulled her knees to her chest. Anger rolled off her in thick, hot plumes. I sat down next to her.

"He lost his job a few days ago," she whispered. "Got fired for his drinking."

I raised my brows. This was the first I'd heard of it. "Why didn't you tell me?" I asked, though I already knew the answer. She was embarrassed. She knew I'd worry. She knew I'd tell my folks, and they'd be offering up any spare change they had to her.

"I've been taking handouts from your family my whole life. For once I'd just love for my dad to get his act together and take care of us himself."

"That dresser was from your grandma, right?"

She wiped her nose and nodded. "Given to me when I was a baby before my parents left home." Sunlight cascaded onto her face as she tilted her head back, highlighting the rain-splatter of tears covering her cheeks. "Why didn't they want me, Claude?"

Her small voice broke me. I slung my arm around her and pulled her close. Words eluded us both. We sat in her barren front yard like that a long while, until I heard the sound of spinning bicycle wheels, and I snapped my arm back to my side.

"Why don't you come over and have dinner with us tonight?" I offered. "We can work on our essays together. Maybe my mom will make some dessert, and you'll forgive me for having to write an essay at all."

34

Kitty stared straight ahead, unreachable, as Vern and Cliff coasted up to the house.

"Romeo and Juliet," Cliff crooned as he dismounted from his bike.

I glared at him, trying to send the message that his lame jokes weren't welcome, especially not right now.

Vern hopped off his bike too and walked over. "Uh oh, you two don't look happy. Don't tell me trouble's brewing in paradise?"

Cliff clutched his chest. "Love's not dead, is it?"

I gritted my teeth and glanced at Kitty next to me, who stared into the dirt. "Can't you bozos see now is not the time?"

Cliff crossed his arms and clucked his tongue. "Guess the honeymoon is over."

I flew to my feet, not as much bothered by the words that he said, but by the fact that he felt compelled to say them at all.

"Shut up!" I shoved him once, and he stumbled two steps. I shoved him again, but this time he shoved in return, knocking me a few feet backward.

"Fly, cut it out," Vern said.

I turned to him. "Me, cut it out? You guys started this."

Cliff messed up my hair and told me to lighten up, but it only made me angrier still. I went at him again, this time with a punch to the gut. But Cliff recovered quickly and yanked my arm, whipping me around until he had me in a headlock. From my position, I strained my neck to look up, and I saw Kitty, still sitting in the dirt, now with her face buried in her hands. I wriggled forward and elbowed Cliff in the ribs until he released me.

Vern stepped in and separated us now. "Cool it, guys. Claude," he said and lowered his voice. He nodded toward Kitty. "Is something actually wrong?"

"What do you think I've been trying to tell you guys?" I

glared at each of them. "Get out of here."

Thankfully, my brothers went into the house, leaving Kitty and me alone again. We sat in silence on the unwelcoming ground. Despite our closeness, she felt a hundred miles away. I yearned to say something that would fix it.

"You know, your dad is missing out," I finally said. "You're the best gal I know, and it's a downright shame he's too stupid to see that."

She looked at me and chewed on this for a moment. Her face seemed to soften, and just as I thought I was reaching into her dark cloud and pulling her out, she hardened again, this time toward me. "He's just trying his best, you know. It's not like he abandoned me, like my *mother.*"

I glared at her. How could she defend the loser who'd just sold her most valuable possession to a complete stranger? And most likely for booze, not bills as he'd claimed. "His best, really? What does he do for you except hurt you?"

The look in Kitty's eyes terrified me. It reminded me of the skunk we'd found in a boxcar last summer. Cornered and afraid, its wild eyes had shone. Then, in the blink of an eye, it had turned lethal. Spraying both of us. We ran, sputtering, shrieking, and gagging the whole way home.

"It's not like he hits me, Claude," Kitty hissed.

"Right. He only stumbles into you and knocks you face first into bookshelves."

"Who are you to talk? You just tried to beat up Cliff over a stupid joke." She rose and furiously brushed the dirt from her clothes, then stomped away from me.

"Where're you going?" I hollered.

"Anywhere but here. And don't you dare follow me, Claude!"

I threw my arms in the air and yelled, "What makes you think I'd want to do a thing like that?"

Kitty broke into a run, retrieving her bike from the side of her house. I watched her go, pedaling away with fury. I marched toward my house and burst through the front door, into the living room, red hot with anger—not toward Kitty and not even toward her useless parents, but wholly at myself. For raising my voice at her, for trying to hurt her with my words when she was obviously hurting already.

"Claude? Everything okay?"

My mother's voice was the final blow to the nail in my tough-guy charade. I lost it.

"Hey, it's okay. It'll be okay." Her comfort only gave my tears permission to slip out all the more.

Cliff must've wisecracked, because I heard Vern smack him and say, "Not now, man!"

"What happened with Kitty?" Mom asked, rubbing my shoulders and guiding me to the couch. "Make yourselves scarce, you two," she said to Vern and Cliff.

They bolted out of the room, but surprisingly enough, they each touched my shoulder as they flew past. Once I heard them outside whooping and hollering, passing a football back and forth, I felt safe enough to talk. But when I looked into my mother's soft face, all I wanted to do was cry.

"I don't get it," I finally said. "Why'd she draw the short end of the stick? Don't they love her? How could they not?"

Mom drew me into a hug. "I don't know, honey. I really don't. People are selfish, that's all. Some people see responsibility coming down the road, and they hightail it the other direction as fast as they can."

"But they're her *parents*. She was just a baby when her mom skipped town. Aren't moms supposed to love their babies?"

She laughed gently, and I couldn't help but feel it was condescending. "Oh, Claude. I don't know what to say. Me? I couldn't imagine deserting my family for *anything*. There's nothing that could take away my desire to raise you kids. But for Kitty's mom . . . I don't know. Never met her. Maybe she was young and scared? Maybe she was just plain selfish?"

"Jeb just sold the most important thing Kitty owned. Sold it right out from under her. We saw him finishing the transaction when we came back from school. Can he even do that?"

She hesitated. "It's wrong, but it is his house."

"But it's her stuff!" I felt anger heating my chest again. "That lush is just gonna spend it on liquor. Can't even buy her a nice dress to wear. Can't even hold down a job."

"Jeb lost his job?" Mom rubbed her temples.

I nodded, capitalizing on her concern. "They have nothing, Mom. And by 'they' I mean Kitty. I could give a rat's ass what Jeb Ralph has."

"Watch your mouth, young man."

"The thing I can't figure out is when I told her what a jerk her dad is, she started defending him! Like he's this great guy all because he doesn't lay a hand on her."

"Your caring heart for your friend is one of the noblest things about you," she said. "But I want you to consider where Kitty's coming from. She didn't have a mom—"

"She *did* have a mom," I interrupted to make a point. "But she chose to abandon her."

"Alright, well she grew up without a mama at home, right? And her dad doesn't exactly get high scores for his parenting. But Jeb . . . when he came to town and moved in next door, he was so in over his head. Had a baby he couldn't feed and didn't know how to care for. Had no money, no hope. But he stayed."

"He stayed and continues to piss away all their money, all their hope . . ."

Mom sighed, and I shut up. She continued, "I'm not asking you to excuse Jeb's choices. I'm asking you to consider Kitty's perspective. She grew up in a home where she feels unloved and unwanted. Do you know how badly Kitty probably wants him to love her? To truly see her and invest in her? How hard she clings to the hope that if she can tiptoe around quietly enough and stay out of the way enough, he'll continue to stay? That he won't leave her and will truly choose her?"

I ruminated, putting myself in Kitty's shoes the best I could. My love for Kitty shouldn't be overshadowed by my disgust for her father. I felt sick. "And I just insulted that, didn't I? Blasted a hole in the middle of her hope, though I don't see Jeb Ralph changing anytime soon."

"You're not going to fix her family. And it's not your responsibility to try."

There it was again. *Responsibility this, responsibility that.* Just as Mrs. Newton had droned on about this morning.

"Then what *is* my responsibility?"

"Being her friend. Making sure she feels respected, safe, loved."

I thought of Kitty, out there alone and hurt, feeling unwanted by the two people who ought to want her more than anyone else. What I was about to say broke my heart, to think that a child should express gratitude for such a thing, but I wanted to make sure my mother knew. "Thanks, Mom. For loving us and choosing to stay. For being a mom to Kitty all these years too."

Her eyes glistened. "You're growing into a good man, Claude. I love you."

My heart sang and lingered on that word: *man.* This was the first time I'd truly considered that I wouldn't be a kid much longer. "I need to get started on my homework," I said with sudden clarity. "And then I need to find Kitty."

Hours later, once my essay was polished and complete, I left the house. At this hour of the day, if one paid close enough attention, there could be heard a dull whistling of the wind as it lifted sand and dirt and trickled over the blackbrush. The sound was as if the sun itself was yawning, ready for its descent.

I walked to Kitty's house, and another sound filled my ears as I neared. A rumbling cry, deep and broken, drifted from behind the waving curtains that covered the Ralph's open windows. I listened outside the door a moment, the sound of the tiring desert and this wistful lament entangling and dancing together in the air. I knocked.

The ballad didn't stop, even when I knocked a second time. No answer seemed like a bad sign. I knocked once more, and when that failed to bring someone to the door, I took the liberty of opening it myself.

I took a few steps into the living room and had a clear shot of Jeb sitting at his kitchen table, head resting in his palm, that sorrowful song continuing to pour from his lips.

"Excuse me? Is Kitty home?"

He looked up, eyes red and wild, and it took a moment for him to remember who I was. "Thought she was with you?" His words slurred together. The bottle on the table was empty, and I deduced he'd taken to it to numb whatever pain it was that brewed inside of him. Though it didn't seem to have done the trick. All his brokenness bubbled up and spilled over right in front of me.

I took two steps toward him. The biting whiff of alcohol stopped me in my tracks. "I wouldn't be here disturbing you if she was, Jeb."

He ran a hand over his dark hair, so grown out and matted down that it reminded me of hardened molasses. He gazed around me, and it seemed like he was empty, scraped out fine like the marrow I'd watched my mother clean from beef bones dozens of times in my life. I turned to go, but something about the sight of him so unhinged held me in place.

"What's wrong?" I dared to ask.

His fingers wrapped around the neck of the empty bottle. I couldn't help but notice the nub of the finger chopped off long ago trying to keep up with the rest. "The well ran dry. That's the problem."

The way he said it made me bristle. Was that his primary concern? His liquor and not his young daughter who had yet to return home? I turned to go, wondering why I'd bothered prying into his darkness at all.

"Don't ever set your lips to this, kid," Jeb called after me.

I turned around. "Do you wish you never had?"

He focused on me and grimaced. I studied his face and looked for any indication of regret, any potential to change, any sign of Kitty in this broken man. But he relaxed, and she could only be found in the gentle slope of his nose and the dark forest of lashes that shadowed his eyes.

"Lot of things I wish I'd never done," he grumbled.

Behind his words was deep pain, but they only angered me. I sincerely hoped—more for her sake than his—that he wasn't talking about Kitty. "Have a good night, Jeb. I'm heading to look for your daughter."

"She'll turn up soon. Always does. Girl just got upset."

I let the door slam behind me for good measure as I left and was on my bike in a flash. My wheels churned beneath me. Worry that she hadn't returned home gnawed me raw, but if I knew anything about Kitty Ralph, I knew where she went when she was sad. So that's where I headed.

When I arrived at our hiding place, I leaned my bike against a boulder and approached the rusted, old Model T. The vehicle had been on the outskirts of town, decaying and falling apart, longer than we'd been alive. My pant leg snagged on a sagebrush, and I shook myself free. I eased open the driver's door. It screeched loud enough to agitate the wild burros grazing nearby. I watched them scatter lazily, puffs of dust left in their wake.

"You're going to frighten away my entertainment," Kitty grumbled.

I hopped into the cab. A mixture of dust and rat urine hit my nostrils. "Sorry. You been watching them long?"

"They came out a while ago. Lost track of how long that's been." She glanced at me. In the weak light of dusk, her face wasn't pink and tear-stained anymore. All I saw was peaceful sadness.

"Sorry about earlier," I said. "I wasn't trying to make you mad."

"I know," she murmured. "Everything you said was true. But that doesn't mean it felt good."

I reached into my back pocket and handed her two folded pieces of paper.

She unfolded them. "What's this?"

"My essay."

"You're mistaking me for Mrs. Newton."

"Just read it, please."

She gave me a calculated stare and smoothed the papers in her lap. "My Essay on Age and Responsibility, by Claude L. Fisher." She glanced at me and wiggled her eyebrows, a giddy little smile curling her lips.

"As a kid of thirteen years old, I haven't had too many run-ins with the word 'responsibility.' I have chores, sure, and expectations of behavior during dinnertime or the Sundays my family used to make it to church. I used to be the first to say that the responsibility of a kid is to be a kid, to enjoy the little things before they fade away and turn into the back-breaking worries adults carry on their shoulders. And while I stand by that still, I do

believe I've been looking at things all the wrong way. Because the truth of the matter is that I am responsible for the man I'm becoming. And that man, whoever he might be, will grow to affect the people I love. So, the question I must answer is this: How does responsibility look to the man I want to be?

"It means doing the best I can with what I have, seeking to be a benefit as opposed to a burden. It means living with intention, serving, and doing right. It means stepping in to aid a kid being roughed up on the playground. It means seeing an injustice and striving to rectify it. It means accepting the many unexpected gifts that life offers. Not with closed hands and crossed arms, but with an open embrace.

"Responsibility, I believe, is wired into each of us. But it is also like a wind churning within. Unless we reach out to wrangle it with purpose, it may escape us, leading us to indulge in ourselves and the glimmers of pleasure that are not lasting but fleeting. So, while it may be easier to turn our faces away from hard work, I feel it is my responsibility to do the opposite. To turn and face it head on, to do what I can with what I have. And what more do I or any of us have than the love in our hearts? Shouldn't our responsibility be to love?

"I will grow, my clock will tick, and alongside it will always be my heart. Through any adventure and obstacle, any triumph and trouble, my heart will always lead me. And in my heart, at the very center, is my best friend. As for her, I will love and never abandon, because my responsibility and desire

are to love her until she sees herself as I do. Because her light has shone so radiantly that it's frightened the weak away. Yet like a moth, her light draws me in. And because of her, I want to be a better man."

Kitty stared long and hard at the paper. When she finally looked at me, her whiskey-colored eyes shone. I prepared myself for another wave of anger, but she leaned into me suddenly and buried herself into my side. If I'd had any sense at all, I would have lifted her chin and kissed her delicate lips. But instead, not knowing what was to come, I simply held her in the cab of that rat-piss-smelling Ford Model T, my body buzzing, feeling like I was the luckiest guy in the world.

4

MRS. NEWTON GAVE me an A on my essay, the first really good mark I'd received all year. She even called home to sing my praises to my mother. Something changed in Mrs. Newton that day. Knowing smiles hurled my way. An occasional wink. So much so that I began avoiding her as much as I could, being the first out the door to recess or lunch or home, although I couldn't escape her entirely. Unknowingly, I'd set myself up to become teacher's pet.

"Claude," she called out to me during class one day. "Might you be a dear and run this note down to the office for me?"

This particular request I didn't mind, for it meant I could wander the halls freely for a while. I never headed straight for the office, and today was no different. Instead, I slipped out my classroom door and around the corner, going up the stairwell to the third floor to spy on the upperclassmen and catch a glimpse of my brothers. Goldfield had a single schoolhouse to serve all the grades.

Note in hand, I hunched down in front of a classroom door, listening to a robust discussion happening on the other side. Just as I had the courage to stand and peek through the small window, the door opened. I jumped out of the way.

"Fly! What are you doing?"

Vern. I narrowed my eyes at him. "You first."

"What are you, the hall monitor?" He held up his palms in surrender. "Please don't hurt me or throw any marbles at me, Mr. Hall Monitor. I'm simply using the bathroom."

"Funny guy, you are." I rolled my eyes.

"What are you actually doing?"

"Oh. I'm, uh, delivering a note for my teacher."

"All the way up here?" He shot me his signature smile, all lopsided and goofy. I couldn't resist smiling back. "You'll get your bottom handed to you if you're caught up here when you shouldn't be. Mr. Vaughan will tan your hide for breaking the rules."

"I'm going, I'm going." I gave him a wave and shuffled back to the stairs.

"Speaking of going, you're going to the game tonight, right?" He said it as though this hadn't been the topic of discussion at our dinner table every night for the past week.

"I'll be there." I pretended to throw a football and said, "My brother, star quarterback. Maybe you'll end up playing ball in college or something."

"Now that's a jolly good dream," he said, head in the clouds. "Navy?"

"Army! Come on!"

He pretended to choke. "Never in a million years, kid." He pounded his chest and grinned, flipped around, and headed for the john.

A door slammed somewhere down the hall, lighting a fire beneath my feet. I flew to the stairs, taking the first few two at a time. I slid down the banister the rest of the way and stumbled into the hall, getting my feet underneath me to jog to the office, making up for lost time. I handed Mrs. Newton's note to Miss Dunlop, the secretary.

"Thank you, Mr. Fisher," she said, smiling sweetly at me. Miss Dunlop was a short, nice woman, very young and always made up with layers of powder and lipstick and strong perfume. My brothers said all that product was to cover the gnome that lurked beneath her sweet front, but I didn't think that was true. Miss Dunlop had only ever been kind.

"Help yourself," she said, holding up a glass dish of Tootsie Rolls. My mouth salivated instantly. I took two, stuck one in my pocket for Kitty, and unwrapped the other right away. I popped it into my mouth.

"Thanks, Miss Dunlop."

A commotion coming from Principal Mathew's office brought my ears to attention. A voice resonated within the walls that I didn't hear often, but it was one I knew without mistaking: Jebediah Ralph. I lingered at the desk.

"Say, Miss Dunlop," I said, moving to the side to get a better angle of Principal Mathew's office. Though with the door closed, I still couldn't see anything. "You going to the game tonight?" I stalled.

Miss Dunlop answered, but I didn't catch her words as Principal Mathew's voice broke through the walls and overpowered hers.

"For the last time, Mr. Ralph, you need to leave. We don't have any work for you, and quite frankly, you reek of liquor."

"Please!" Jeb's voice cracked, outlined in near-hysteria. "I just . . . need something to get me through. I'll sweep, clean toilets! I'll do anything!"

"Come back when you sober up, Mr. Ralph."

Jeb said a slew of words I couldn't quite hear nor decipher, followed by a hearty thump and shattering glass.

"Oh my!" Miss Dunlop leaned forward and touched my

arm, trying to break me from my trance. "Why don't you head back to class, dear?"

The men shouted over one another now. When Principal Mathew's door flew open, Jeb came staggering out, muttering under his breath. Just as he looked up, I took off.

—

"Come on, Mom! Dad! We're gonna be late!" I sprinted out the back door and headed for Kitty's. I hopped up onto her porch, ready to knock, but she opened it before I even had the chance. I'd decided I wouldn't utter a word to her about what I'd overheard at school earlier in the day. Partly because I didn't want her to feel embarrassed or upset. Partly because I wasn't sure how to feel about it. Something akin to compassion for her dad had stirred inside of me—he was out there at least *trying* to find work. I didn't like the feeling; it didn't mix well with the rest of me which loathed him.

The four of us walked from our houses on Columbia down to the makeshift football field to watch Vern and Cliff's unofficial game against Beatty. Central Nevada currently had no organized high school sports league, but at least it was something.

"Oh! There he is!" Mom yelled as she spotted her firstborn. "Come on, Vern! Kill 'em!"

Kitty shot my mom, who was normally a woman of great reserve, a look of concern.

I leaned over and whispered to her, "You know how excited she gets at events, especially ones any of us are competing in."

"Yeah, I'll never forget her during last year's Fourth of July races," Kitty muttered. She joined forces with my mom, making a battle cry of her own. "Kill 'em good, Vern! You too, Cliff!"

Mom burst out laughing and reached across my lap to slap Kitty on the thigh. "That's my girl!"

Dad clapped his hands. "Pretty soon, Claude, you'll be out

there too. Maybe they'll have an actual league next year when you're in high school."

I shrugged. "I don't know if I could play. Maybe?"

Dad sat down and looked at me, concerned. A grease stain between his thick eyebrows made them look connected. "Maybe? Sure, ya will!"

I enjoyed football, but I was doubtful I'd fill out enough to enjoy the sport in an actual game. Vern and Cliff both had the stocky, buff genes that graced my father. Thus far in life, I'd taken after my mother's side of the family. Lean, slim, and nimble. To be honest, I'd seen some of the hits footballers took and was scared of being snapped in half like a twig should I ever be tackled like that. Maybe I'd buff up one day, or maybe I could just be the kicker. Every team needed a good kicker.

Both teams gathered in their huddles to discuss their plan of attack once more, and then the game began.

Mom let out a blood-curdling scream of excitement, and Kitty nearly fell off her chair.

Vern impressed us all, showing off his throwing abilities and once running it in for a touchdown himself. Cliff played well in his role on the line. But in the end, triumph evaded our eight-man team, and Beatty sang out their victory instead of us.

The loss hadn't deterred Vern's happiness, though. He bounded over to us after the game, his pants a dusty mess, sweat dripping from his golden hair like rain.

Mom jumped out of her chair and threw her arms around him.

"There's a rumor the drugstore has a shipment of soda. The team's talking about going there after we get cleaned up," Vern told my mom. Then to my surprise, he turned to address me. "Wanna join us, Fly?"

I stared at him a moment, unsure if I'd heard him correctly, and not just about the soda. Vern was asking me—his nuisance kid brother—to hang out with his friends, the upperclassmen? He smiled as though he could read my mind. "Come on. It'll be fun! I want you to come hang with the guys too."

I glanced at my parents, who nodded approvingly. But then I thought of Kitty. I couldn't ditch her.

Reading my mind again, he said, "Kitty, you should come too."

"You guys go on without me," she said. "Ginny and I have plans to paint our nails tonight."

"I'll walk home with them and get my bike," I said.

"Sounds good. We'll meet you there in a bit, Claude!" said Vern.

"You get him home by nine!" Mom hollered as Vern ran off.

He turned around, jogging still, and yelled, "9:30?"

Mom shrugged, and he gave a thumbs up without even slowing down.

We never saw Cliff before we started walking home.

"You sure you'd rather stay home and paint your nails?" I asked Kitty, wrinkling my nose. "How boring."

Mom bopped me on the head. "Don't you call us girls boring. We aren't boring. Are we, Kit?"

"Not at all."

I begged to differ, but certainly wasn't going to voice it again. As soon as we got home, I hopped on my bike and sped back across town to the drugstore. Sure enough, the whole team was there, rowdy and still smelling like sweat and dirt. The inconceivable rumor of soda turned out to be true. Soda had been a rarity in our town since the war started. Seeing the bubbly liquid here was further proof that life was beginning to return to normal. Vern smacked me on the back and pulled me between him and Cliff at the counter. He motioned to Phil Ficklin, the store owner, to pour a root beer for me too.

Phil slid the frosty mug of soda to me and said, "A boy among men, eh?"

Cliff clinked his mug against mine. "Kid's gotta grow up sometime."

I rolled my eyes, wanting to remind him we were only a few years apart and drinking the same thing. I wanted to be mad at him—both of them, really—for patronizing me so blatantly. But honestly, for once I felt like I truly belonged amongst my brothers. I sucked down my drink and let them goad me into a heated conversation about sports with their pal, Willie.

"My Cubbies are winning the whole shebang!" Willie proclaimed. "I can feel it. There's something tingling in my bones that just says so!"

"You sure you aren't just thinking of Jenny too much?"

Willie howled with laughter. He leaned around Cliff and asked, "Who you got winning the Series?"

"Claude's usually right about this type of thing," Vern said. I straightened at the compliment. "Call it luck or a gift, but he has a way of analyzing and predicting."

"That's true," Cliff said. "He always bets on me to crush Vern when we wrestle, and he's always right."

Vern whacked Cliff upside the head, and Cliff whined, "What the heck, man?"

"That's right, you sissy. Can't even take a wee little slap."

Willie laughed so hard he sounded like an accordion. "Is that so, Claude? In that case, say the Cubs are gonna win," Willie pleaded. "Come on. Tell me what I want to hear."

I thought about it a moment before answering. "I'm partial to Detroit." My voice wobbled. I cleared my throat, embarrassed because I wanted so badly to prove that I belonged there. I went on, my voice intentionally lowered, "But honestly, from what I hear 'bout the way the Cardinals have been playing, and considering the momentum they have from last season, I think they'll end up champs again."

"More like chumps." Willie shook his fist at me, a grin just under the surface of his taut face. "Them are fightin' words, Fly."

"Guess we'll find out. Hopefully we can get a signal next game."

We moved on from baseball to football and then somehow to girls. I kept my mouth shut and only listened, learned, and I'm sure grew red as I thought about Kitty.

Finally, just after nine o'clock, Cliff slid off his stool and clapped me on the shoulder. "We gotta get home. Where's Vern?"

I hadn't even realized Vern was gone from beside me. He'd moved to a booth by the door, two other guys sitting across from him and a girl at his side. Maisy Thomas, his longtime crush and possibly the prettiest girl anyone around here had ever seen. Every feature on her face seemed to be carved with care from the world's finest clay, painted on with the steadiest of hands. I still didn't think she held a candle to Kitty, though. No one could.

We watched Vern, animated and the center of attention, gesture wildly and say what must've been the punch line to a joke because the small group of friends simultaneously burst into laughter. Maisy, her face aglow, smiled at Vern. His lopsided grin, which truly was like that of the happiest retriever dog, flooded his face.

Cliff and I interrupted the group, telling Vern we needed to leave. Vern looked bewildered. "Right now?"

"Yeah, well Mom told you to be home with him by 9:30, right?" Cliff nodded in my direction.

"I'll get myself home; it's alright. You guys stay." Suddenly, I felt like a burden. Like a helpless little kid who needed to be escorted home.

Vern held up a hand and scooted out of the booth. "Nah, let's go."

Part of me still felt odd, like I was intruding on my brothers' evening out with their friends. But underneath that feeling I was still flying high with the thrill of being part of it, with having been invited at all.

We biked home. We hadn't been a trio like this for years. My brothers were always a pair—built-in best friends less than a year apart in age. And I was the tagalong, only when necessary. The nuisance. My second half came in the form of Kitty. Thank God for Kitty.

But thank God, too, for this night with my brothers.

We whizzed down an empty Main Street, the September night air crisp on our cheeks. We weaved between streetlights in a line. Vern was in the lead, and I brought up the rear. Suddenly, Vern took a detour. I was glad. I didn't care if we ended up home late. I just didn't want the night to end. Not yet.

Cliff popped a wheelie and proposed a race to the school. The three of us took off, pedaling our hearts out. Except for Cliff who barely had to work because he had a head start. Time flew by as we rode through town. When we began our official journey home, I lagged slightly behind, reluctant, hoping they'd slow to my pace. Every moment on these streets with my brothers was absolute bliss.

A considerable distance grew between us. Up ahead, Vern rounded the corner onto Columbia, followed by Cliff.

Suddenly, the sound of metal against metal cut through the air. The hot squeal of brakes disturbed the night. Someone screamed.

I pumped my legs to catch up with my brothers and turned the corner to see the mangled frame of a bike twisted into the grill of a sedan on the wrong side of the road. The nearest streetlight glinted off both the bike's shining metal and the silver Chevy emblem on the automobile.

I dismounted from my bike and ran toward the collision, the gravity of what had just happened hitting me hard. "No! No! No!" I yelled, my voice already choking in my throat.

I found Cliff bent over Vern, frantically searching for a way to stop the blood from pouring out of his head like the soda fountains we'd just left at the drugstore. I watched Cliff's face twist in a cry for help. But I couldn't hear him. I was caught in the sudden, swirling vortex of everything I loved being taken from me.

The door of the Chevy that had collided with Vern opened. I looked at the driver's face, my body flooding with a hatred I'd never felt before. The man stumbled around the door. I lurched toward him, propelled forward by a force of rage, and tackled the man to the ground. His head smacked against the pavement with a crack.

I'd never imagined hurting another human the way that I pummeled Kitty's father that night.

5

A FEW DAYS had passed since I'd witnessed my brother lose his life. A few days since Jeb Ralph had stayed briefly at the hospital then went to jail. A few days since my world had been flipped upside down.

My parents, through their grief, tried assuring us that it was simply Vern's time. That we ought to trust God through this disaster. But I couldn't ascribe to their sense of consolation. Where was God and all His mercy? If He was so good, why didn't He protect Vern? All I knew was that Vern was gone, and it wasn't right.

People flooded in and out of our house—neighbors and friends and some people I'd never seen before in my life. The influx was too great a burden for my poor mother to bear, so she locked herself in her bedroom most of the day. She only emerged at night, like a cat, searching desperately for the comfort, affection, and company of what family we had left.

Kitty attempted to lock herself away too, though not from the townsfolk, but from my family. The shame she felt on account of her father's inebriated mistake was too great to bear.

The confusion of losing both her father and Vern in one fell swoop overtook her and pushed her to recede into the shadows. It took a lot of coaxing to bring her out of her darkened home and into ours.

One afternoon, Kitty and I sat listlessly playing checkers on the floor when a woman I didn't recognize poked her head through the front door. She hadn't bothered to knock.

Dad rose from the couch, brows raised with concern. "Can I help you?"

The woman did a quick scan of our home before replying. "I'm looking for my niece . . . She either lives here or next door." The woman gasped when she spotted Kitty next to me. "Kitty? Oh, my! Look at you, all grown up!" She stepped into the house boldly and held her arms open, a stupid smile plastered on her face like she fully expected Kitty to run into her arms like a toddler.

Kitty stood and squinted at the woman, who had a bright red scarf tied over her dark hair and a pleated matching skirt. "Aunt . . . Peggy?" Kitty asked hesitantly.

"Who else would it be, sweetie? Come here!" Peggy bustled over to us, and I caught the whiff of cigarette smoke. She wrapped her arms around Kitty, who stiffened at the gesture. "You poor dear." She pulled away, holding Kitty by the shoulders and giving her a once-over. "You look awful. Let's go and get you cleaned up, hmm?"

Kitty looked the same as she did every day. Beautiful. Her sandy hair bounced around her shoulders in soft waves. Her clothes were hand-me-downs, but my mother made sure to keep them carefully mended and clean. I disliked this woman already. I scrambled to my feet.

Dad stepped in and asked kindly, "Who did you say you were? Kitty's aunt?"

The woman nodded and offered a smile. "Yes. Peggy

Littleton. Jeb Ralph's younger sister."

"Littleton? You live around here?" Dad asked. It was clear he knew nothing about this woman either.

"Tonopah. Been there the last few years."

"Then why aren't you there now?" I crossed my arms. Something told me not to trust this woman.

Peggy looked at me and frowned, her carefully drawn eyebrows forming a V between her eyes. "You must know what happened?" Her voice changed as she addressed me, regarding me like a small child. "With Kitty's daddy in that accident and him hitting that poor kid, he's asked me to come take care of her while he's away."

"That poor kid? That kid?" I stood up straight and looked around, bewildered by her ignorance, trying to gauge if this was a sick joke. "That kid was my brother!"

Peggy's mouth moved several times like a fish out of water as she tried to formulate a response. Did she truly not know it was her brother who had killed mine?

"How come we've never seen you before this?" I questioned and moved closer to Kitty, feeling cagey and protective. "I don't know you from Adam. You're closer to an intruder than you are an aunt."

"Claude, let me handle this," Dad warned in a low voice.

But a simple word of caution from my father wasn't enough to rein me in. My body buzzed as anger inched up my spine. The past few days had been a mess of chaos and events that I couldn't control. Who was this stranger to show up without welcome and threaten to further fracture our lives?

"Kitty doesn't need taking care of," I declared. "Especially by someone she clearly barely knows and who knows nothing about this situation. So, why don't you just go."

Peggy laughed at my audacity. "Honey—"

"Get out!" Something snapped inside of me. "You're not

welcome here! Go!"

"Claude!" Dad slid his hand around my arm, trying to calm me down.

Mom emerged from the bedroom, rubbing her temples. "What's all this commotion about? Everything okay?" She stopped when she saw Peggy. "And who are you?"

"Kitty's shrew aunt. Fresh in from hell."

"Claude!" Mom shrieked as Dad gripped my arm harder and yanked me backward.

"Enough! To your room. Now!" he bellowed.

I stomped away, white-hot and spitting with rage, leaving the lot of them to duke it out without me. But there was no duking, only talking, and soon enough, Kitty and her stranger aunt were gone.

"You let Kitty go with her?" I asked, aghast.

"Claude, she's her aunt."

"She's a stranger."

No one argued with me on that.

"You don't have to like her, Claude. But if I hear you talk to or about a woman in that manner again, I will make sure you regret it. Got it?"

"Excuse me for defending my murdered brother." The moment the words left my mouth, I instinctively ducked and shut my eyes, bracing for the smack that never came. I cracked an eyelid and peered at my father. He was staring blankly at the floor, all hint of life drained from his face.

Mom promptly turned and walked away. I barely breathed as I waited for Dad to respond. He finally said, "You defend your brother by being an honorable man." He walked away then, and I stood there confused, because that's what I thought I was being.

A while later, after listening through our paper-thin walls to Mom weeping in the next room as Dad whispered promises that everything would be okay, I hopped out of my bedroom window. I wanted to find Cliff, who'd made himself scarce all day. Lights were on in the Ralph house. A bad feeling gnawed at my gut, and I only hoped Kitty was okay in there.

I looked at my bike leaning against our house. I couldn't yet stomach the thought of riding it, so I took off on foot toward the school. The early evening sun hovered low in the sky, warning me that it wouldn't stay hung up there much longer. I didn't have a lot of time. Mom would have a cow if I weren't home by nightfall at a time like this. But I wanted to discover where my brother had disappeared to all day and why he wasn't home floundering in misery with the rest of us.

I walked the perimeter of the school but saw no sign of Cliff. As I finished my circle around the grounds, I spotted Richie Garrison walking toward me.

"Hey, Fly," he said, awkwardly raising a hand in a lame sort of wave. "I saw you poking around here from my house." He jerked his head and nodded toward his home just across the street. "Sorry about your brother."

"Thanks," I muttered, unsure what else to say. Death, I was quickly learning, made for many uncomfortable conversations. "Have you seen my brother Cliff around by chance?"

"No, sorry." Richie cradled a football under his arm. He tossed it to me. "Wanna play catch for a bit?"

I glanced at the sky, the sun still hanging on, and then looked around in case Cliff had materialized out of nowhere. "Sure," I said.

We didn't say more than a few words, but over the next hour, until it was too dark to see, we threw that ball back and forth. And for a brief while, something inside of me loosened up.

"Claude!"

I turned toward my dad's voice, the outline of his figure

cutting through the darkness as he headed for me. "Over here!" I yelled and turned to hurl the football to Richie, who stood waiting about twenty-five yards away. He caught it with a grunt and threw it back.

Dad stood beside me. "We didn't realize you'd left. Your mom is wanting to have a proper family supper. Have you seen Cliff?"

"Nope. That's who I came out looking for." I extended the ball to him. "What kind of arm you got nowadays?"

Dad took it and juggled the ball back and forth before sending it flying toward Richie. "Oof!" Dad grunted, rubbing his right shoulder.

"Nice throw, Mr. Fisher!" Richie called out. He jogged over to us and held out his hand. "Sir."

Dad shook his proffered hand but said nothing. I had no idea if he knew Richie's name or not. Richie seemed to be debating whether to say something else, but Dad reiterated our need to head home, so he and I took off.

Cliff was seated at the fully set table when we walked in, staring down at the plate of food in front of him.

Mom stood at the sink, meticulously cleaning the tin foil she'd just cooked with to reuse another day. Something palpable hung in the air. It was different than the heaviness that had been present the past few days.

Dad and I took our seats. When Mom joined us, I noticed her blotchy and swollen face. Fresh from a cry. It hurt to look at her.

My nose suddenly zeroed in on Cliff next to me. "You smell like smoke."

He shot me daggers, then sheepishly looked at Mom through his lashes.

Mom pointed a finger at me. "If I catch you smoking too, you'll never leave this house again."

I sat up straight and peered at Cliff, who again wouldn't meet our eyes. Dad cleared his throat. "What exactly is going on?"

"Cliff showed up tonight sucking on a cigarette like he's been doing it his whole life."

"So?" Dad said.

"So?" Mom gasped, borderline hysterical. "I just lost one son! I'm not gearing up to lose another!"

Dad set his fork down and rubbed his forehead. "Smoking did not kill Helen's son."

"You don't know that!"

"Working in the mines did him in."

"He smoked like a chimney! Helen told me that special doctor they took him to said it was the cigarettes. It's not as safe as everyone thinks!"

"Then tell me why every other doc in the country smokes and puts their faces on all the advertisements, huh? If it's so bad? It's just a cigarette. Let the kid off the hook, Ginny."

Mom's voice heightened to a wavering, screeching pitch. "I will never—"

"Virginia!" Dad matched her decibels. "Enough!"

Mom rose from the table and took her uneaten plate of food to the counter, setting it down with a clatter. Dad went to her, and she fell into his shoulder, sobbing.

Cliff and I exchanged glances.

Dad led her to their room. By the time he reemerged, Cliff and I had finished eating and cleaning up after ourselves. "Take it easy on your mom, guys," Dad said. "Stay out of trouble, please."

A light in Kitty's house flickered on, catching my eye. I turned and watched her rummage around her kitchen, her sandy hair illuminated in the pale-yellow light.

She looked up and caught me watching her, her face

solemn.

I pointed to her and made eating gestures with my hands.

She shrugged and shook her head.

I held up a finger and nodded toward my porch. She gave me a thumbs up and disappeared.

"You two are something special." Dad stood watching me, hands on his hips. Cliff had already disappeared to our bedroom. "I don't want you going out anywhere. Got it?"

I nodded my head. "Yes, sir."

I broke off a chunk of a Hershey's bar my mother had hidden in the cupboard a few weeks before. I didn't know how she'd managed to get her hands on such a rare commodity. Maybe she'd traded for it or used some special stamp, but even still, I hadn't seen a full candy bar in over two years. Whatever the case, I doubted she'd mind if I shared some with Kitty. I headed outside with the chocolate.

In the soft glow of the porch light, I waited and heard Kitty's door open, then close. The sound of her footsteps approached, and I watched her step over the red paint that peeled up from my porch's wooden planks. She adjusted the blanket draped around her shoulders and sat down in a rocking chair beside mine.

"Here," I said, handing her the piece of chocolate.

"Thanks, Fly," she murmured and took a nibble, savoring the treat as we stared into the darkness.

"So, how's your aunt? Is that really who she is?"

She sighed. "Yes. My dad's sister. Never really knew her."

"Why's that?"

"Don't know. She lived somewhere back East most of her life, until the war when she moved to Tonopah. Dad and I visited her only once a few years ago. I guess she was too caught up in her own life to be part of mine. Kind of like everyone else in my family."

I wanted to tell her I was sorry that she came from such a lousy family. Instead, I said, "It's cold out here. Let's go inside. We have a fire going." I started to stand, but Kitty grabbed my hand, pulling me back down. "What is it?"

"I don't . . ." Her voice faded. In what little light the moon provided, I saw her eyes fill with tears. "I don't want to see your family right now. I think they could probably use a little space from me."

"Don't start saying those things again."

"It's kind of hard not to." She pulled her blanket tighter, folded her legs beneath her. "I feel like it's my fault. I could have stopped it."

I stiffened. "What do you mean?"

"If I hadn't been over here with Ginny, well, I could've been home to stop him from leaving. Hid his keys at the very least. I'd gone home once, but when I saw he was drinking—heavily enough to not even realize I was there—I came back over here."

This lightless pit of self-blame that Kitty had fallen into was the same one I'd grown familiar with over the past couple of days too. "You're not your dad's babysitter, Kitty." My voice was thick with gravel. I cleared my throat. "If anyone should feel responsible, I'm afraid it's me. I was the tagalong. The kid brother who made them leave the party early. If it weren't for me, they would've stayed out with their friends later. And none of this would've happened."

Kitty gently touched my arm, her hand warm from being inside her blanket. She shook her head. "Claude, Vernon invited you. You weren't tagging along. He wanted you there with him."

Her words ricocheted off me, leaving no impact upon my deaf ears at all. I couldn't help but feel I'd failed my brother. I guess she couldn't help but feel the same too.

"I don't want to talk about this anymore," she whispered. "Please."

"Fine by me." The problem was, I didn't know what else *to* talk about. All the unsaid things on our minds stretched out before us, floating away into the night sky, too far away for us to even catch if we tried. After a while, talking felt more difficult than staying silent. So we sat, the only movement between us an occasional shiver, until the creak of Kitty's front door piqued our attention. We turned to see Peggy, illuminated by the houselights, pop her head out.

"Kitty May? You out here?"

Kitty waited a beat before speaking up. "Over here. With Claude."

I sensed Peggy's eyes on us, felt an odd chill of scrutiny. "Time to come in, sweetheart."

"Why? You need somethin'?" Kitty hollered. Under her breath, she muttered to me, "I'm a stranger, not her sweetheart."

"It's getting late," Peggy said, a bite to her tone now.

I gritted my teeth and mumbled, "It's only eight o'clock."

"I'll be there in a minute." Kitty cut through the darkness with an icy stare of her own until Peggy retreated inside, leaving the door ajar.

"Who does she think she is? Bossing you around like she's your mother? Don't listen to someone who has no authority over you. She doesn't even know you."

Kitty went quiet. I recognized the distance in her eyes as she wrapped her blanket more tightly around herself, slipping away from me. "It's okay, Claude. I'm pretty tired anyway."

"Don't go yet. At least, don't go because she told you to. Go on your own terms."

Kitty's lower lip quivered. She looked away from me, then stood and hopped down the porch steps. "We should both get some rest. Your family probably needs you anyway."

I need you, I wanted to say. But instead, I let her walk away. Back to her house, to her odd, bitter aunt, knowing I'd see her again come morning time anyway.

6

THE NEXT MORNING, I fumbled with my tie. I circled the ends, wrapped and looped them every which way with no success. Normally I'd ask for help with this type of thing, but Mom could hardly muster the willpower to leave her bed, let alone dress herself. I couldn't burden her with my stupid tie, not today of all days. Dad either. So, I gave up, stuffed it back into the drawer, and headed out to look for Cliff.

"Your brother isn't here," Dad said. He sat at the table, staring through the window at what appeared to be nothing. The words packed a heavier punch than he intended, even though we both knew he'd referred to Cliff. "He left twenty minutes ago. Wanted to go down to the field, toss a ball around."

"He couldn't have invited me along?" I couldn't help but think that Vern would have invited me. My anger surrounding his absence suddenly changed course, targeting Cliff. My stomach clenched. Maybe he'd learned his lesson about inviting me places.

Dad sighed and shifted. "I suppose he should have included

you, Claude. Try not to be angry with him. He needed to distract himself . . . let off some steam."

"He's not the only one who needs that," I hissed.

Dad went quiet, too tired to argue, too dumbstruck by the upheaval of our lives to entertain my sourness. My pain.

I went to Kitty's. She opened the door, still in her nightgown, hair disheveled as though she'd just gotten out of bed. "Hi." She frowned.

"Why aren't you dressed yet? The funeral starts in twenty minutes."

"I'm not going."

"What do you mean you're not going? Of course you are."

She shook her head, and her hair fell over her face like a shield. "I can't, Claude. I'm so sorry."

The door shut in my face. I stumbled backward, caught off guard by her abruptness. "Kit!" I called but received no answer. One minute passed. Then two. Surely, she'd snap out of whatever mood she'd just fallen into and open back up? I waited. Counted to thirty in between knocks. Another minute passed. Nothing.

I turned and stormed back into our home through the back door.

"Kitty not home either?" Dad said.

I stopped to face him. "She's home. Says she's not going to Vern's funeral. She *can't.*" I emphasized the word. *Can't* indicated she had another obligation or perhaps was forbidden. I knew neither of those things could be true. *Didn't want to* was more accurate. How could she skip this?

Dad got up, concern clouding his face. It was the most expression I'd seen from him all day. "What do you mean she isn't going?"

"Dunno. Go ask her yourself." I went to my room and slammed my door behind me. I immediately regretted it; I knew Mom couldn't stand such a thing.

I sat on the edge of my bed, staring at Cliff and Vern's bunk bed on the other side of the room. I could imagine Vern lounging on the top bunk, tossing a bouncy ball at the ceiling. Or scribbling in his journal, no doubt writing about college, Maisy Thomas, or sports. Perhaps all three. He'd look up to tell a joke or tease me at some point about Kitty. *Trouble in paradise? Wife kick ya to the curb?*

In the volatile spirit of the day, I rose again and headed straight back to Kitty's. I needed to get through to her. But as I rushed through the house, a sight stopped me short of bursting through the screen door. Out on the back patio knelt my dad, holding Kitty in a tight embrace. Both of their shoulders jiggled as they cried together. Tiptoeing, I crept closer until I could hear.

Dad held her squarely by the shoulders now, saying with sternness, "It is not your fault, you hear me? You are not your dad's mistake."

Kitty cast her eyes down, her profile turned to me. Tears and snot glimmered in the sunlight. Her cheeks were a swampy pink. Her lips moved, mumbling words that were too quiet for my ears.

But Dad's voice came out penetrating and clear in response. "Don't you know you're part of ours? Vern thought of you as a sister. You're our family, Kitty. You have nothing to be sorry for."

I watched her fold into herself and eventually into Dad's arms. It was a scene I could only stand to watch for so long before I lost it myself. I backed away and sat down at the dining table. My elbow caught Cliff's cereal bowl from the morning. His leftovers pooled onto the tabletop, dampening the sleeve of my suit with spoiled milk.

———

Our community church was overcapacity. People squished into

the pews, bumping elbows with one another until every seat was taken. The rest of the funeral-goers spilled outside, congregating in a huddled crowd near the door. All five hundred-something members of our small community gathered together to pay respect to Vernon. Well, all five hundred-something minus one, because he was being held at the county jail.

The organ player began a melancholic tune, signaling the start of the ceremony. Whispers were hushed behind me. The church fell silent, sans the groaning breaths vibrating from the organ. I turned to Kitty, the sound of her hiccups bringing everything into focus. They weren't hiccups, I realized, but sobs. Her shoulders shook as she sat hunched forward, her arms wrapped around the backsides of her knees.

The music stopped. The pastor welcomed us all. I reached over and rested my hand on Kitty's back, noticing the dried and crusted milk on my sleeve. She moved closer. I pulled her against me, feeling in that moment much older than I had ever felt before. For a brief moment, I was transported back to the front seat of the Model T, fighting the urge to turn Kitty's face toward mine. I wanted to wipe the tears from her eyes and press my lips against hers.

But Vern's casket in front of us brought me back to reality, the morbid image of my brother lying inside killing any and all romantic flutters within me.

Cliff sat on my other side and slung his arm around my neck.

Compelled by a force of brotherly love, I reached over for his hand and squeezed it. He squeezed back. We sat like that for the remainder of the service. I chanced a glance or two at my parents. Mom was buried into Dad's side, hidden from view. Dad looked plain numb. Absent. When the service concluded, Cliff and I stood. We joined Dad and a few other men to move the casket.

We proceeded to the cemetery. Most of the town accompanied us to watch his body be lowered into the ground. The wind picked up soon after we arrived and stirred up the dust, making an already miserable day even more unpleasant.

Mom lost it when the cemetery worker scooped the first heap of dirt onto Vern's casket. Dad had to hold her back from diving into the plot. With the image of my father pinning my flailing and screaming mother down, her fists wildly thumping against his chest, her cries enough to puncture lungs, I took off in a run in no particular direction but away.

An arm shot out to stop me. I didn't even bother looking up to see who it belonged to. I was just focused on getting out of there.

Phil Ficklin from the drugstore said, "Let him run." Whoever held me let me free.

Undoubtedly, everyone could see me for a while as I sprinted away, the flat desert land not keen on hiding much from view. I changed direction, the wind at my back pushing me along more quickly now. A few miles later, I slowed. My chest burned. My suit clung to me, soaked through and ruined with sweat.

I shed my jacket and unbuttoned my shirt, letting it flap with the wind. I picked up a rock and chucked it as hard as I could into the brittle desert air. I picked up one rock after another, working myself into a frenzy until I tasted nothing but salt when I licked my upper lip. At that point, I couldn't tell the sweat from the tears.

The wind whistled a haunting melody through the stiff, reaching leaves of the surrounding Joshua trees. It slipped through them as easily as my own life seemed to be slipping through my aching fingers. I yelled, my voice whipped away by the tumultuous waves. Howling along with the wind, I asked the incredible force to carry my pain far, far away.

7

OF ALL THE things I expected to happen in the days following Vern's death, the least I was prepared for was another goodbye. I leaned against my bedroom door, eavesdropping on my parents' midnight conversation, appalled by what I heard.

"She can't be just taken away. Shouldn't she get a say in this?"

I heard my dad's resigned sigh, the one he only did when he faced utter defeat. "She's a minor, Ginny. She doesn't get a say in anything."

"I know that, Leonard," my mother snapped. "But how well does she even know that *woman*? In all the years we've known Kitty, she's never had a visit from her before."

"She's her aunt."

"We're more family to her than Peggy!"

"But it's not our decision. It's Jeb's."

"I thought Peggy was just coming to stay with her. Check in for a time, see to it that Kitty's alright . . . Not take her away. It's like losing another child." Mom's voice wavered. "We raised that little girl. You remember when they were babies? It was like having twins."

"Claude and Kitty," Dad said. "Kitty and Claude. Always two little peas in a pod."

"Remember setting up their bassinets in front of the stove to keep them warm enough on winter nights? Kitty slept here, tended to by me. Not by her father. Certainly not by her aunt. Where was Peggy when Kitty needed a mother? Hmm? Where was Peggy then? She should have no right to Kitty. None."

"I know, Ginny. You don't have to convince me. I agree with you."

"How long will she be away?"

"I reckon until Jeb is finished serving his time."

A long pause. I held my breath.

"Isn't there something we can do?" Mom said. "Anything at all? Can't we write to the county judge and ask him to overrule, or at the very least, let her decide? She can stay here with us. The girl has lost everything already."

"I suppose it's worth a shot. I'll head down to the courthouse on my break tomorrow and see what I can figure out, but I think it wise for us not to get our hopes up."

"How do you think Claude will take the news?"

"To lose your brother and best friend in the same week? He's going to be crushed. But it's not far. We can drive up every few weeks. They'll still see each other."

"It won't be the same for them. They mean everything to each other!" Mom's voice lurched, signaling the start of a good cry.

"*Shh*. I know, honey. I know," Dad spoke softly. I pressed my ear harder against the door to hear. "I want to change all of this. I'd give myself . . . I'd trade anything."

"I don't recognize our life anymore, Len. I don't know how we'll ever get through this."

I didn't want to hear anymore. I slipped back into bed,

knowing full well I'd be unable to sleep. Cliff snored softly on the other side of the room. I was tempted to wake him, to confide in him everything I'd just learned. But I stopped myself. Who knew how much peaceful sleep any of us would get in the days and months to come? The least I could do was grant it to him now. I rolled over, wondering if Kitty was miserable and awake like I was. Did she already know we'd be saying goodbye?

Fire crawled from my stomach to my throat, and I curled into a ball on my side to keep it at bay. *I don't recognize our life anymore.* My mom's words filled my mind. Never had she spoken something more relatable in my life. Would I ever feel remotely normal again?

———

I woke to the smell of bacon. At first, I salivated, excited for a meal not from a box, until my memory stirred, and my appetite vanished. Cliff's bed was empty but made. I got out of mine and haphazardly smoothed out my blanket, not yet ready for today's disappointments. I found Mom moving around the kitchen with gusto I hadn't seen from her in days. When she saw me, she plastered a big smile across her face. But the tears brimming in her eyes betrayed her.

"Morning, Claude," she sang. "Biscuits are almost ready if you want to have a seat."

I plopped down, feeling like a prisoner about to be served his last meal. Mom set a plate of biscuits, smothered in gravy, and two thick strips of bacon in front of me.

I looked at the empty chairs around the table. "Is no one else here?"

"Dad had to go back to work this morning."

"Did Cliff go to school?"

"No. He joined Dad at the shop." She sat down across from me, her hands wrapped around a cup of coffee. "Well, eat up."

My stomach revolted. Too heartsick to eat. But I knew she'd spent good time and money making this specially for me. I glanced at her, the fragility in her face making me ashamed. I picked up my fork, ignoring the growing knot in my gut, and took a giant bite, unwilling to pop the bubble in which my mother currently existed.

"Kinda nice not having to ration anymore, huh?" She nodded toward my heaping plate of food.

"Yes ma'am. Thank you." I took another bite. "When do you go back to work?"

Pop. There went Mom's bubble. She stared sadly into her cup, deflating in front of me. In the last few years, Mom had gone to work bright-eyed and bushytailed every morning at the county courthouse as a file clerk. "I don't think I am, actually."

I began to ask her why not—though who was I kidding; we both knew why—but the sound of fists pounding on our back door shot us out of our seats.

Mom winced. She knew as well as I did who was out there. Kitty flew through the door before either of us had a chance to answer it. She ran straight into my arms and pressed her tear-stained face deep into my chest. I walked us to the living room and sat on the couch. Mom sat down too. Neither of us asked what was wrong. The painful truth carved itself into each of us, leaving its knowing mark like initials on a tree.

"When do you leave?" The hollowness in my voice surprised me.

Her bloodshot eyes bore into mine. "You already know?"

I glanced at my mom. "I overheard."

"Peggy wants to leave today."

"Today? As in *today* today?"

She nodded. "Today. I don't know why I can't just stay here. This is my home! My school! My friends! What do I do?"

Mom swooped in and knelt down in front of Kitty, resting

her hands on Kitty's knees. "Sweetie, Leonard's going to talk to some people today, see what strings we can pull, if any. We don't want you to leave either."

"Peggy's determined to get home today. Says she can't afford to miss any more work and that she misses her cat and a bed with real sheets." Kitty rolled her eyes. "She doesn't want me missing any more school and won't shut up about how much I'll like Tonopah. How many times have I been to Tonopah? Ain't much different than this." She looked back and forth between me and my mother. "Don't make me go with her, please."

I'd do anything in my power to keep her here with us.

Mom popped up to her feet and clapped her hands. "You hungry? We have biscuits and bacon." She fluttered away to make Kitty a plate without waiting for an answer. "Eat up. Get your strength. We're not waiting for Len. The three of us are going down to the courthouse to sort this out ourselves."

—

Mom begged and pleaded with everyone she knew, everyone she'd worked with. But it didn't seem that anything could be done. Kitty was a minor. Peggy was her next of kin, willing and insistent on taking her in at Jeb's request. *And besides, she'd only be twenty-six miles away*, they said.

Kitty stomped along the road in front of us, seething. She flipped around and walked backward, talking a mile a minute. "I'm not going! She'll have to take me kicking and screaming. I'm not leaving! How can they expect me to go with a woman I barely even know? *Only twenty-six miles away!* If it's so close, then how come Peggy has never bothered to visit me before? You know I've only met her twice? Well, supposedly, because I can't even remember one of those times!"

When we got back to our houses, Peggy was sitting on Kitty's front steps with a cigarette in hand. She sprang to her feet. "Where have you been? You knew I was ready to get on the road!" She made a grand swooping gesture with her arm, directing Kitty, who looked up at me with a defeated expression, to the house. "Get the rest of your things and meet me in the car."

All traces of zeal and fury fled from Kitty's face. In an instant, she shifted into total submission, doing as she'd been told, making herself small and agreeable. Just as she'd done her whole life. Even without her old man around, she still found herself to be the doormat.

Mom and I watched Kitty be scolded and ushered into her house. Once Kitty had gone inside, Peggy turned and gave us a tight smile.

"I'm so sorry about your son and brother," Peggy said before walking away.

The condolence left me unsettled. I watched her climb into her car, glaring at her with corrosive hatred all the while. But she ignored me and began to carefully apply lipstick as she gazed into the rearview mirror.

"I'm sorry, Claude. It's just a little ways north. We drive up often enough. You won't lose your friend forever." Mom gave my shoulder a tight squeeze and blinked back tears. "Why don't you go check on her?"

I bounded up to Kitty's door like I'd done countless times in my life. But never before had it been to say goodbye. The word lodged in my throat. *Goodbye.* Of all the things I'd ever wanted or planned to say to her, this had never been on the list.

She opened the door before I could reach for the handle. We stood in the doorway face-to-face, our lifetime of memories stretching between us. Years of laughter, fights, and secrets rumbling beneath our feet, a grand orchestra only we could hear. A tear rolled down her cheek.

Our hearts beat the same rhythm. *Don't. Go.*

"I'll find a way to see you every chance I get. I'll drive up, bike, ride the rails if I have to. But I'll get to you."

"They're shutting that down, Claude. That's part of why my dad lost his job to begin with. Drinking just accelerated the process. The war's over, the army airfield is all but shut down. People are moving on. Gasoline isn't rationed anymore." Hope drained from her eyes. "That railroad won't be operating much longer at all. And it's too far for a bike, and you don't have a car. Not that you can drive yet anyhow."

"I'll be getting my license soon." The more I tried to convince her, the less I convinced myself. Even still, I wasn't about to let the last strands binding us together slip through my fingers. "Mom and Dad can drive me up. Maybe even Cliff. If I have to, I'll hitchhike."

She shook her head. I wiped the soft pads beneath her eyes with my thumbs, tracing the spray of freckles that graced her nose and cheeks. The tiny speckles would forever make me imagine that a ladybug had stepped in brown paint and skittered across her face.

"Come on," I said. "Don't be so down. It's gonna work out." I didn't fully believe this myself, but I sure as heck wasn't going to let Kitty in on that.

Peggy honked her horn, but I could only hear the pain that drummed within my chest. I pulled Kitty into me and held her. Peggy honked again.

Kitty reached down and picked up her small basket of belongings. "Don't tell me goodbye." She clutched her basket tightly, put on the bravest face she could muster, and walked out of her house.

My crying mother wrapped her in a tight hug and whispered urgently in her ear. I stood in the doorway of the Ralph home, watching as my entire life unraveled before me. In a blur, Kitty left Mom's arms and went to Peggy's car. The sight of her pitiful wave burned itself into my brain.

And just like that, she was gone.

—

I excused myself halfway through dinner. Mom tried her best to cheer me up by cooking my favorite meal. For twenty minutes I pushed the meatballs and potatoes around on my plate, only managing a few bites. Something about wasting my food felt oddly satisfying.

I left my parents alone at the table and went to my room. Cliff was off somewhere, probably playing sports with his friends, running around in a desperate attempt to keep his mind from holding still long enough to feel Vern's absence. In the midst of all the Kitty drama today, the reason she was being forced to leave at all had almost slipped my mind. But it came rushing back to me now in one giant affirmation that all my joy had been stolen right out from under me.

My parents spoke in low voices at the table, oblivious to how well sound carried back to my room. I cracked my door open cautiously and listened, curious if Dad had gleaned any new information that he'd been withholding in my presence about Kitty's situation. I held my breath. Desperate. A dog begging for scraps. Something. Anything to get me through.

"How was it seeing Kitty off today? Claude barely spoke a word all evening."

"It was so hard, Len. Broke my heart. But you know what?"

"What?"

"As much as I don't want Kitty anywhere but next door to us, a little distance might be good for them after all."

I could practically feel Mom wince from here.

"What do you mean?"

"Well . . ." she began. I didn't dare to breathe. "They were awful close before she left. I got the impression that there's more than just a friendship brewing there."

This blow I hadn't expected. Betrayed by my own mother.

Dad let out his breath. "Well, I can say I'm a little disappointed. Can't say I'm surprised. Did any of us truly *not* see this coming? If anything, that makes me feel bad for them all the more."

"We should drive up to see her soon. She's got to know we won't abandon her too."

I perked up. *Hope.* Perhaps it wasn't entirely gone?

"Absolutely. By the way, Big John called, asked if we would be up for company next weekend. What do you think?"

Big John, Dad's best friend who lived in Hawthorne. He was practically family, like Kitty. It would be nice to see him again.

"That's fine," Mom said.

They continued talking. I stepped away and stared at the two empty bunks. Vern didn't have a choice in his being vacant, but Cliff did. Where was he? I climbed into Vern's bunk and lay down.

What would Vern have to say about all of this? Could he tell me how I ought to begin sorting this out? I stared at the ceiling as if the answer might be written up there. Everything about hope I'd known—the ripe passages of Scripture Mom would read to us when we were younger—was blurred now. Too fuzzy to remember, too far from my grasp—or perhaps, more likely, I was too hardened right now to entertain any thought about the God who could've stopped all of this from happening and didn't.

But even so, I considered what Mom had suggested about visiting Kitty soon. For a moment, I let the promise of it scoop me from the enemy's hands and deliver me into a place of hope before I fell into a much-needed deep sleep.

8

LIFE CHUGGED ALONG at a record slow speed over the following week. With each day, I discovered a new low, a new pocket of bitterness to sink into.

Dad, solemn and tight-lipped, resumed his regular hours at the shop, working long days, coming home beat tired with a newfound preoccupation with hygiene. I watched him stand at the sink, scrubbing his hands with a bar of lye soap, taking unusual care in ridding himself of the grease and oil that stained his skin.

Mom, when she managed to make an appearance, feigned smiles and spoke in unusually chipper tones, busying herself to keep from unraveling. Most days when I got home from school, I'd find her asleep, some chore in the house half-done, as though midway through she'd lost all vigor and had no other choice but to buckle beneath the weight of her exhaustion. One day I found a pile of sopping wet laundry, still in the wash basin, forgotten and beginning to mildew. I rinsed each article and hung them on the line to dry. Another day I found the rugs she'd taken outside for a beating hanging off the porch, collecting more dust than they'd started with.

Cliff all but dissolved into his friend group, doing everything to avoid being home or being still enough to miss Vern, his best friend. My resentment toward Cliff festered. Why wasn't he seeking me out, the only brother he had left?

At school, I was avoided. A wide berth was given to me in the halls. Averted gazes met me in the classroom. Deep down, I sensed that my classmates and friends only felt awkward, but that didn't stop me from feeling like a dangerous disease no one wanted to catch. *Don't go near that Fisher boy or else your entire life will derail too.*

When the bell rang on Friday, dismissing school for the weekend, I ducked out of my classroom as quick as I could, hoping to avoid Mrs. Newton and the talk she'd asked me to stay late for. I zipped down the hallway, the heavy, wooden doors at the end beckoning to me. *Faster. Almost there. You've nearly made your escape.*

Richie clapped me on the back out of nowhere, making me jump. "Fly. You're moving faster than you have all week."

I slowed, wary of this friendliness. "And?"

"I'm just saying. You gotta wake up, my friend."

"I am awake." I shrugged his hand off me.

"You know what I mean. You lay your head on your desk all day. I think I've seen you pick up your pencil twice. And you've barely uttered a handful of words in five days. I don't know where you are, but you ain't here."

I gritted my teeth.

"All I'm saying is this," he continued. "Mourn your whole life if you need to. Just make sure you don't quit living while you're still alive."

His frankness startled me. Everyone seemed so afraid of saying the wrong thing that they said nothing at all. Yet here was Richie, telling me all kinds of things I didn't want to hear.

What business did he have telling me how to feel? How to be? I didn't respond, hoping my silence would get my point across. But he stuck with me, his stride matching mine the whole way home.

Mom was slumped down amid the couch cushions, her feet propped up on the coffee table, hands folded in her lap. She lazily opened her eyes at the sound of our arrival. "Oh, hi boys," she said sleepily. Then, realizing the time, she shot straight up. "What time is it? School's out already?"

"Yep, just barely," I said.

"I didn't know I'd fallen asleep," she mumbled, shaking her head to get rid of the fog. She swayed as she rose to her feet and went to the kitchen. We followed. "Richie, it's nice to see you."

"You as well, Mrs. Fisher. It smells great in here," Richie said.

Mom smiled, and it almost seemed genuine. "Pot roast. Been cooking all day. There'll be plenty if you'd like to stay for dinner. We do, however, have Pastor James coming over too."

"Pastor James?" I questioned.

"From the church. He spoke at Vern's funeral."

I rolled my eyes and almost laughed. "What's P.J. coming over for? You realize Vern's funeral was the first time we'd stepped foot in that church for, what, two whole years? Why clamor for God now?"

Mom let the empty pan she was holding clatter onto the counter. She crossed her arms as she faced me. "Please don't call him that. It's disrespectful." Mom sighed and rubbed her temples. "We used to go regularly when you boys were younger. I don't know why we stopped. At any rate, your father and I asked him to come. We think it'd be good to have a little support during all this."

I bristled. First, I had Richie inserting his advice where it wasn't welcome. Now a pastor was coming over to do so too. "I don't want support. I just want my brother back. Can he do that?"

"Claude, please."

"No resurrection, no meeting." I crossed my arms, and my nastiness spewed from a place inside of myself that I didn't recognize.

Richie shifted uncomfortably next to me. "I don't want to intrude on your plans. Thanks for the invite, Mrs. Fisher."

He was only trying to be a good friend—something I wasn't sure how to be at the moment—but I wanted him gone. I didn't want him at the dinner table, taking the chair that belonged to Vern. I didn't want some pastor I hardly ever saw doing the same, either. I didn't want anyone trying to pull me out of my slimy darkness. I just wanted to be left alone.

"I'd better get home." Richie made for the door. "Let me know if you want to play ball or something tomorrow. And don't forget what I told you earlier," he called over his shoulder as he left.

I sent him off with a wave.

"What'd he tell you earlier?" Mom asked.

I looked her straight in the eye. "Just offered me some words that don't truly change anything. You know, *support.*"

Wounded, she looked at me, all traces of light gone within her gray eyes. She walked away, giving me what I'd asked for— to be left alone.

The isolation only helped to confirm the rottenness that oozed from my every pore. Out of habit, I glanced out the kitchen window, spying into Kitty's empty home. Who are you supposed to go to when the one you always went to is gone? I spun around, overwhelmed by the groping anger within me, searching for a plate to smash, a fork to throw, any way to displace my frustration.

I grabbed a wooden spoon and hurled it at the back door.

But in the split second of it leaving my fingertips, the door opened, and I watched in horror as the spoon nailed Pastor James in the eye like a dart.

Dad, who was right beside him, looked at me like I'd lost my mind. Maybe I had.

"What'd you do that for, Claude?"

"It was an accident, I swear!" I wanted to dive out the window. The last remaining crumbs of my pride would surely land on the floor if I did.

Pastor James waved Dad off as he tried to get a look at his eye. "I'm fine," he said. A chuckle rumbled from his thick chest. "There's a reason God made us with two of these things, right?"

Dad laughed with him uneasily. He came over to me and set a hand upon my shoulder. "You alright there, buddy?"

Thick crevices outlined every feature on Dad's face. He'd seemed to age a dozen years in the span of a week. For some reason, that frightened me into telling the truth. "Honestly, Dad, I don't think I am."

He wrapped his arms around me and told the truth too. "Me neither."

Life rarely rocked my father's boat, but the look on his face convinced me that he was clinging to a deflating life raft. Much like myself. The notion was disquieting. I glanced at Pastor James, then back to my dad. "Can I be excused tonight?"

He deliberated, knowing both Mom's wish for the evening and my opposing one. For whatever reason—I chalked it up to the embarrassment and pain he surely saw painted on my face—he gave me the okay. Maybe deep down he doubted the impending 'Fisher Family Support Session' too. Maybe he knew it would take more than a miracle from God for this collective aching heart of ours to heal.

9

NO ONE QUITE knew what to say when Big John arrived from Hawthorne the next morning. Because, well, he wasn't so big anymore. He hadn't shrunk in height. He still needed to duck when he walked under the ceiling beam in our living room. But otherwise, he was unrecognizable. His skin hung over his skeleton like a wet sheet on a coat rack, his face sunken like a corpse. He embraced us with hugs far less thick than I'd remembered. While the rest of us tiptoed around his strange appearance, he went about the day like nothing was different at all.

After dinner, Dad finally looked him dead in the eye, told him not to lie, and asked what was going on.

That's when Big John told us he had cancer. Even though we could all see the proof right there in front of us, we looked at him in disbelief.

"How bad is it?" Dad asked.

Big John took a sip of his coffee. The cup shook in his hand. He set it down and smiled. "We're not here to talk about me."

"Yes, we are." Mom rested her hand on his. "John?"

"Well, it ain't good." He tried to smile, like the whole thing was a joke. But now that the truth was out, he faltered and cracked.

"Where?" Dad asked.

"All over." Big John motioned across his entire midsection. Then he slowly brought his hand to his forehead and tapped it with one finger.

Dad covered his mouth with his hand and rubbed the scruff on his face. "How long?"

"How long have I had it? Doc first found it, oh, a few months ago."

"You know what I meant, John."

Big John had always been an anomaly to me. Larger than life, filling up a whole room with his presence both physically and soulfully. And now, as tears splashed into his mug, I realized invincibility didn't exist in this painfully mortal world.

Cliff excused himself from the table, no doubt to avoid this deathward discussion, and I couldn't blame him.

I went after him, finding him in bed, his back to me. I sat down on the edge of my bed.

"I'm so tired of this, Fly." His voice cracked. "Not Big John. It doesn't make sense how life can change so fast."

"I know." I wanted normalcy. For life to be good, what it had been. I wanted both of my brothers and me to be wrestling in our living room or catching horny toads together outside. For Kitty to be waiting in front of our house, ready for an adventure. For Big John to be big again. But instead, we had loose ends forever left untied, business unfinished, pieces of life and love suddenly dropped and left to rot, to slowly fade away until they would one day become bleak reminders that only existed in our memories.

"You know what I just keep thinking? Why him? Why Vern? I came around that corner right with him. Why wasn't I the one Jeb hit?"

"I could say the same thing. I keep thinking that if I didn't tag along with you guys that night, none of this would have happened."

"Don't think that. It was no one's fault but Jeb's."

Deep down I knew this to be true, but I wondered if he really believed it. Perhaps he felt so far away from me lately because underneath it all he blamed me? The nuisance kid brother who messed everything up. The thought made me shudder. I longed for his forgiveness, for Cliff to tell me this wasn't true—that he held Jeb at fault, not me. But I wouldn't stoop so low as to grovel for that validation, as badly as I needed it in this moment. I left him be. Big John and my parents too. It felt better to leave everyone alone after the turn the evening had taken.

I kept waking to nightmares throughout the night. No sooner would I drift to sleep than I'd wake again, cold with sweat, gasping for air and the overwhelming urge to check on my family, to make sure they were all right where they needed to be—safely tucked in their beds, their covers rising and falling with their breath. A shuffling in the hallway caught my ear. I hadn't any idea what hour it was, but someone out there was awake. I rose to find out who.

The kitchen was empty. In the soft glow of lamplight, I found Big John in the living room. His nightshirt drooped sadly over him. He sat on the couch—his interim bed for the night—his hand inside a paper sack beside him, a book splayed open on his lap.

"Can't sleep either?" he said, regarding me as I sat down in the armchair and pulled Mom's afghan, draped over the back, onto my lap.

"Not so much."

He popped something from his bag into his mouth, then

extended the entire sack to me. "Care for a lemon candy?"

I looked at him quizzically, then glanced at the wall clock above his head. "Lemon candy at three in the morning?"

"Helps with the nausea," he said, and my stomach sank. "Hard to eat much these days. Guess the tumors are blockading my innards. Lemon candies don't help much, but they take the edge off some." He shook the bag, proffering his precious goods a moment longer. In solidarity, I took one.

"I'm sorry you're sick." It felt lame, but what else was there to say?

"That's alright." He worked at the candy in his mouth and looked upward. "These things happen. And I've had a good run."

His coolness struck me. Here was a man facing a certain and soon death, and what had he but a bag of lemon drops and nonchalance? "Does it bother you?" I asked.

"Does what bother me?"

"Knowing . . . you know . . . your time is . . . almost up."

He popped another candy, and it prompted me to eat mine too. "Time's limited. That's a fact we all gotta accept sooner or later. At least our time here is. Our time on the other side, well, that's another story." Big John attempted to laugh, but it quickly dissolved into a coughing fit. He slipped yet another candy into his mouth. "Helps with this throat tickle too," he croaked and pointed at his neck. When the coughing subsided, he said. "I've got a confession to make." He closed the book on his lap, and I saw that it was a Bible. He set it aside.

I must've looked panicked, because Big John fell into another coughing fit sparked by laughter. He sputtered and cleared his throat. "Lighten up, little Fisher. It ain't no ghastly deathbed secret."

"The way you said it made it sound like something big and serious you have to get off your chest."

"More like off yours." He laughed some more, having completely confused me now, but I found myself laughing alongside him. "Let me explain. 'Member that time you guys visited me, and your brothers moved the bed over top of ya?"

I remembered well. "Yeah, we were sharing your spare bedroom. They were taking the bed, and I was sleeping on the floor. I woke up to them having moved the bed over me."

"You didn't just wake up. You lost your marbles!"

"Well, wouldn't you if you found yourself suddenly trapped under something in the dead of night?" At the time, I was scared out of my mind and furious at my brothers afterward. But the comedy of the prank wasn't lost on me now. I'd give anything for Vern to be here, orchestrating pranks with Cliff. Even at my expense.

"Well, this is what I gotta confess. It was my idea!"

My mouth fell open. "All this time I thought you were an ally."

He slapped his knee and hooted.

"I'm bigger now," I said, shaking a finger in jest at him. "And not above retaliation, so you'd better watch it. You're in my territory now."

"Cliff won't turn on me. Least I hope not anyway. Then I'd be in big trouble!" He sighed, and it came out with a wheeze. "You boys are sure a special crew. Every onea'ya."

The life went out of my lungs, removing all traces of whimsy in the air. Big John picked up on it and dared to venture further down that road. "Your folks tell me Kitty's living in Tonopah now. Bet that's pretty hard, huh? There has never been hardly a moment during all my visits here that Kitty wasn't around too."

"I don't know how much they told you, but yep. She's gone. Living with some aunt she barely knows."

"You talk to her since she left?"

"No."

"Well, you call her up in the morning, alright? Tell her we're meeting for lunch before I leave town at that deli I like up there. That's still open, isn't it?"

"Babby's? I'd think so."

"That's right. Babby's."

"Will you even be able to enjoy it?" I pointed to his bag of candies, referring to the nausea which they attempted to curb.

He winked. "Absolutely."

"Why do I feel like you're just trying to make up for that prank?"

He barked out a laugh and said, "Well, would it work?"

"I'd forgive you for anything if it meant seeing Kitty." This made him smile. I got up and placed Mom's afghan over the back of the chair where I'd found it. "We'd better try to get a little shut eye, wouldn't you say?"

"Suppose we ought to try. Goodnight, Claude."

Before I left him alone with his Bible and his candy, I stopped. "Hey, Big John?"

"Hmm?"

"Is there anything you wish you would've done?"

"Done?"

"You know . . . differently? Or . . . more of?"

Big John regarded me with an intensity that let me know he'd understood my question. "Prayed," he answered. A pensive cloud settled over him. "Been more grateful. Things change when you look death in the eye. I had so much to be thankful for in life and never really took the time to tell the Big Man thanks."

"Do you feel thankful right now? Even though . . . you know . . ."

He laughed. "Even though I'm dying? I feel more thankful now than ever."

90

I felt a tug in my chest. "By the way, there's a candy store in Tonopah that sells lemon suckers. At least they used to. You might like those."

"All the more reason for a stop there."

—

I tried calling the Littleton residence so many times the next morning that Miss Bianchi, the operator, asked me if everything was alright. But no matter how many times I tried, every one of my calls went unanswered. Big John encouraged me to try again and not give up. But finally, once we'd put off lunch as long as possible, I had to.

We followed Big John out of town—he and my dad in Big John's 1937 Plymouth pickup and Cliff at the wheel in our LaFayette, my mother riding shot gun and me in the back—Tonopah bound. The town's population had ballooned throughout the last handful of years, much like Goldfield's. When the new air base was built, military and civilian workers flooded the city, spilling into Goldfield due to the housing shortage during the war. But with the war over now, both towns were deflating, trickling back down to their usual runty volumes.

If luck were on my side, we'd run into Kitty. She'd magically be at Babby's Deli, sitting at the counter when we walked in. I daydreamed about it the whole drive, so much so that I nearly believed it could happen.

The bell on the door jingled when we walked in, and my heart skipped a beat when I saw a group of girls somewhere around my age squished together in a booth. But one quick glance brought my hope crashing down. None of them were Kitty.

Big John hardly ate a bite, and I knew the nausea he'd told me about must have been acting up. Though because I could hardly eat either, I wondered if it secretly was in solidarity with me this time.

We walked over to Henry's Sweets when we were through so Big John could stock up on sour candies. He paid for two bags, full to the brim with sweets, and handed one to me as we walked out. "Maybe these'll help with your troubles too."

"Thanks," I mumbled. "Why don't you take them? They're guaranteed to help you more than me. I'm afraid I'm a helpless cause."

"Can't be any worse for wear than I am." Big John nudged me in the ribs. "You hang tight, okay, Claude? There're seasons for everything in life. Things will change."

Would they? I looked around at the broken lot of us. Cliff, one hand shoved in his pocket, the other clinging to the comic book he'd just purchased at Henry's. He was walking three feet from me, though he might as well have been in another galaxy. Mom, leaning against the front end of our Nash LaFayette, eyes downcast at her black Oxfords, watching the ruffling of her long skirt in the ankle-nipping wind. And Dad, arm slung around his oldest friend, a man I'd once thought too big for death. But perhaps, I considered now, was actually too large for life. The two of them were in what looked like a battle of stoicism. Of not being the first to say goodbye.

"Not long enough of a visit. You sure you can't stay another day?" Dad asked.

Big John looked over the four of us. "Wish I could, but I've got an appointment in the morning. Leila's coming in from Utah for it."

Leila, his only daughter.

"Okay," Dad resigned. "Please tell her hello from us. We'll make it up to visit you soon. Let me know if anything changes." He looked him squarely in the eye and made him promise.

But the promise Big John made felt paper-thin. Because as he'd only just said, things will change, and I hoped with all my might that they could for him.

We all hugged him. Dad had a hard time letting go. I had to look away. I noticed Cliff did too, though he took it a step further and climbed into the car.

I followed suit and hoped for Cliff to offer me a sliver of solace, something to patch us together if only for a moment.

But Cliff thumbed through his *Captain America* comic and let the air grow stale between us.

Mom got into the car next, followed minutes later by Dad.

I looked out my window as we pulled away, just in time to see Big John wipe his eyes.

On our way out of town, Dad made a sudden turn and pulled into a gas station.

"Something wrong, honey?" Mom asked, leaning over to look at the dash. "I thought we had plenty of fuel."

He whispered something to her, and then said to me, "Come out with me, Claude."

I figured there was going to be a lesson to teach me something about pumping gas or something about the car. Instead, as I rounded the rear bumper, he asked if I happened to have an address for Kitty's aunt.

I eyed him with suspicion. "No."

"Alright then. We'd better start asking around." With me flanked at his side in a state of disbelief, he asked the first man he saw if he knew a Mrs. Peggy Littleton.

The man looked from Dad to me and back again. "Ah, yep. Sure, I know Peggy." He adjusted his dirty cap and barked out a husky laugh. "Every man in this town knows Peggy."

Dad grimaced. "Do you know where she lives?"

"Sure do. Right by St. Mark's. Ain't that some irony." The man snorted.

We thanked him. As we walked back to the car, I asked Dad what the man had meant by his flippant comment.

"I don't care to speculate," Dad said. "And I don't want you repeating what you heard."

"Do you think Peggy's a bona fide hooker?"

Dad immediately stopped walking, and I ran into his backside. He turned around and faced me. "I don't know, son. She's a lost person; that much is clear. But you'd best be respectful when we see her today. Got it?"

"Got it." But truly, I didn't. It felt like I didn't get anything anymore. Like why Kitty was being forced to live with her harlot aunt and why it was disrespectful to point that out. "Before I get my hopes up here, are we really heading to find Kitty?"

"Gonna give it our best shot."

My stomach cartwheeled, and I slid into the backseat.

Cliff glanced up from his comic as Dad turned north out of the gas station, away from Goldfield. "Aren't we going home?"

I grinned when Dad said, "We're making a pit stop."

We weren't sure which house belonged to Peggy, but we decided to try the house closest to St. Mark's. Just like most of the surrounding homes, an American flag was pitched out front. My family waited in the car at my insistence. I walked up to the house alone and climbed the concrete steps to the door. I knocked. When it opened, I had only a moment to brace myself before Kitty flung herself at me. We stumbled backward, almost falling down the steep steps.

"What on earth are you doing here?" Kitty peeled herself off me, but the grin plastered across her face, matching my own, remained. She looked past me to the LaFayette, where my family was waving to her from within.

"I tried calling all morning."

"You did?" She frowned. "Peggy dragged me out this morning. To church of all places!"

"Is that such a bad thing?"

"I'll explain later. I'm so sorry, Claude! So, what's going on? Why are you here? Gosh, I've missed you so much."

"Can you come with us? To get ice cream or something?"

She immediately shut the door, ready to go, looping her arm in mine. We made for the car. "Peggy left not too long ago and will be gone awhile. I can't believe you're really here, Fly!"

Mom and Dad got out when we drew near, and they each took turns wrapping her in a hug. I opened the back door, and she scrambled in, sitting in the middle between Cliff and me.

"Hey, Kit," Cliff said, putting an arm around her and kissing the top of her head like a brother would a little sister. "Good to see you."

We ended up back at Henry's Sweets. As we pulled up, even with Kitty bouncing in her seat right next to me, I almost choked up when I saw that Big John's truck was truly gone. Part of me hoped he'd still be right where I saw him last, parked behind the wheel, weeping.

Inside, we sat at the counter and ate sundaes while Kitty chattered away, filling us in on her new life. She hardly took a break to eat or breathe. "You know what she told me when we left Goldfield? Just as we were driving away, me in a fit of tears, she says, 'I'm not gonna let you turn into one of them. Your mama at least had the brains to get out of this god-forsaken desert when she had the chance. Them folks would keep you here to rot all your life. Even your daddy wasn't doing you any favors. Can't believe he never got out of here too.'"

"Oh, sweetie," Mom whispered, her voice aching. "You know God hasn't forsaken this desert, don't you? There's nowhere His presence can't be found."

"You really think so? Even in a house such as Peggy's?"

"Even in a house such as Peggy's."

"Do you want to know why she's here? In this *god-forsaken desert?*" Kitty asked.

"Why?" I wasn't sure I really wanted to know. The more I learned about Peggy, the more I disliked her.

"I first heard rumors at school . . . just little whispers. Crumbs here and there. But one day Peggy up and told me the whole story herself. I will say, I learned more about my dad from two minutes with her than I ever did with him my whole life." She grew quiet a moment.

"For starters, they were from Missouri. And my dad watched his own dad die in some freak horse accident on the farm when he was about eight and Peggy was four. Guess they never had a mother, because theirs died giving birth to Peggy. They never really had much, lived with relatives all their lives until my dad married his bride at twenty-five. Peggy left the first chance she could, when she was only fifteen. So, she drifted this way and that all over the states, figuring out how to follow the money. When the war broke out and the air base was built, people flooded into town for work, and she came too. Got a job at a brothel." Kitty wrinkled her freckled nose in disgust. "That's why she's here. In this desert. To prostitute her body for money. My bloodline is topnotch, I'm tellin' ya."

I shot a glance at my dad. He leveled my gaze, warning me to keep my trap shut.

She continued, "That's where she met an airman. Somehow, believe it or not, the two fell in love. Guess he came from some sort of money back East. He scooped her up out of that brothel, married her, and bought the house of a civvy who died the week before in an accident. Her whorin' days were behind her, she told me. But then he went and got killed in a training accident.

"And now, Peggy's too heartbroken to move on, to get out of here, go someplace she actually likes. I think she's just too bitter to go. Shriveled up and bitter. She's waitressing at the hotel, though kids at school say they've heard she still works the red-light district. But I don't know if they're teasing me. When my dad went to jail, he called her up. He knew she still lived in Tonopah, though she never visited, mind you. He was hoping she'd pay his bail. But she didn't have the money and told him he deserved to pay his time anyway. She offered to take me in while he was locked away. And why Dad took her up on that is beyond me.

"He's made a lot of grandiose promises. About how he's gonna straighten up his ways. Gonna take care of me and Peggy like he wishes he'd have done in the first place. I think Peggy's just trying to cling to what she can right now. Distract herself at my expense. I think she believes she's doing me a favor. But all I want to do is be home, to live next to you guys. It's awful with her."

I could hardly stomach the things Kitty said. More than anything, I wanted to shield her from all of it. Next to me, Cliff whistled and muttered something under his breath. Mom rested a hand on Kitty's forearm. "I'm so sorry, dear. Oh, how I wish you could come home with us."

"Do you think there's any possibility I could?" Kitty looked back and forth between my parents.

Dad scooped out the last spoonful of melting ice cream from the bottom of his bowl. "It's doubtful. Not yet anyway." We all knew the words he didn't speak and why he didn't speak them . . . *Not unless your dad gets out of jail. And we all know that won't happen anytime soon.*

As much as I wanted Jeb Ralph to pay forever for what he'd done to our family, if it meant Kitty could come home, I *almost* didn't mind the thought of him walking free. Even if it meant him living next door to me. I shivered at the thought.

"What if you talked to my dad yourself? You know, ask him to give your family the rights, not Peggy?" Kitty's voice faltered with hesitant hope.

Dad slowly nodded his head, mulling over the idea. Could he really bring himself to speak with the man who'd killed his son? "I hadn't considered that."

"It's so hard to be around her. I feel bad for her in a way. Honestly, I do. But I don't know how much longer I can handle her contempt of life. Not to mention stave off her coming at me with rouge, lipstick, and curlers."

"Hang in there, honey. Your aunt probably has as much experience with kids as a fish does with walking," Mom said, though her voice was ripe with worry. "It might take some adjusting on both ends, but I'm sure it'll get better. And you know we're here for you. You can always call."

"Peggy told me I can't make long-distance calls. And besides, I don't have your phone number." Kitty smiled sheepishly at her.

Mom's face softened. "I guess you never before had a reason to. 3423. Just ask Miss Bianchi to transfer you to the Goldfield Fisher's. If you need us, you call. I'll send money to make up for the cost if need be."

"How's your new school?" I asked. "Mrs. Newton has called your name by accident twice since you've been gone."

"School is okay. Not really good, not really bad. Just different . . . you know?"

"At least you probably don't have any troublemakers who cause the whole class to write two-page essays."

"Sadly, none of those. But I wish I did." Kitty took a bite of her now-melted sundae. "How's home?"

We told her about Big John's visit, but for some reason, all of us failed to mention his death sentence. I don't think any of our hearts could bear discussing it again nor putting the weight on Kitty's already burdened shoulders.

On the drive back to Peggy's, Kitty slid down in her seat, not yet ready to return.

"I'm sorry this isn't a longer visit," Dad said. "How'd it be if next weekend we come up again, Kitty? Maybe you and Claude could catch a movie."

"Really?" I perked up and caught his eye in the rearview mirror.

"Sure. How's that sound, Kitty?"

I caught her looking at me out of the corner of her eye. "That sounds fantastic."

When we got back to Peggy's house, she was sitting on the front steps, smoking a cigarette.

"Oh, great," Kitty muttered. "I thought she'd still be gone."

Mom followed Dad's lead, getting out of the car ahead of us. Cliff, for whatever reason, got out too. Kitty and I followed. We hung back, behind my parents with Cliff. That was the only way I figured I could remain as respectful as Dad had warned me to be. I didn't yet trust my mouth around Peggy Littleton.

Peggy stubbed out her cigarette and stood, crossed her arms. "Sweetheart, I was worried sick."

"We were in town for lunch, so we stopped by and took Kitty for an ice cream," Mom said.

"Well, she's my responsibility now, Mrs. Fisherman. I need to know where she is. Jeb might've been fine with her taking off at her leisure, but I'm not."

"It's Fisher," Mom corrected, an edge in her voice that wasn't present before.

"With all due respect," Dad said, "Kitty has been part of our family her entire life. She's like flesh and blood to us. We've really missed her and wanted to take her out for a short time."

"You ain't related to her, Mister," Peggy shot back. The cruelty in her tone made me bite the insides of my cheeks raw. It was the only way I could keep my trap shut.

But Kitty, in a moment of boldness, took a defiant step toward her aunt. "Peggy, this family is the closest thing to family I've ever had. You're not my mother. Certainly not in charge—"

Peggy snorted and interrupted her. "And what would you know about having a mother? About the same as me. Come on. Let's let these people be on their way."

I couldn't hold it in any longer, or else I'd bite my tongue right off. "*These people?* You think we're so much lower than you, don't you?"

Peggy ignored me and climbed her cement steps to the door. She held it open. "Come on, Kitty."

Kitty turned to me and whispered fiercely, "Do you see what I mean? Find a way to save me from this."

Cliff leaned in, offering his own advice. "You can't stay here, Kitty. Just leave with us. Who's she to stop you?"

"Kids," Dad said, evidently having overheard us. "This has to be handled the right way."

Peggy barked for Kitty another time.

"Peggy!" Kitty yelled. "This isn't fair!" But the slapping of the screen door only punctuated Peggy's senseless dislike for us, for her niece. Before my eyes, I watched Kitty deflate, going belly-up, transforming into the obedient, tiptoeing-around-the-broken-glass girl I'd seen so many times. I grabbed her hand and tugged her toward the car, but her feet remained planted.

"Come on," I said. "We'll deal with the repercussions later."

"No, Claude. I wouldn't put it past her to go after anyone who crosses her. She's that bitter and angry since her husband died. Least that's the talk I've heard. I don't want to make things worse for myself here. Just come back for me next weekend," she pleaded. "The movie, right? Just keep coming back for me, okay?"

"Of course." It was an easy promise to make.

10

THE FOLLOWING SATURDAY, I woke at dawn's first light and stared at the wooden slats above me. Cliff had decided to move into the top bunk, which left the bottom open—mine for the taking. Dad had sold my old bed and bought a desk to fill its space next to the window.

I almost whispered to Cliff above me to see if he was awake too, but I stopped when I remembered he wasn't there. He'd stayed the night with a friend. I rolled over and dangled an arm over the side of the bed, fished through my stored belongings, and pulled out my newest one—a gift.

When we'd returned home from Tonopah after seeing Big John off and visiting Kitty, I came into my room to discover Big John's Bible laying on my bed. My first instinct was akin to panic. Big John had forgotten it. But deep down, I knew the placement in my room was not to be mistaken for negligence. It had been a wildly personal and hefty gift.

I lay on my stomach with his Bible open in front of me, its breaking spine making me wonder how it even stayed together at all. I felt intimidated, perhaps inferior, as I rifled through the pages. Mom had always been the one to read Scripture to us—Dad only on the rare occasion. On my own, I had no real clue where to start. I finished my quick flip-through and in the back of the book discovered a piece of cardstock paper. It was a scribbled list of verse citations filling up the sheet.

Were these significant to him? I skimmed the list and picked the last tag—*EX. 15:2*—to see what it had to say. It took me a few minutes of flipping backward and forward and back again, each minute more flustering than the one before, to come to my senses and use the table of contents. I scanned. *EX* stood for Exodus. Of course. I found it quickly after that and read.

The Lord is my strength and song, and he is become my salvation: he is my God, and I will prepare him an habitation; my father's God, and I will exalt him.

The old stories recounted and read to me as a child came back to life. God had just parted the Red Sea and brought the Israelites safely to the other side, out of the clutches of Pharaoh's army, which had been swept away into the sea. So, they sang praise to God for their rescue and for being their strength.

I closed the Bible. If the Lord could push back the waters and divide a sea, if He could give His people a way out from something so harrowing, then why couldn't He free John from his cancer? Why didn't He swoop in and protect Vern? I swallowed the thought the best I could, but in my inability to understand, a pipe threatened to burst somewhere within me. I knew the leak would prove impossible to stop once it started to gush.

I clamped my eyes shut, allowed a full minute to pass, and then I got up to start the big day I had before me of taking Kitty to the movies.

—

102

Dad and I pulled up to Peggy Littleton's home at one o'clock. The car hadn't even come to a complete stop before I was out the door and up the steps. To my disappointment, Peggy answered, cigarette in hand, after my second knock.

"Hello, Mrs. Littleton. Is Kitty home?" I looked over her shoulder, her small frame not blocking much.

"Oh." She clucked her tongue. "I'm afraid not. She's off with a few of her new girlfriends."

Something felt amiss. "Well, when will she be back?"

"They're having a sleepover."

"But we had plans. Surely she didn't forget?" Kitty wouldn't let this slip from her mind, I knew. "We're supposed to see a movie today."

Peggy set a hand on my forearm, as though to comfort me. I feared my skin would be seared when she finally let go. "She wanted to be with her friends today. I'm sorry, honey. But truthfully, and I know you might not see it now, it's better off this way."

My throat went dry. What's better off, and for whom? What had she done with Kitty? Where had she sent her in order to interfere with our plans? Through gritted teeth, I attempted to be polite. "I know we got off on the wrong foot, and I apologize for that. But I think you have the wrong impression of me. You see, Kitty and I, we've been inseparable since we were babies. She's my best friend."

"Yes, I understand that you were neighbors for a long time—"

"Neighbors? We're more than that. Peggy, you know nothing about our lives. Yet, you seem to hate me for no reason."

"Honey, look. I'm sorry for what happened to your brother. Truly. Death is, well, it's terrible." Her eyes moistened and gathered with pity. "The love of my life exploded in an airplane not long ago. When I saw the smoke far off in the sky that day, I knew right away. I always said nothing good comes out of the desert. Haven't been wrong yet."

"So then, why don't you leave? Move someplace else?" I studied her. Smoke curled from the end of her cigarette. She closed her eyes as she held it to her lips, and I yearned to break through to her.

"Believe me, once I get the OK, I'll be on my way, even if that means Kitty in tow. I think she'd like the East Coast. The rain. The green."

I stopped breathing. I hadn't considered losing Kitty forever.

"Kitty! You in there?" I called out into the silence behind Peggy, praying with all my might she was in the house. "Kitty!"

"She's not home."

Dad skipped up the steps, coming to my aid. "What's the hold up?"

"Kitty's not home," Peggy informed him. "I've told your son here this several times, but he hasn't the manners to leave when he's been asked."

"We made plans to pick her up today," Dad attempted to explain. If only he knew his efforts were futile. "Though I suppose we can pick her up wherever she is now if you'll tell us where to find her."

She closed her steel eyes. When she opened them again a few moments later, she regarded me. "I know a thing or two about heartbreak, 'bout not being able to let something go. But Kitty's learning, and I hope you do too, to cut it off before it gets even more painful."

She gave me no time to formulate a reply before shutting the door, a single wisp of smoke left in her wake. Dad knocked, but he had to know as well as I did that the door wouldn't be reopening.

We left and drove up and down the streets of Tonopah in search of Kitty. I hopped out at the Butler Theatre to see if she was waiting for me there but had no luck. She wasn't at Henry's or the grocery stores or the school. After an hour of searching, my dad made the decision to go home.

I'll keep coming back for you, Kitty. Just like I promised.

11

"COME ON, FLY! Cheer up! You're really that desperate to see her?"

I threw the football back to Richie, but my lackluster throw put him in a tizzy. He stomped over, the ball wedged under his armpit. "Alright, if you're that hung up on this, then I guess it's my job to help ya out."

"And how do you figure you'll do that?"

"One thing you might not know about me, Fly, is how good I am at hatching plans."

"One to bust Kitty outta her aunt's place?"

"I don't know about that. Sounds against the law. But maybe a plan for you to see her?"

"What're you thinking?"

"You said it'll be impossible to see Kitty when her aunt's around, right? Well, what time of day isn't her aunt with her?"

"When she's at school?"

"Bingo!" he said. "We'll ditch school and drive up during the day. We got an extra car parked round back of our house. Never gets used. My parents wouldn't even know it was missing."

"You knucklehead. That's all illegal too."

"Yeah, well, it's better than making Kitty a fugitive, isn't it?"

What he proposed made me pause. His ridiculous idea elbowed its way into my brain and grabbed hold of me. "Do you think it could really work?"

"Sure. Look, here's what I'm thinking. We fake sick as soon as we get to school and get sent home. Then bam! Tonopah bound!"

"We won't be able to fool Mrs. Newton. There's no way. She'll see right through us."

"Fine. Then we target Miss Dunlop. She's afraid of germs, and she's too sweet to know the difference since she doesn't have kids of her own. Less experience with these shenanigans."

"How do you know she's afraid of getting sick?"

"Remember when Buddy Clark puked during the assembly last year? Miss Dunlop shooed him out of the gymnasium so fast. Sent him straight home. Didn't want the rest of us sick."

"Alright, genius, so how're we gonna do this?"

He thought about it a moment before raising one finger. "We walk into school and linger outside the office, just in her view. This part's a little gross, but before we walk inside, we stuff our mouths full of water and chewed up cereal or something. Pretend vomit. Then we let it spew there in the hallway. Act miserable, you know. All that. She'll have to send us home before anyone else gets a look at us."

"You don't think she'll send us to the nurse?"

"We'll be home free. Trust me."

"What about calling home? Won't they notify our parents? Or have them come get us?"

"My parents will be working. What about yours?"

"My mom doesn't work anymore. But on Thursdays she always goes to a friend's for tea."

"Then we go on Thursday."

"I don't know if I trust you in making this work, but let's do it." The excitement within me almost made me forget the second half of the plan. "Wait. What about Kitty? She'll be in school. There's no way we'll be able to sneak in there or bust her out."

"Shoot." He rubbed his neck. "I guess I hadn't thought that far ahead."

"Catch her at lunch recess?"

"Now you're thinkin'!"

With our less-than-fool-proof plan in place, I strutted home surer of myself than I'd been in a long time. My mind focused on one thing and one thing only—Kitty May Ralph. Maybe I was hung up on the thrill of skipping school and flying out of town in a car we had no business driving. But only just a little.

———

When I got to school Thursday morning, I found Richie leaning against the side of the many steps leading to the front doors. "Alright. Here," Richie said, dropping into my palm a fistful of cereal and nuts. "Chew it up real good and put a little of this in your mouth." He pulled out of his bag a bottle and pressed it to my lips to drink.

I nearly spat out my mouthful and tried my best to hold it in.

"Don't worry," he said through a fit of laughter. "It's just water, vinegar, and a bunch of spices from my mom's cabinet. Just to make our puke look a little more . . . pukey. Work your cheeks so you don't look like a balloon." I did as he said. "I'm going to go in, wait in the bathroom a minute, and then come out puking. You stay out here a minute or two, and then come inside doing your own thing. So it doesn't look like we're doing this together."

I nodded, and he left me. I leaned against the side of the

stairs, my mouth full of mushy fake barf that I feared would turn real any moment. One thing was for certain; my gagging wouldn't be fake. I counted to 120, praying with every number that no one would come up to speak with me. But everyone was inside by now, already in their classrooms.

By the time I opened the heavy door, Richie was already in the hallway, near Miss Dunlop's desk, doubled over. His hands clutched his stomach, and a horrible retching sound came from his mouth. He spewed all over the floor. His moan echoed down the hall. Miss Dunlop flew out of her chair, her hands covering her mouth.

I stumbled away from the door and let my feet slap loudly against the wood floor to gain her attention before I dropped to my knees and let it rip. I moaned and wiped my brow when I was done, giving the best performance I could.

"Oh, my! Oh, dear!" Miss Dunlop rushed to my side, rubbing my shoulder as I stayed on all fours. "Oh, my! Claude! What's come over you boys?" She rested the back of her hand on my forehead a moment. "You do feel warm," she murmured then walked over to Richie and felt his forehead too.

He wiped his mouth with his sleeve dramatically. Still clutching his stomach, he said, "We're going to be late for class. Mrs. Newton will paddle us."

"Oh, no. You boys aren't going to class. We can't afford to be passing this bug around. You're going home. Now." She sidestepped around the piles of faux vomit, grimaced, and turned her head away. "We'll get Mr. Mulligan to clean up this mess. Let's get you boys out of here. I'll go phone your folks to come pick ya's up."

Panic inched up my spine. "Oh, Miss Dunlop," I moaned. "I can get myself home. My dad's at work, and my mom's not really in a position to come. She's . . . you know . . . with my brother and all." As the words came out, I crossed a line I never thought I'd cross. I knew I was the biggest loser in the world. But I was a desperate guy, walking a tightrope, grasping at whatever I could to keep from falling further into failure.

Miss Dunlop pursed her perfectly lined lips together. Sadness knitted between her brows. "Sure, sure. I'm sure she has enough stress on her plate as is. No sense in making her rush down here, considering you only live a short walk away."

"Me too," Richie moaned. "Just across the street."

"Right." She looked around, deliberating. "I want to make sure you boys get there okay. I'll drive you. I'll let Mr. Mathews and Mrs. Newton know when we get back. Come on now. I don't want your germs floatin' around here."

She shooed us out the front doors. Richie and I panicked but kept up our ruse. We loaded into her Woodie wagon. She dropped Richie at home first, then me. Thankfully, Miss Dunlop didn't insist on coming to the door and speaking to our mothers. Not that either of them were home, but that fact alone would have made her worry all the more. I waited, a rattlesnake nest of nerves in my belly. An hour later, Richie finally pulled up.

I ran out and climbed in the car. But after taking one look at Richie's pale face, I asked, "What's wrong? You really getting sick?"

He shook his head. "Just . . . just a little nervous is all."

"How come?"

Richie looked sheepishly at me and winced. "This is only my second time."

"Second time what?"

"Driving."

"You mean to tell me you decided to take a car you don't even know how to drive?"

"I got over here, didn't I?"

"You drove, what? Half a mile?"

"Well, do you know how?" he retorted.

"Sure. Dad's let me behind the wheel a couple times."

"Alright, then switch me. You drive."

The blood drained from my cheeks. This was much different than Dad letting me loose on mountain roads.

A knowing look spread over Richie's face. "Thought so. I can do this. The one time my old man took me out, he gave me the full rundown. I just gotta remember."

"Step one. Turn the key."

He shot daggers at me and started the engine. When we finally got on the road, his driving wasn't so bad. Other than his knuckles blanching white as snow and a few awkward lurches here and there. But it was nothing worse than how my driving would've been. Once we got onto the 95, Richie's death grip on the wheel relaxed and the knots in my stomach did too as each mile brought us closer to Kitty.

That is, until Tonopah actually came into view.

"Drive straight, man!" I hissed. "You're gonna get us pulled over."

"Sorry." Richie's white knuckles were back. He pulled the bill of his hat lower and sat up as straight as he could, no doubt trying to make himself taller, older. The car puttered along, us jittery in our seats. We parked across the street from the school.

"When do you think their lunch is? Same time as ours?"

"I'd reckon so. How much longer?"

I looked at my watch. "Maybe fifteen or twenty minutes?"

Richie stretched out his arms and rested against the window. "So, what's the deal with you two?"

"What?"

"You and Kitty. You guys madly in love or something?"

Were we? I couldn't speak for Kitty. "She's, you know, one of my closest friends."

"Friends, huh? So, if my evil aunt dragged me away, you'd

ditch school and risk a lot of trouble to come visit me too?" He grinned big and toothy, knowing he'd cornered me.

"Maybe if you were as pretty as her."

He laughed. I stared at the school, imagining Kitty sitting at her desk, taking notes as her teacher scribbled across the blackboard. Was she paying attention? Thinking of me? Could she sense me out here waiting for her?

Twenty minutes passed before we saw any students exit the building. In the course of five minutes, the field between us and the school was peppered with pickup games of football and kids hunting for horny toads.

"Let's go," I said. We got out of the car.

I crossed the street, my heart rattling my ribcage with its pounding. I suddenly didn't care if a teacher saw me. Kitty was here somewhere, so close. We jogged onto the school's property and received puzzled stares from some of the kids. I asked a group of them if they knew where I could find Kitty Ralph. They pointed us in the right direction, toward a group of girls lined up and leaning one-by-one against the brick wall of the school.

I could've picked her out from miles away.

She stood second from the end, her face turned away from me as she gabbed to the girl with the black bob beside her. I approached her, while Richie lagged behind. The friend tapped Kitty on the shoulder and pointed my way. Kitty turned and studied me, unmoving. My confidence waned, but I kept walking. She pushed off the wall and met me in the middle.

"Claude . . ." She spoke my name with an air of disbelief. "What on earth are you doing here?"

My tongue twisted. All the words I wanted to say tripped over themselves. "I just had to see you."

"You're gonna get us both in trouble."

Of all the things I expected from today, Kitty's animosity

wasn't one of them. "After what happened last weekend—"

"You mean when you stood me up?"

I searched her face. Was she joking? "No, I didn't."

"You . . ." Her forehead wrinkled. "Peggy answered the phone that morning. You . . . you called and bailed."

"And you believe something Peggy said? Kitty, I never called. I showed up Saturday, and you weren't there. I'd never cancel on you."

She huffed and crossed her arms. "You really stopped by?"

"Yeah. Peggy said you were off with friends, spending the night with some girls from school."

"I was, but only because I was hurt that you weren't coming."

"She lied to you, Kitty. She also told me she might be moving the two of you away."

Tears brimmed in her eyes. She looked away. In her indignation, it felt like she'd unfastened herself from me entirely.

"Kitty, talk to me. Please."

"What do you want me to say?" She glanced backward, toward her friends who stood at attention, curiously watching our exchange.

"I don't know. Anything would be nice. I came clear up here to see you. Risking my literal hide."

"You shouldn't be here."

"Why?"

"Because it makes it harder. There's no changing this separation. You're there, and I'm here—"

"We're both right here, right now."

"You know what I mean. Peggy is bound and determined to get out of here. Remember what you said about ending up facedown here in this desert dirt? As soon as she hears from my dad—what will he care—that she has permission, we're gone,

Fly."

"You have to fight this, Kitty. Call your dad and—"

"And what? I'm at the mercy of people who have never truly put me first a day in their lives. You think they'll listen to me? That what I have to say matters? It's so easy for you to tell me what to do when you aren't the one living it."

I suddenly felt like she saw me as the bad guy when all I ever wanted was to protect her. "You told me to come back for you, Kitty. To keep coming back for you. That's what I'm doing, and that's what I'll continue to do."

"Well, stop it. I shouldn't have said that."

I couldn't believe the words that were falling from her mouth. This strange twist of events made no sense at all. Kitty wiped beneath her eyes with her knuckle. "I'll always be your friend, Claude," she said. "But you really ought to go home before you get us both in a world of trouble. It's not worth it."

I heard her version of the truth behind her words: *I'm not worth it.*

"You're giving up?"

Before I could reach out to stop her, she stepped away and rushed past her friends, disappearing into the school. Richie touched my shoulder and whispered that we should go. It was then that I realized we'd attracted quite a crowd.

Another nail in my coffin. I couldn't move. Richie dragged me away to the car. My legs only worked by some involuntary force. A pounding in my ears drowned out everything around me. The whistles from a teacher. Richie starting the engine. His nervous, incessant jabbering. Even the siren of the policeman, pulling us over. The pain carved me from the inside out, robbing me clean, all my useful and shiny bits seized, leaving me a dusty, depleted pit, much like the surrounding hills.

12

GOLDFIELD TEENAGERS, CLAUDE Fisher and Richard Garrison, were caught bringing mischief to town on a school day, having stolen a car belonging to Mr. and Mrs. S. V. Garrison and going for a joyride rather than attending class. Neither child has a driver's license.

We made Tonopah's paper. As if being caught and reprimanded for our misbehavior wasn't bad enough, small-town news reporting ensured that our reputations were smeared with a hearty helping of mud. Not that word wouldn't have gotten around anyway, but still, the newspaper mention didn't help.

For our truancy from school, Richie and I received a week's worth of in-school suspension. Rather than joining our peers at recess or lunch, we were ordered around by the cantankerous old custodian, Harry Mulligan, who capitalized on our folly by making us do everything from scrubbing toilets to wiping down inches of dust in the gymnasium.

Outside of school, our punishments were quite different. I honestly wasn't sure which one of us got it worse. Richie's parents grounded him for one month solid. His mom even took to walking him to and from school every day, dropping him off like the youngsters, checking him in at the front desk with Miss Dunlop, who couldn't quite look at us the same once she'd learned how deeply we'd tricked her.

But my parents didn't ground me or treat me like a six-year-old. They didn't yell or pile on chores or whack me with a belt like I probably deserved. I wished they had. Because my dad's silence in the car when he picked me up from the county jail was bad enough. And the tears—the weight of knowing I'd made my father cry—were far worse than any other punishment I could've ever received.

I begged him to talk to me, to hear how sorry I was and to forgive me, to understand my lapse in judgment and my desire to protect Kitty.

He finally looked away from the road toward me and said, "Tell me what to do, Claude."

"I thought you're the one who's supposed to tell me."

"Tell me what to do to help you accept this. I understand why you wanted to check on Kitty, but that doesn't make it right. Do you need help? Do you need to talk to someone?"

"You sound like Mom," I muttered. The suggestion rattled me. Like no one heard me the first time. Like he didn't understand me after all. "I don't need someone's useless words. I need the two things I can't have."

"You can't have Vernon or Kitty back," he snapped. "And not being able to accept either one is turning into a problem. A big problem that could've gotten you killed or arrested today." Dad rarely got heated, but his voice filled the car.

For some reason, that old pipe deep down inside of me was preparing to burst again. I looked away and tried to hold myself together. "I'm so angry, Dad," I admitted.

He blew out a deep breath and reached over to squeeze my shoulder. The warmth of his touch soothed me. "Being angry isn't wrong, Claude. I'm angry too."

"With me?"

"Life. Circumstances. Vern being taken too young . . . Jeb's carelessness. Kitty moving away. John's cancer. Him not telling me about it sooner."

"Are you angry with God?"

Dad moved his hand back to the wheel and answered slowly. "Sometimes I want to be. But no."

"Well, I am." My blood ran with fury, and I wished I had something to sink my fists into right then. "How could you not be?"

He waited a moment and said, "I just keep going back to this—no tragedy in all of history has ever come as a surprise to God. Not one. Not even Vernon's. Not Kitty's."

"And that makes it all the worse," I muttered.

We pulled up to our house. Dad killed the ignition, though neither of us moved to get out.

"What do you mean, Claude?"

"I just don't get it." I looked at him, exasperated. "In all God's sovereignty, His all-knowingness, why didn't He stop these things from happening?" I asked.

Dad rubbed his chin, and I noticed the weathering of his hands, the deep crevices blackened over the years with oil and grease. "I used to tell you boys a lot of stories when you were young, didn't I?"

"Yeah." I furrowed my brows. "What's that have to do with anything?"

"I'm just thinking . . . As fun as it was to make up spook stories or tell you about this town when I was a kid, maybe I should've spent more time telling you about the things I went through."

My breathing slowed, the fire in my veins cooling as I feared what he might say.

Dad licked his chapped lips and said, "I used to ask myself that same question you just asked when I was a kid growing up with no dad, no sister. My memory's fuzzy after all these years, but I can still to this day remember my mother up one night, fit to be tied, shaking her fists and asking God why He was punishing her. Why He stole her baby girl away. Why He couldn't have helped my dad slip out of the mine in the nick of time. And after that night, I was good and convinced that God didn't actually care about us at all.

"I saw the hardships around us. The death and disease. The crime and greed. How were Mama and I going to survive? Make ends meet? If God wasn't going to protect us, I decided that I didn't need Him. I'd step up and take care of us myself. But little did I know at the time, He was protecting and providing for us all along. He sent us miners and families, all good people, who rented out our spare room and gave us income. He sent Mr. Brooks next door," he said as he pointed to our house.

"You know," he continued, "I grew up in the same house Kitty did. That's where your grandma and I lived. And when Mr. Brooks moved into the house we live in now, well, he took me under his wing and gave me a job at his new auto shop. He talked to me about God sometimes while we worked, and he taught me all the things my father would have. In fact, Mr. Brooks became some sort of father to me. And that's why when he passed, he left his home and business to my name. God was working; He was good and faithful even when I'd turned my back and written Him off."

Dad paused, and his face softened. "Claude, bad things are inevitable—it's a fallen world, after all. But you have the choice to carry those bad things with you all your life or not. If you allow anger to consume you, oh boy, it will. It will morph you into something unrecognizable and swallow you whole, so you end up bitter and depressed like Jebediah Ralph. But I've found it's a heck of a lot easier to lay it all down and let the Lord carry the weight. Trust in Him to sort everything out in His way, on His time."

I stared my father down. Why, in all my years, hadn't he told me these things before? I glanced at our home, thinking of this generous Mr. Brooks. Then I looked toward Kitty's, where Dad had cried over his father, where Kitty had cried over hers.

"It's hard to trust in God when I want Jeb to pay for what he's done," I said.

"I know. But Claude, it's not your job to seek justice on behalf of Vernon or Kitty. That falls on God. He sorts it out. Not you."

I shook my head. "So, then what is my job? Twiddle my thumbs and wait around for God to punish him? Go to the jail and give Jeb a big ol' hug, maybe thank him for ruining my life?"

Dad chuckled. "Who knows, your mercy and forgiveness just might be what makes him seek repentance."

"Repentance!" I snorted and slapped the dash. "You think someone like Jeb would ever change?"

"If God led me out of my darkness, who's to say He can't do the same for Jeb too? And who's to say He can't use you like He used Mr. Brooks to help me?"

I thought about this a moment. I wasn't sure I wanted to be used in that way.

"Once you understand the grace that God has extended to all of us, everything changes, my boy," Dad said with finality. "You want rest? Peace? I'll tell you what Mr. Brooks told me—look to the cross."

"Look to the . . ." I scratched my head. "What the heck does that even mean?"

Dad chuckled. "I have faith that you'll figure it out one day, just like I did. Just don't look too long. Jesus isn't hanging up there anymore."

My head spun. I didn't understand. I think Dad could tell. "I need to get back to work. Go inside and face your mother. She's worried sick, I'm sure," Dad said. He nodded toward my door, cueing me to head inside. "I love you, Claude."

In all the world, the myriad of children throughout time unlucky enough to grow up without fathers, God had looked at me and decided to exclude me from that sad list by giving me Leonard Fisher.

"I love you too, Dad."

—

Dad worked a later night than usual, making up for lost time spent dealing with me. We'd no sooner sat down at the table as a family when a gunshot cracked outside, followed by another, and another. All four of us shot straight up and ran to the window. The sky, though brilliant hues of orange and purple, couldn't veil the man approaching from up the street.

"What on earth . . ." Mom took one look and made for the door, none of us able to stop her from marching outside. "What's going on?" she yelled, the three of us at her heels.

"Pretty sure that's the beast that killed my girl the other day!" Bob Dunn, who lived on the corner, hollered as he triumphantly paraded closer. His rifle was slung over his shoulder, his round belly jiggling with every step. Bob's whistling cut through the air, a happy little out-of-place song.

My eyes caught sight of a lone coyote, laid out dead in front of Kitty's old house. I nudged Cliff. He grimaced when he spotted the lifeless animal, its silver coat speckled with blood.

"There goes my appetite," he muttered and headed back

into the house.

"Bob!" Dad hollered and waved. "What's with the late hunting?"

Bob Dunn adjusted his belt as he strutted toward us.

Mom hopped off the porch in a huff and met him face-to-face in front of the Ralph's old home.

Dad and I stayed on the porch—front row seats to this showdown. "Aren't you gonna help Mom?" I asked him.

He laughed. "Does it look like she needs help to you?"

"No, but Dunn might."

"This is unacceptable!" Mom shrieked at him. "What are you thinking?"

"What?" he asked and truly seemed confused.

"You can't be aiming your gun at people's houses!"

He pointed to the empty home with the muzzle of his gun. "No one lives here anymore, do they?"

"That's not the point." Mom threw her hands to her hips and glowered.

"Alright, alright. I'm sorry." He held up his hands in defeat. "But this mangy beast killed Wilhelmina."

"Who's Wilhelmina?" Mom lifted a hand to cover her mouth, her brows knitting together with worry.

"Who's Wilhelmina? Who's Wilhelmina?" Bob looked at her with total exasperation. "My hen!"

Mom's face contorted. She drew in a deep breath. "You mean to tell me, you shot over here, towards my home and my family all to avenge a dead chicken? A *dead chicken?*"

"Come on, Virginia. You act like I was shooting at your family. I've been looking for that coyote for days. There I was sittin' on my porch when I spotted him slinkin' around. Couldn't believe my eyes at first. I had a clear shot. I had to take it." Bob sighed and rubbed his bald head. "I swear I wasn't tryin' to upset ya."

"I know, Bob. And for the millionth time, you can call me Ginny." Mom hugged herself against the chill of the evening and took a moment to compose herself. "I just don't want any more accidents. I'm glad you got your coyote," she said, tone clipped, hands trembling. She spun on her heels and stalked past me and Dad, back into the house.

Dad followed her, but I remained.

Bob moved toward the coyote. Out of curiosity, I did too. "Somethin' not quite right in this one's head," he mumbled as he bent over and lifted it by the scruff of its neck. "Better he's out of the way now, 'fore he caused any more trouble." He slung the dead coyote over the shoulder opposite of his rifle. "See ya around, Claude." He walked away, whistling the same tune as before, leaving me alone in front of Kitty's old home. The same home my dad was raised in.

I looked at the front door in all its rundown glory, the portal through which my favorite person used to skip out to meet me every day. The smooth finish of the aging wood wore thin. Within the rough, exposed grains, I saw Kitty and myself, where we'd started and what we'd been reduced to. Out of habit, I skipped up the porch steps and knocked. Almost called out her name just to remember what it felt like. I tried the knob. The door gave way, inviting me into the vacant space.

I walked inside. The first thing that struck me was the chill. The house wasn't warm and inviting. The Ralph's stove sulked in the corner; no fires had filled its empty belly for weeks now. I moved through the living room and into the kitchen. Dust as thick as snow covered the valance above the window. I looked out the window and into mine, smiling as I realized this had been Kitty's view of me for years. But the knowledge that we'd never look out our windows and see each other again extinguished all tenderness.

I walked away and down the hallway. The home had two bedrooms, just like ours. I opened one door and peeked inside.

Left behind belongings of Jeb's were strewn around the room. I closed it and went to the other, pausing. Was this a violation of Kitty's privacy? I twisted the knob before I'd made up my mind.

Save for her bed and a wicker chair that looked like it would crumble with the weight of a penny, the bareness of Kitty's room only accentuated my loneliness. One single item hung by a nail on the wall—a calendar made by hand. It still displayed September. Taking the liberty, I ripped off the top paper, revealing the current month of October beneath. Circled in black pen, the date of the ninth had *Claude* written across it.

I blinked. That was tomorrow.

I took a seat on her bed. *So, this is where she slept. This is where she laid her head every night and slipped into the palm of nightfall, which held her and listened to her as she prayed her prayers and thought her thoughts.*

I lay down and tried to picture what it was like for her. *Was she ever cold?* I would never let her go cold. *Was she ever lonely?* I would always be there for her. *Was she ever scared?* I would protect her for all time. All the things I'd pledged to her before our worlds flipped upside down were still true. Though I couldn't help but realize I'd already failed. I couldn't keep her warm, couldn't keep her company, couldn't keep her safe. I couldn't even keep her here.

On the eve of my fourteenth birthday, I closed my eyes and cried in Kitty's bed. How did my heart still beat so strongly for the impossible? And how would it ever stop?

13

I LEFT EARLY the next morning before daybreak and before anyone had risen. I mounted my bike for the first time in weeks and sped away from my house. My tires hummed as they spun, harmonizing with the morning breeze as the rest of town lay still. Claude, the lone rider.

The darkness pushed me along. I sped up, the sense of solitude churning my pedals. Light stirred above as I went. A new day was dawning. A tall sign, unreadable in the dim light, soon came into focus. I already knew what it said: *Goldfield Cemetery*. I parked my bike at the entrance and proceeded by foot, weaving around the quiet, dusty graves until I reached Vern's.

"It's my birthday," I muttered. I sat down in the dirt and hugged my jacket around me. "But you probably know that already, don't you? You probably know everything now." I stared at the rock marking his grave and the small wooden cross erected beside it.

Look to the cross, Dad had said.

I was looking. Now what? "You know, I used to think I had

it all figured out. Turns out I know diddly-squat." I wiped my eyes with my sleeve. "I miss you, brother. We're all so lost without you." I thought of Mom and her feeble attempts at normalcy. Dad and his fractured, passive nature. Cliff and the quiet distance unspooling from within him.

"Vern, I don't want to run from this pain my whole life. But the truth is I am. I wish at every turn I could trade places with you. I'm getting a little nervous that this is how it's always gonna be." The more thought I gave to everything, the more hopeless it all seemed. And the more hopeless it seemed, the more I resigned. "Remember those soldiers you told me about? The ones who lost their arms or legs, but still felt pain in their missing limbs?" I swallowed hard. "Is this pain ever going to end? Can't you talk to someone up there for me? Pull some strings? Tell 'em to make this better?"

Minutes stretched out before me, waiting patiently for me to fill the air again. But the words wouldn't emerge. I looked up. A hawk soared overhead, its body a dark silhouette against the awakening sky. I followed the bird until it disappeared from view, briefly imagining that it had picked me up by its talons and taken me with it.

Everyone at home ought to be awake by now, I figured. Maybe they were wondering where I was? Maybe no one had noticed at all? I didn't want anyone to see me here, label me as the town weirdo, coming out and talking to the dirt. So, I stood and brushed the dust from my clothes, unable to bring myself to say goodbye.

I left. The morning breeze was brisk and stung my wet cheeks as I whizzed home. The sun continued to rise. The town continued to wake.

A basket of eggs sat on our porch when I got home, a note slipped inside. I plucked the paper from the basket and read, "Wilhelmina's final dozen. Sorry again. Bob." I carried the basket inside and found my family sitting at the kitchen table.

"Claude." Dad sighed with relief when I entered. "Where've you been?"

"See, I told you guys he was fine," Cliff quipped.

Mom turned away when she saw me, bustling from the table over to the stove. Her nervous energy set our home abuzz as she fluttered around the kitchen like a gnat and refused to acknowledge my presence. Probably too fed up with my disappearance, yet again.

"Sorry, Dad. I had something to do."

He lifted his brows, waiting for more. I set the basket of eggs on the table.

"Someone to visit," I mumbled, sheepishly turning my face away. "I, um, went to the cemetery."

He glanced to my mother and back to me, nodding with understanding now. "Let someone know next time."

"Okay, I will." I went to my mom and set my hands on her shoulders. "I'm sorry."

She looked at me, the anguish so clearly visible in her eyes, and offered a tight smile.

"Mom," I pleaded. "I really am sorry. I'm not trying to make this harder on you guys."

Reaching up, she pressed her warm hand to my cheek and whispered, "I know, honey. I think we're all trying our best."

For a split moment I wondered if I truly was. *Was the person I was on track to become matching up with the person I wanted to be?*

We all sat and ate breakfast together, which I couldn't help but realize was a rare occurrence these days. Everyone always seemed to be going separate directions now. Our schedules and our waffling degrees of grief kept us apart. Had it not been for my noted absence this morning, this fellowship around the table might not have happened.

No one made a comment about my birthday. I don't think anyone had the brain power to even remember. So, it remained for the time being a secret between me and Vern, which somehow filled the cracks in my spirit. With the renewed sense of togetherness, it was all I could have ever asked for anyway.

—

The school day passed. When I hopped on my bike to head home, a glint of silver against russet dirt caught my eye. I leaned down, and when I picked up the quarter, I could've sworn that Mr. Washington winked at me.

"Looks like today's my lucky day after all," I murmured, shoving the quarter into my pocket. I glanced skyward. "Thanks for putting in a good word to the Big Man, Vern."

My route home changed, suddenly including a detour to the drugstore. There, I robustly asked Mr. Ficklin for a cola. He said I was lucky; he only had a limited supply left. He handed over the cold soda. I laid my quarter in his palm, telling him to keep the change.

"You sure about that?"

The change would've been nice. How many things could I have purchased with the remaining twenty cents? Several things floated into mind, but I nodded my head anyway.

"Looks like we're both having a good day," he chuckled. My quarter clattered into his cash register. "What's the special occasion?"

I let the soda pool in my mouth, fizzing and popping and delighting my taste buds in every way. The liquid was so sticky sweet and satisfying that it took everything in me not to chug the whole thing in two seconds flat. But I wanted to savor it. Or at least try. "Not sure how special it is, but today's my birthday."

"Your birthday, huh?" His eyes twinkled. "Birthdays are always special, at least when you're young. When ya get to my age, well, you stop having birthdays."

"You can't just stop having birthdays."

"Sure ya can."

"Because you don't wanna get older?" I took another long, unhurried drink.

"No, because ya lose count!" He grabbed another glass from under the counter, filling it to the brim with dark, bubbly goodness from the fountain. He set the full glass in front of me, watching my eyes widen. "On the house. Happy birthday, Claude."

Alright, Vern. You're two for two.

"Just don't get too sentimental about it. You already overpaid for that first one." He laughed and winked. Then his gaze drifted out the window. I followed it, and together we watched a lady, her dark hair pinned up on her head, her long coat grazing the ground as she pushed a baby carriage along the wooden sidewalk.

"I think I've seen her walking around town before. Who is she?" I asked.

"Refugee." He stooped over, leaning his elbows on the counter. "Poor gal doesn't speak a lick of English, though maybe that's a blessing in disguise. Can't understand the nasty insults that come from Roy Davies, that wretch."

Distance grew between her and the store. I studied her back until she was out of sight. "Refugee? The war is over. Why isn't she home?"

"How can you return home when there ain't a home to return to? Hers is probably a pile of rubble. According to Miss Bianchi, she left right in time . . . before they stopped letting people into the States. Spent a stint out East, maybe Tennessee? Pennsylvania? Can't remember now. Rumor has it that she had other children too. Whether through circumstances or death, they ain't together now. Somehow, she quietly slid into town with her baby a few months ago."

I chugged what remained of my first soda and started on the second, feeling a twinge of guilt as I enjoyed my treat while that woman padded along, uprooted and alone. I imagined myself running after her, tapping her on the shoulder, holding up my palms in peace, if only to be near another's grief, one different from my own.

"Claude?"

I snapped out of the trance I wasn't aware I'd fallen under. "Sorry. What's that?"

"I said, you got any big birthday plans?"

Lifting my glass, I nodded to him. "This count?"

"Sure does." He knocked on the counter and set himself to tasks around the store. I gulped down my soda, suddenly wanting to return home. Thankful I had a home to return to at all. I opened my mouth to thank Mr. Ficklin, but the loudest belch I'd ever heard roared out instead.

He started laughing so hard he had to wipe his eyes. "Good thing you're the only one in here right now or that might've scared everyone away."

"Excuse me," I mumbled, still a bit shocked at myself. "I've gotta get home. Thanks, Mr. Ficklin."

"Tell your folks hello. Cliff too."

I told him I would and headed out. I continued my detour by stopping by Dad's auto shop. But the place was locked up, the *Closed* sign on full display. I peered in the windows and thought it odd but headed home. My parent's car was gone when I arrived. I found Cliff at the table, scratching away at his homework.

"Where's Mom and Dad? The shop's closed."

"Dunno. They weren't here when I got home."

I took a seat across from Cliff. "I've got a load of math and history to study. You're lucky. Only one more year after this one."

"Maybe," he said. "Adam Bates dropped out last year and is doing alright for himself up in Reno from what I hear. Plenty of kids don't finish school."

"Wait. You're thinking of dropping out? Mom and Dad won't have that." I was convinced he'd do anything to get out of here.

He glanced up at me briefly and shrugged. That's when I noticed his eye.

"Hey, what happened?" I leaned forward to inspect the wound.

Cliff touched his eyebrow and dried blood flaked onto his finger. "Just a little scuffle."

"You got in a fight? With who? What happened?"

"It wasn't much of anything, really. You know Wilson?"

I shook my head no.

"Tall guy? Vern's age? Super hairy?"

I shook my head.

"No? Well, he grabbed Maisy where he shouldn't have." He went on to explain how a group of them had been chatting in the hall when Wilson joined the circle and edged in next to Maisy. Cliff, standing directly across from her, noticed her face suddenly pale. It had twisted into disgust and panic right as he noticed Wilson's arm fall back to his own side.

Cliff had shot forward. "Did you touch her?" he asked Wilson, who set his jaw and shook his head. He turned to Maisy. "Did he touch you?" She nodded once. Cliff shoved Wilson out of the circle. But the circle moved, surrounding the two as they duked it out.

Wilson's knuckles had smashed into Cliff's brow, but Cliff cracked Wilson's nose with his fist. It had run like a faucet, blood splattering all over the worn hallway floors.

I shot out of my chair, blood pumping with excitement. "I

can't believe I missed that! Wait, what happened next?"

"That was it. Mr. Vaughan broke it up and escorted Wilson down to the nurse."

"Did you get in trouble?"

"Nah. Maisy told him I was only standing up for her."

"What about with Mom and Dad?"

"Dunlop called home and told Mom. They'll probably ground me." He didn't seem concerned. "I figured you might've been called out of class to mop up Wilson's blood."

"My suspension ended yesterday. Otherwise, I guarantee you, it would've been either me or Richie."

"Mulligan really took advantage of you two, huh?"

"I swear he didn't do his job at all while he had us at his disposal. We worked double time and double speed to catch him up on his duties every day."

"Why work when you can have a couple of students do it for you?"

The back door slapped open behind me. A cool gust of wind rushed inside. But when I turned around, no one was there. I started to get up, grumbling about the faulty latch when my parents appeared from around the corner. Mom led the way inside, carrying something small and pan-shaped with a sheet draped over the top. Dad brought up the rear, a guitar in his arms, his fingers plucking a slightly disheveled and out-of-tune version of the birthday song.

Cliff glanced at me and winked.

Mom set her mystery object down on the table. She whipped off the sheet, revealing a delectable-looking screwball cake.

"Happy birthday, sweetheart."

I was so fixed on the cake that I hadn't realized Dad had stopped playing the guitar, let alone considered why he had one at all.

He slipped the strap over his head and held the instrument out to me. A few scuff marks graced the front, but it seemed in relatively nice condition.

Cliff whistled and reached out to run his finger along the smooth wood grain.

"Go ahead," Dad said, extending his arm out farther.

Hesitantly, I took the guitar from him. "This is for me?" I hiked my leg onto the chair, propping the guitar on my thigh and giving it a few out-of-key strums.

"All yours. I can remember a few chords I picked up when I was younger, if you want me to show you?" Dad offered.

"Please, by all means."

As Mom cut the cake, Cliff and I watched Dad fiddle with the guitar, adjusting the pegs until it was in tune and then rearranging his fingers over and over again on the strings until he found the sound he was searching for.

"Where'd you learn to play guitar?" I asked. *And where'd you get this, and how'd you afford it?*

Dad chuckled. I couldn't tell if it was at my question or out of the glee of playing music for the first time in decades. "My dad had one. He wasn't around to teach me, obviously. But I always loved to mess with it. Then one of my teachers at school showed me a few things. The rest I picked up on my own."

He moved his fingers with more assurance, muscle memory waking up from years of slumber. He formed shapes that didn't yet make sense to me and plucked at the strings in spider-like motions.

For the first time in my life, I realized where Vern had gotten the big, lopsided grin that had always managed to enliven me. From my father. I'd just never seen it until now.

14

IN THE WEEKS that followed, I did a lot of thinking about anger and justice and God because of the talk with my dad. Could it be true that I was seeking justice and immediate retribution where I ought to be seeking grace and forgiveness? Fighting for control rather than handing the reins to God? Despite how badly I wished it to be so, I knew that Vern couldn't be awakened from the dead. Kitty wouldn't be moving back home. I wasn't so far removed from reality that I couldn't understand these unfavorable truths. What, then, could recompense my loss? The questions swirled in my mind, weaving around and around themselves until they were a snarl of knots that I grew too tired to untangle.

On Thanksgiving Day, Dad got the call that Big John had passed away. He hung up the phone, his face mute and ashen, and left the house for refuge at the shop. No one heard from him for hours.

Mom finally asked Cliff and me to head down there to check on him. We could hear clangs and crashes almost a block away. When we got there, Cliff peered through the window, hands cupped around his face. I watched him stop shivering from the cold. His eyes pinched. The corners of his mouth drooped. He turned and held out an arm to prevent me from looking.

But I wasn't the small, shrimpy brother who needed protection anymore. I pushed him aside and looked for myself, my breath fogging up the window. I saw our father, sweat dripping down his forehead in thick beads as he threw wrenches, pry bars, and anything else he could get his hands on at the steel garage wall.

I looked away and mounted my bike, not bothering to wait for Cliff as I knew he'd be right behind me. Neither of us spoke the whole way home. We told Mom that Dad would be home soon, which thankfully he was. Good and steady Dad, even when he was broken.

The days passed slowly, yet somehow, they turned into weeks, and the weeks into months, and eventually the new year. Vern's absence was hardly spoken of during these stuffy winter months. We all held our breaths, afraid to say his name, afraid to be the one to break the silence, afraid to remind each other.

Snow carpeted the ground a handful of times in meager attempts to bring us cheer, or despair, depending on how we looked at it. Most folks, including myself, didn't mind. I liked a nice change of scenery. A bright, distracting splash of ivory where otherwise nothing but sand and dust existed. Snow was a good way to excuse the bitter cold.

And as it melted in the spring, the four Fishers who remained fell into a collective lull, each of us bursting at the seams with vacancy. In the desert, the season of spring was nothing more than a tiny precursor to summer. It arrived with no vibrant show, no big magical blooms, no spectacles. Only quiet dissolve.

—

One March day, I sat at my desk playing guitar. A knock on my bedroom door interrupted me. I called out, "Come in."

The door opened. Mom padded inside and took a seat on my bed. "Mind if I bother you for a minute?"

"Sure." I leaned my guitar against the wall and turned my attention to her.

"How are you doing, honey?"

Something had long ago dulled inside of me, tamping down my life and my joy. I opened my mouth like one of Edgar Bergen's ventriloquist dummies and the words, "I'm fine, Mom," slipped out automatically.

Her gray eyes seemed to plead with mine, begging me to soften. "I'm just worried about you. How are you really, Claude?"

How am I? The simple question could breezily be answered: *I'm fine. Good. Not too bad.* But I wrestled with these dismissive responses because I knew they didn't reflect the truth. For some reason, the truth felt like less of a burden than a lie.

"I wish I knew," I finally said. "I don't mean to sound, well, melodramatic, but time is passing, and I feel like I am too. Like I'm walking around with no life left inside me."

Mom's eyes never left me. Her concern prodded me on.

"I guess I feel hollowed out. Or forgotten? Like I'm stuck in limbo. Turning my wheels and going nowhere. That's where it feels like I'm headed. Nowhere. I do what needs to be done each day. Then somehow, I end up in bed at night wondering how I got there, unable to remember hardly a single thing about my day. And at first, that was okay. A lot of my anger slipped away, but nothing filled its spot." I paused. "The absence helped at first. You know, each day didn't feel as painful as the last. But now that I want to feel something again, I can't. It's gone."

"I think we all feel like that to some degree. I'm sorry,

honey. What do you mean, though? What's gone?"

"Sometimes I wonder if it's God," I murmured. I knew this couldn't be true—look at my dad and everything the Lord had brought him through. But I kept wondering where He was and when He was going to bring me and all of us through these troubled times too.

"He's not gone," she said softly.

"Then why does He feel so far away?" The wind tapped on my window. I looked its way, catching the tail end of a dust cloud being carried past. "It's like somehow I slipped through the cracks, and He forgot me."

Mom's shoulders sagged. "Oh honey. It's impossible to fall through the cracks. Though I think . . ." Her voice trailed off. In a few beats, she picked it up again. "I think we can experience distance within our relationship with Him though. I think sometimes we don't want to see Him in all the intricate details—the boring and mundane ones and the easily overlooked ones. We expect grandiose moves from Him, but a lot of times we don't have the patience to wait for the grandiose. Or the trust."

"And what if the grandiose never happens?"

"Then that's okay too. But He promises that He works all things together for good. And you know, the hope we have in what lies beyond this side of eternity . . . that's mighty big, wouldn't you say? Not sure how much more grandiose a gesture we could ask for."

"It's hard to imagine it." I'd tried, more times than I could count, to imagine what comes next. What had Vern felt as he walked into the other side? What did Big John see when he closed his eyes for the final time? But my pea-sized brain failed me every time, unable to render even a vague vision of heaven.

"To trust in something you can't see or understand, well, that's faith," she said.

Faith. The thought of it took my breath away. Trusting that all of this heartache would be stitched together for something good, that there truly was a great city waiting for us in the sky, that we could be healed while we wait for our time . . .

"Mom?" I said.

"Yes, honey?"

"Do you know who else feels far away? Cliff."

Mom tried to smile. "I know. But he'll come back around. I really believe that." She pointed to my guitar and said, "You're improving. You sound really good."

"Thank you."

"I ran into Jane Keller at the store yesterday. Sweet old lady, she is. We got to talking, and I told her about you learning to play guitar. She told me that if you ever need an audience to practice for, there's a group of older ladies who meet at the church on Thursdays to quilt or crochet. *Wilted and Quilted,* they call themselves." She laughed. "Apparently, Gabriel Freeman used to stop in and play hymns for them while they met. You might remember him? He's a little older than Vern. She said they sure miss the music."

I couldn't help but laugh at the proposal. I picked up my guitar and strummed a chord.

"I know it seems a little silly," Mom said and smiled.

"I'm even less of a singer than I am a musician."

"Well, it's something to think about anyway."

I could count on one hand the hymns I knew. And even then, I hardly knew them. But still, I found myself strumming now, fumbling between chords, finally finding a progression that gave some semblance to Amazing Grace. I stumbled through it over and over, half-heartedly singing what words I knew by heart, the whole performance increasing in gusto as it grew in familiarity to me.

For a brief moment, I forgot my mother was still there until her gentle voice laced itself with mine. I looked up and realized it had been a long time since I'd heard or seen her cry. She now leaned against the lower post of my bunk, silently releasing tears that had been lurking all winter. My fingers continued to play, though my mouth went still. We stared in sadness, speaking a multitude of words without uttering a single one of them.

I finally stopped and set the guitar aside, rose from my chair, and wrapped my mother in my arms.

15

SPRING TURNED INTO summer. Mom went back to work. Not at her former job in the courthouse, but this time in a seasonal position at the post office. She teased me that she only did so in order to afford all the clothes I kept growing out of. In the span of a few months, I'd shot up four inches. My quickest growth spurt so far in life.

Dad continued his work at the auto shop, but once school let out for the summer, he enlisted me as an official part-time employee. The two of us would turn up at home after a day's labor, a filthy mess. *A couple of grease monkeys*, Mom called us and claimed her added income would also be used to cover the extra costs of laundry.

Richie grew closer to me—as close as a brother as my own slipped away. The rope that tethered Cliff to me loosened a little more each day. It wasn't as if I was gripping it as tightly anymore either. I let it slip through my fingers, gentle and continuous, gradually growing less fearful of when the rope might come to an end and my hands would be entirely empty. Mom said he'd come back around. I attempted to trust that he would.

Outside of working for my dad, I tore around town with Richie, getting into trouble where and however we saw fit. Small forms of rebellion packaged within dry afternoons. Exciting thrills that pumped my blood, reminding me that I was still alive. He'd show up to my house every afternoon when I was done working, ready to find something to get ourselves into.

One morning, Dad gave me an unexpected day off. I phoned Richie to let him know. By the time he was done with his morning shift at the drugstore, I had drifted back to sleep on the couch and only woke when he pounded his knuckles on the door. Mom wasn't home, or else she'd have already answered it and told him to quit it with that racket and just come in.

"It's open," I shouted from the couch, my voice hoarse. I shook the grogginess away. "Richie! Come in!"

He finally quit his pounding long enough to hear me and let himself in. "Long morning doing nothing, Fly?"

I peeked at him through the slit of one eye. "One of these days you ought to join us. See how real men work. We don't sort candies at the drugstore."

He snorted, sunk into the armchair, and rifled through the newspapers on the side table. "The *Tonopah Times Bonanza . . . and Goldfield News.* I like how we're a little afterthought in the title." He laughed. "Man, you ever read these headlines? *'Police Search For Gun Thief.'* Golly, I hope they find him. *'Single Glove Found Outside Mizpah.'* A single glove? Police better get on that mystery too. Oh, listen to this one. Good grief. *'Local Brothel Sponsors Boy Scouts.'* Only in Nevada, huh? Wonder if Kitty's aunt was behind that?"

I glared at him.

"Bad joke?" He set that newspaper down and picked up another. "Sorry, man. Here's some good news to cheer you up. *'Police Nail Thief, Recover Missing Guns'*. Well, it's about time those thugs were busted." He flipped the page. "Oh, here's a good section. It's called *'Teenage Times.'* Let's see what's going on with our peers, shall we? Oh good, Johnnie and Pat— whoever they are, must be from Tonopah—visited their grandparents over the weekend. And the Smith family went camping and saw two bears. Oh my! Sharon Parker has decided to attend college in Reno. Good for her. And —"

Richie suddenly stopped. I peered at him as he held the paper up to his face, still not speaking. "What is it? Someone we know?"

The jiggling back door handle brought my ears to attention. I heard it open, then a low whisper. The utility room door opened and shut. I scrambled to my feet to find Cliff peering down the hall between the kitchen and the living room, bewildered and chagrined at the sight of me.

"You're home?" He spoke with surprise. Then, more coolly took a few steps toward me and said, "You guys finish early?"

I wondered if Richie also sensed the charged atmosphere, the sudden nauseating smell of deceit. "Dad gave me the day off. What're you up to? Not working today either?"

He shrugged noncommittally, but in the brief pocket of his silence, a floorboard in the utility room creaked. I caught Cliff's nervous eye. I tore down the hall, past the bedrooms and through the kitchen, shoving Cliff out of the way. I ripped open the utility room door, and there, right next to the laundry sink, was Maisy Thomas.

I shut the door on Maisy and turned to Cliff. "What do we have here? Sneaking girls in when you think everyone's out of the house?"

Cliff hung his head back and gazed at the ceiling. "Fly, it's not . . . I swear to you we weren't doing anything like that. We just wanted to hang out."

"Maisy? Maisy Thomas? Really, Cliff?" I pushed my way past him.

"Come on, Claude!" He pleaded, hot on my heels. As though my approval were important. As if he really cared about me at all. Sometimes, it felt like I'd lost both of my brothers instead of just one. "That's why I was trying to be sneaky. Because, well, I know it's a little weird, but just . . . just hear me out, okay?"

"Date whoever you want, Cliff. But why does it have to be Maisy? You know how Vern felt about her."

"In case you haven't noticed, Vern isn't here anymore," he spat.

Of course, I knew what he meant. Vern wasn't here and was never coming back. I had to stop treating things like he was. But in the moment, all I saw in front of me wasn't Vern's best friend, but a dirty rotten traitor. I stormed out the front door, a wall of heat smacking me in the face.

Richie followed behind. We hopped on our bikes.

"You gonna fill me in? Tell me what the heck just happened?"

We rode a half mile before I calmed down enough to speak. "My brother's an idiot," I grumbled. Richie, I knew, wanted more. "Maisy and Vern were unofficially dating before, you know . . ."

"So, Cliff is dating the same girl Vern was sort-of dating before he died?"

"Yeah. And he's crossing him."

"Oh." Richie fell into an unusual silence as we slowed. Minutes went by, the crunching of gravel beneath our tires the only sound between us.

I finally couldn't take the quiet. "What is it?" I barked at him. "If you have something to say, just say it."

"I just think you're being a little too harsh right now. I don't know Cliff all that well. And it's not like I really knew Vern. But I can tell they don't seem like the type of brothers to hurt the other on purpose. Wouldn't you agree?"

I gritted my teeth. Of course, I agreed. They'd been best friends.

"I don't think Cliff is trying to hurt Vern or his memory. Honestly, Fly. Vern shouldn't get dibs on a girl he ain't even around for. It doesn't make sense to hold that against him. If Cliff and Maisy like each other, then what's it to you?"

The heat slowed me down. Or maybe it was his logic. Either way, I didn't like it.

Richie slowed down too and suddenly came to a full stop in front of the old hotel.

"What?" I hollered, then circled around and stopped next to him.

"There's something you should know."

I shielded my eyes against the sun and studied him. "If it's bad news, I don't want to hear it right now."

Richie grimaced but let whatever it was drop. He looked at the towering red-brick hotel before us. "You know this place is haunted. Let's get out of here."

Everything here is haunted, I thought. "It's not haunted unless you believe it is. You've never been in there, have you?"

"No way, man. But everyone I know who has been swears they've seen ghosts."

I shook my head. "There were officers from the army air base that slept here during the war. None of them got spooked or saw any ghosts, did they?"

"Maybe they did, and we just didn't hear about it."

I hopped off my bike and leaned it against a stone pillar.

"Let's see for ourselves."

"Won't we get into trouble?"

I turned around and looked him dead in the eye. "Richie Garrison scared of trouble? Call the Bonanza! This is the headline of the century!"

He threw his shoulders back. "I think there's something wrong with your brain right now, Fly. But if you want to go in, then fine. Let's go."

We walked around the building and found a door with a broken lock. With a little pushing, we popped it open. Daylight streamed in, dust surfing the streams of light. But where the light couldn't quite reach, darkness remained. Shadows groped for us; something lurked just out of reach, waiting to snatch whoever strayed too far or too close.

"You go first," he said. "This was your idea."

I slipped into the shadows and moved down a side hallway toward the front lobby where daylight spilled in through dingy windows. Little white and maroon octagon tiles decorated the ground. They were filthy, but I could still make out the building's name, *Goldfield Hotel*, written across the floor. The room was grand—grander than I'd ever suspected—and I could see how in its heyday this place had been so wildly popular. Behind a dusty, mahogany front desk, a large safe stood erect, its doors open, its insides bare. What valuables those shelves had held back in the day, I couldn't even imagine.

I heard Richie's footsteps finally enter the building, each one slicing through the silence. "Fly?"

I crept behind the desk and squatted down. Surely, he had to see this coming, right? Still, I stifled my childish giggling as I heard him draw near. I searched the inner shelves of the desk, finding an old pencil with teeth marks around its middle. I peeked over the desktop.

Richie stood near the front entrance, his head craning back

to get a good look at the heavy beams across the ceiling.

My moment. I launched the pencil toward the staircase behind where he stood. The poor kid jumped three feet high. I ducked and clamped a hand over my mouth to keep my laughter in.

"I know that's you, Claude! Knock it off! Get out here!" His yells echoed, but so did the tremble in his voice. I searched the desk for something else to throw but only came up with old matches. My fingers were caked with filth.

As I emerged from my hideout, I bumped my head on the ledge of the desk. Richie told me it served me right. Couldn't argue much with that. We turned in circles, taking in our surroundings.

"What a place," he muttered. "Not much of a looker now though."

"You just gotta look past all the dirt and dust."

"And boarded windows and ghosts."

"Those too." I shuddered. "Come on."

Richie hesitated for only a moment. To be honest, I didn't know where my fearlessness, or perhaps carelessness, came from. I forged onward. What else had I to lose?

We climbed to the second floor, the stairs moaning beneath our feet. Most of the doors were shut. I stood outside the first one, ready to turn the knob, but something held me back—the notion that maybe I didn't want to know what was waiting on the other side after all.

I backed away and followed Richie down the hall until we came to an already open room. Furniture awaited guests that would never again come. The bed, naked of sheets or blankets, looked like it held secrets no one would want to know.

A noise from somewhere in the hotel stopped us in our tracks. We exchanged glances, our 'fraidy-cat faces mirroring each other's.

"You hear that?" he asked.

"Probably just the building settling. Or rats."

Neither one of us moved. I'm sure neither one of us fully believed that explanation. We high-tailed it back downstairs, turned a corner, and passed what used to be the kitchen. We found ourselves in a large, empty room with a staircase in the floor, descending into the basement.

"You know what this is, don't you?" I whispered. "I think this was the gentleman's lounge."

I looked around, scanning the room for any evidence of my assumption. "Dad used to tell us spook stories about this hotel until Mom made him stop because we'd get too scared to sleep. He said there was rumored to be a gentleman's room. Only men were allowed in here under the excuse of gambling and spending time with their friends.

"But what they were really doing . . ." I stepped closer to the staircase and squinted down into the darkness. "They'd sneak down these stairs into the basement where a secret, underground tunnel brought them to the red-light district. Then they'd sneak back up and go be with their families. Their wives were none the wiser."

Richie, now standing at my side, peered into the abyss and grimaced. "I get the feeling something real bad happened down there."

"Dad said there could've been some murders in the midst of all that secrecy. He told us a story once about the ghosts of those poor women coming back to haunt the men that disrespected them. I remember him telling a story about the owner getting a prostitute pregnant and keeping her chained to the radiator because he didn't want his wife finding out. That's about when Mom shut down Goldfield Hotel story time."

"So, you're telling me there're spirits of whores flying around down there?"

"Dad always said that maybe some of these women were straight up Jezebels. But a lot of them? Well, he plumb felt sorry for them. What must you think of yourself to subject yourself to that kind of life?" No sooner had I recalled this than I felt a punch in my gut, remembering all the nasty things I'd thought about Peggy Littleton.

What sounded like a heavy object slamming against cement reverberated up to Richie and me from somewhere deep within the basement. Goosebumps crawled down my spine. We fixed our eyes on the dark down below.

Richie sucked in a breath. "I think we made someone mad down there."

An overwhelming chill wrapped around my chest, sucking the life from my lungs. I gulped for air, two forces competing for my breath. Expansion and contraction. I sensed something come over Richie too. Our legs couldn't pump fast enough to get us out of there. We tore around the corner, back through the kitchen, and into the lobby.

I slipped, my knee taking the brunt of my fall. Richie grabbed me and pulled me up by the collar, back to my feet. When we finally tumbled through the side door and into the bright light of the sun and hot summer air, our chests heaved at record speeds.

We sprawled out in the dirt for a good ten minutes, catching our breath.

I propped myself up on my elbows, staring at the building that had just spit us out. "Maybe that wasn't my best idea," I admitted.

Richie sat up and shivered in spite of the blistering heat. "Do you think . . ." He shook his head. "Never mind."

"What?"

"I don't want to say it out loud."

"Do I think that was a real ghost down there?"

He nodded.

I'd never believed in the idea of ghosts, but we'd encountered something. That much was sure. "I think whatever it was, I'm glad as heck to be on this side of it." And whatever it was, I wanted nothing to do with it.

"Let's call it a day, huh, Fly?" he said.

I agreed and stood, ready to mop away the nervous sweat that now bled through my clothes, ready to sit in the safe confines of my home.

"If that was a ghost—and I'm not saying it was—why do you suppose it hasn't moved on? Why do you think it'd linger around, haunted and haunting?" Richie mused.

A fearful thought clutched me, the notion of Vern being stuck somewhere in limbo, somewhere in between, unable to break free of the confines in which he was bound. I closed my eyes, shutting the wretched hotel out of my view. I asked God to make sure Vern was up there, accounted for in Heaven.

"I've got to see someone," I blurted out and fetched my bike. "I'll see you tomorrow."

Richie scrambled to his feet. "Where're you off to all of a sudden? Church?" he joked.

Little did he know, I actually was. I mounted my bike and took off.

He shouted after me as I pedaled away, "Read the paper, Fly!"

The paper? I didn't have long to figure out what he'd meant, because in a matter of minutes, I coasted up to the church where Vern's funeral had taken place. The same church where my parents currently attended every Sunday service. Where they used to bring my brothers and me every week when we were children. I flew off my bike and stumbled through the doors, filthy and panting, not taking into consideration who might be gathered inside.

Suddenly, wrinkled hands moved to cover gasping mouths. Fabric fell to the floor. The door swung shut behind me as I entered the small room outside the church's sanctuary. Though I didn't realize it right away, I stood there before the old ladies of *Wilted and Quilted.*

"Gracious sakes," the lady closest to me mumbled, her hand pressing against her heart. She set her quilting materials aside and came to me. "You look like you've just seen a ghost."

I almost told her I had. "I'm here to see Pastor James. Is he around?" A bead of sweat trickled down from my forehead. I swiped it with the back of my hand.

"He's in his office." She pointed across the room to a closed door. "You want some water, honey? Matilda, get him some water, would you? Look at your leg!"

I glanced down to see that the skin on my knee was busted open and a stream of blood was dried on my shin.

A woman with curly, white hair and thick, cat-eyed glasses shuffled away and reappeared with a cup of water. She pressed it to my lips, giving me no choice in the matter. I downed it in a matter of seconds. As I wiped my lips, Matilda mopped my forehead with a damp rag. Suddenly, with these ladies so close, I became aware of my own stench, though they didn't seem to mind.

"That's the little Fisher boy," I heard one of the seated women say.

"He ain't so little anymore," another muttered.

I looked up to see several of them sitting at tables, nodding their heads in unison.

I walked across the room and knocked on the pastor's office door.

Pastor James opened the door and didn't hide his surprise. He gave me a once over, clearly concerned by my disheveled appearance. "Claude Fisher? Is everything alright?"

"I apologize for interrupting, sir. Can I, uh, come in and talk? Please?"

"Absolutely." He stepped aside and allowed me into his cramped closet of an office. I slid into the only spare chair. Dust billowed from my clothes in a puff.

He shut the door, though the murmurs of the old women on the other side couldn't be silenced. "What brings you here today?"

"Where do the dead go when they die?" I blurted out.

His weathered forehead wrinkled. "Wow. Well now, that's a very good question." He reached for his Bible, flipped through the delicate pages, and scanned them up and down. "Am I mistaken to assume you're worried about your brother? Where he's gone off to?"

"I just want to know he isn't a ghost." The idea that my brother's spirit could be lurking around suddenly felt stupid.

"A ghost. I see." He paused, pursed his lips, and looked at me. "Do you believe in ghosts, Claude?"

My mind replayed that horrible sound in the hotel, the innate sense that something was wrong, the fear that had pulsed through my veins. "I don't know anymore."

"You wouldn't necessarily be wrong if you did. Spirit beings in this world are very real. However, disembodied spirit beings of deceased loved ones are not."

"So, people can't be ghosts?"

"Correct."

While somewhat relieved, I wasn't satisfied. I needed further proof. "Why not? What *are* ghosts then?"

"Ghosts are"—he chuckled and shook his head—"often a figment of people's imagination. The wind rustling a paper just so . . . Light shining on an object just right . . . But, perhaps occasionally, what people think are ghosts could be an encounter with a spirit being, which we've established couldn't be a dead loved one." He skimmed a page. A flock of brown spots on his bald head stared at me while he did. They matched all the others that peppered his skin. "Have you ever heard that to be absent from the body is to be present with the Lord?"

"You said that at Vern's funeral." I surprised myself with the memory from that day, long ago suppressed.

He smiled. "That's right, I did. Now, hear this: 'Then shall the dust return to the earth as it was: and the spirit shall return unto God who gave it.' When we die, we return to our Maker, and we fall under judgment. We don't linger here."

I picked at the dried blood on my leg, anything to keep from meeting eyes with Pastor James as I formulated my next question. Giggling erupted from beyond the office door, the women hooting about something. I swallowed and shook their voices out of my head. A hundred snapshots flittered through my mind. Vern standing so proudly after his football game. The view of my brothers' backs speeding ahead of me on their bikes as I lagged behind. Briefly, Vern's lifeless body on the side of the road. The verse in Exodus I'd read in Big John's Bible.

"Why do you suppose God let this happen to Vern?" I asked quietly. "He could stop the Israelite's enemies from reaching them. He literally swept them away in the sea. Why couldn't He stop the car from hitting my brother?"

"Well . . ." he said slowly as he folded his hands, "I can't answer that for you. But what I do know is that we live in a cursed world filled with people who exercise their free will to the detriment of others. And I also know that we all have a date with death at some point. There's no getting around that. Sometimes, I believe, the Lord allows hard things to happen for reasons we can't begin to understand with our limited minds. But what you ought to realize, Claude, is that while the Israelite's salvation at that time was from a physical enemy and from a physical slavery, the Lord also delivers us from an unseen enemy and slavery into an eternal salvation through the finished work of Jesus Christ."

Another round of laughter came from outside the door. Pastor James paused and continued when the ruckus died down.

"You came in here asking about the spiritual world. Well, I'm here to tell you there's a spiritual battle happening all around us, one that only He can shield us from. Through Jesus, we have hope. Not just in the physical sense of the word in this earthly lifetime but hope that transcends all of time. He died for my sins. He died for yours. He died for Vernon's. We have eternal life, and what a joy it is to know that, in spite of hardship and tragedy here, we have an eternity of peace to look forward to. Sorrow not, Claude."

My eyes moistened. Pastor James handed me a handkerchief. I clutched it in my hand, keeping the tears I couldn't explain at bay. One of the ladies laughed loudly again.

Pastor James looked their way and smiled. "Those are the ladies of *Wilted and Quilted*."

"My mom told me about them." I set the handkerchief on the desk. "I guess someone asked if I'd play music for them or something."

He chuckled. "Sounds about right. Would you like me to introduce you?"

I knew I'd have to pass back through the lot of them to leave, so I said, "Sure."

I was introduced to the six members of *Wilted and Quilted*. Ada, the woman who'd first greeted me when I stumbled inside, was the graying, long-haired chairwoman of the tiny crafting society. Then I met Matilda with the cat-eyed glasses. Jane, Margaret, Edna, and Beulah.

"You know, I knew your grandma," Jane said, smiling fondly. "We were good friends, Elsie and I. Been in this town a long time. In fact, I used to babysit your daddy sometimes."

Beulah cleared her throat, flicked her dark, sliver-snaked braid over her shoulder, and sat up straight. "It's mighty grand to see a young man rushing in to see his preacher. Too many little miscreants running around town these days, stirring up mischief." She clucked her tongue and then nodded in approval at me.

I opened my mouth, about to set her straight so she didn't get the wrong idea about me. *I'm one of those miscreants.* But Pastor James spoke first.

"I think we were all blessed with Claude's presence today." Turning to me, he said, "My door is always open."

"Thank you," I said, and I meant it.

Jane piped up. "You don't happen to have your guitar nearby, do you? Your mama told me you've been learning."

"I don't have it with me today. I'm sorry."

Pastor James dismissed himself then. I tried taking the opportunity to dismiss myself too. But as I headed out the door, a voice called out, "Now wait just one minute!"

I turned back around. Matilda fixed her glasses and inspected me. "You're just about the same size as my grandson. I'm working on this jacket. See?" She held up a heap of fabric for me. "But he lives in Carson City."

I sensed where this was heading, even before Edna gasped. "He could be your model!"

Matilda smiled, the heavy folds at the corners of her eyes wrinkling like an accordion behind her frames. "That's right, he could. I just want to make sure these measurements are alright . . ."

I thought of the glass of water and the mopping of my brow when I'd first stumbled into the room. "I'd be happy to help."

Once those magic words left my lips, the room sprang into action. And it wasn't just Matilda, but all six women who flocked around me. They spun me first one way and then another, held fabric to my body, flapped my arms out and in like I was a bird.

Matilda came at me, sewing pins stuck between pursed lips, measuring me at odd angles.

All of their voices swirled together, making comments about my grandmother and asking questions about my family.

When I heard Kitty's name thrown into the ring, I twitched. A pin sank into my arm. "Ouch!"

"Now hold still," Matilda mumbled. "My hands aren't as steady as they used to be, so I'm relying on you. Don't be tryin' to get away just yet. We're almost done."

Under their careful eyes, I stiffened, trying to avoid being poked again and straining to hear Kitty's name once more.

Matilda spun me around, looked me up and down. "Done," she declared. I sighed in relief though the ladies didn't immediately fall away.

Ada touched my arm as gently as she could and smiled softly. "You know, for a second, I thought I was the one seeing a ghost when you first stumbled in here today. You look so much like your brother."

She couldn't have meant Cliff, with his dark hair and smoky features. "You knew Vern?" I asked.

"Oh, to a degree. Fine young man, he was." She leaned in and whispered closely, "Maisy's my granddaughter."

I wanted to disappear, to slip out from beneath her delicate touch. This was too much.

"She's been torn to pieces for months," Ada continued, holding me in place. "Funny thing though, not long ago she told me how your other brother defended her in school. Your parents have done a fine job with you boys." She patted my forearm, releasing me now.

Margaret, a woman tall and thick with two missing teeth,

crowded in, demanding sudden attention. "How would your mama like me to drop off a lasagna tomorrow night for dinner?"

I hesitated. How was I supposed to know what my mother would like?

"You let her know Old Margaret's gon' be stopping by tomorrow sometime, will ya?"

I nodded. Maisy. Ghosts. Church. Lasagna. None of the things I would've ever imagined would edge into my day.

16

AS LUCK WOULD have it, Margaret decided to pop by with her lasagna the following afternoon as I practiced guitar. Mom let her in. I moved to hide my coveted possession to the other side of the couch, but Margaret spotted it before I could.

"There's that guitar Jane wouldn't quiet down about!" She handed over the dish to Mom and adjusted the waistline of her skirt as she traipsed over and plopped down right beside me. "Well, come on. I can't be here long. Let me hear a little somethin'."

I blinked. Something about arguing with Margaret seemed futile. I pulled my guitar back onto my lap, edging slightly away from her. I began picking away at a simple tune Dad had taught me.

About ten seconds in, Margaret touched the neck of the guitar, interrupting my ability to play. "Play me a hymn."

"I don't know many," I confessed. "I'm still kinda new at this."

"It's a prime time to learn. I'll sing, you play."

Mom leaned against the wall in the hallway. Her shoulders

jiggled up and down as she silently laughed. I looked at Margaret.

Her brows pitched nearly to her hairline, she waited expectantly.

"Okay. Why don't you start, and I'll try to follow?"

She sucked in a breath and opened her mouth. Where I expected a foghorn came a delightful trickle of wind chimes, a voice somehow both delicate and rugged, reaching and withholding.

I forgot to breathe, forgot to blink, forgot to strum my guitar.

Margaret abruptly stopped and threw a hand to her hip. "You gonna let me carry this tune all by myself? Come on, I think it's in the key of D."

We started and stopped so many times I lost count. She showed me how to place my fingers. Told me the chord I played wasn't a good one.

Then she encouraged me. "Come on now. You got this."

At one point, she asked me to give her the guitar so she could show me how to play something but quickly reneged. "Oh, heck. Too hard. Never mind."

She pressed me to sing with her. "Louder," she commanded. "Ah, that's nice. You got yourself a nice little voice. Hey, Ginny," she called out to Mom. "You know your boy could sing?"

Then she turned back to me. "Alright, one more time through, else Orin might have another heart attack if I forget to come home and feed him."

"Is Orin your dog?" I asked.

"Husband. Some days I wonder though." Margaret slapped her thigh and stood. "Gabe Freeman used to come over to the church a couple times a month and play some tunes for us old grannies as we did our projects."

"I've heard." I quickly looked to Mom, who still stood in the hall, hand covering her mouth.

Margaret waited a moment, seeing if I'd take the bait. Finally, she said, "Well, maybe you and that guitar of yours will stumble upon us one of these days. You know where and when to find us." She winked and went to my mother, giving her a peck on the cheek before leaving.

Mom closed the door, and her pent-up laughter tumbled out.

"I'm so glad you find this entertaining," I grumbled, setting my guitar aside and sprawling out on the couch.

"I'm sorry!" She wiped her watering eyes, and then took a breath, waving at the air in front of her. "It's just . . . the look on your face . . ."

"Mom!" I cracked a smile, the comedy not entirely lost on me. "You don't expect me to actually, you know, go down and play music at the church for a bunch of old women, do you?"

She sat down in the armchair, slung her feet over the side, and bounced them up and down like she was a little kid. "I don't see what it would hurt. Clearly, you're adored there. Think of how much it would bless them. Give it some thought. Could wind up being fun if you ever feel prompted to do it."

I closed my eyes, imagining Margaret throwing aside her knitting supplies and transforming into a choir director, bossing me around with chords, pointing at the other ladies with a crochet hook, telling them when to come in and how. Yeah, sure sounded like fun to me.

"Claude," Mom said gingerly. "There's something I'd like to talk with you about."

My eyes fluttered open, and I regarded her. As her eyes faded from amusement to apprehension, I stiffened.

"It's about Jeb Ralph. We heard his trial is supposed to start next week."

"It's about time, right?"

"And we also got a notice from the county regarding the Ralph's old house. Jeb apparently signed the deed back over to us."

I propped myself up on my elbows. "Kitty's house?"

She nodded.

"Signed it over? Why? What do you mean? It's ours now?"

"Ours now, yes. Ours . . . again. He sent a letter too."

"Did you write back and tell him we don't want his stupid house or his stupid letter?"

"Claude."

"What'd the letter say?"

She already knew I'd reject its contents by default, but she told me anyway. "That he could never repay us for our kindness toward his daughter. That he will never be able to repay us the debt of taking Vern's life. That he's sorry."

I snorted. "He's basically saying, 'Sorry I killed your son. Here, have the house you gave me.'"

"I still remember meeting Jeb." Mom's voice remained hopeful and calm. "Kitty was so little, and it was so cold. He had no clue what to do. I mean, would you? If someone walked in here right now, set a baby in your arms, and walked away? But Jeb stayed. I'll give him that much. I think the easiest thing Jeb could've done was to leave Kitty with us and skip town. But he never did."

"Maybe she would've been better off."

"Well, if that were the case, we'd have raised her as your sister."

And you can't fall in love with your sister.

Mom sadly stared through me, history still zipping past her eyes. "That house was empty from your grandmother's recent passing. When Daddy sold it to him all those years ago, he hardly charged Jeb a penny. Dad knew it was the right thing to do. And then he gave Jeb a job, which he held for a while, until the heavy drinking and accidents began. Then Dad had to let him go. After that, Jeb grew cold, more aloof, and disengaged over the years. He just wasn't a man that had much joy.

"But we continued helping him out by taking care of Kitty, raising her practically as our own, sending her home with food to make sure their cupboard wasn't bare. Even though he never spoke of it, I know none of it went unnoticed with Jeb. Maybe this is him finally growing up and being sorry, realizing he needs to take responsibility and change?"

"A little late for responsibility, don't you think?" I wasn't purposely trying to be confrontational. In fact, for a long time, I hadn't thought about Jeb Ralph and how angry I was at him. But the kettle heated up inside me, beginning to hiss now. "He just knows the house is useless to him, whether he gets out of jail or not. He's too much of a pansy to ever face our family again after what he did, after everything he's taken from us."

Mom stared at the ceiling, her legs resuming their bouncing. "Maybe you're right," she mused, not in the mood to argue. "Whatever the case, the home is now ours."

—

When the trial came, I declined attending. I didn't want to see his face. Couldn't imagine looking into the eyes of the man who'd done so much damage to the people I loved the most. But after all was said and done, I paced in my room, running on fumes of anger, wishing I'd have been there. What good it would have done, I couldn't say.

I imagined everyone in the courthouse, our little town packing those seats full, eager to hear what the judge thought a pitiful man charged with vehicular manslaughter deserved.

When I got home from school, Cliff was just leaving in the car he'd recently purchased. He gave me a curt nod as I coasted up to the house. Through the windshield, I could see the markings of disappointment across his face, could sense the tethers loosening all the more.

Dad broke the news to me, not offering much else besides the cold facts. Jeb Ralph was given a measly five years in prison, whereas my brother was sentenced to a lifetime in the grave. I think Dad was a little stunned too.

And Mom, well, she purposely busied herself around the house with the same fake smile painted on her face that she'd worn when everything first happened. But it didn't fool me. I knew she was reliving every second of it, torturing herself with the memories just as I was. Even worse, she had had to sit through the recounting of events during the trial. Something I couldn't even do.

I sought my mother out, wanting to fall into her arms, for her sake as much as my own. She welcomed me, her touch being the only peace I could find, the only ounce of reassurance that everything would be okay. And it occurred to me, as I was tucked in the comfort of her arms, that no amount of prison time, whether five years or five hundred, would have felt like justice. There was no magical number sufficient enough for me to feel satisfied. Mom squeezed me tighter, and I wondered if she felt the same.

"Was Kitty there?" I asked.

Mom didn't answer right away. I asked again.

"No." She kissed my hair, breathed me in like I was an infant, not her ever-growing teenager.

A million questions paraded through my mind, but one stood out above all the rest. "Mom, do you think Jeb Ralph got what he deserved?"

"Do I think the judge did his job correctly today? I want to say no." Her voice trembled. "But no matter the punishment, it doesn't change the fact that I still can't get my son back. And I just want my son back."

I felt a tear splatter against my skin and looked up, watching more cascade down my mother's broken face. The hardest part about intimately knowing someone's pain was not being able to do a single thing to change it.

"I'm so sorry, Mama."

She released a shaky breath and squeezed me again. "I don't know what we expected from today, but somehow it feels like the outcome would've been a letdown no matter what."

"I know what you mean. Do you think he's truly sorry?"

"He saw us today, Claude. Me, Dad, and Cliff. It wasn't on accident, but because he looked for us. He sought us out on purpose. It was from a distance, but he stared at the three of us, his eyes bloodshot from crying. To answer your question, I think Jebediah Ralph is a lot of things, but sorry? Yes, yes I actually do think he is."

I imagined his red-rimmed eyes pleading for the only thing my family had the power to give: forgiveness. I felt like she'd taken a pickaxe to my heart and split it in two. "It's a shame being sorry can't undo what's already done, isn't it?"

"Yes," she whispered. "But it can certainly change someone's future."

"Do you really think a man like Jeb can ever change?"

She ruffled my hair and sighed. "No one is ever too far gone to get right."

Such immense hope packed into ten words. I would've easily believed them years ago as a kid who didn't know how badly the human heart could break. But I had a hard time swallowing them now.

"I don't believe," she mused, quietly enough that I wondered if it was to herself or to me, "there's anyone out of God's jurisdiction to save."

17

Fall 1946

MAYBE IT WAS because of the weekly lasagna she kept bringing over, but Margaret finally talked me into coming to the *Wilted and Quilted* meetings. The ladies gave no opportunity for timidity. *Just play,* they'd told me. *We made plenty of mistakes when we first started out too,* they'd said, holding up whatever project they were each working on. *If we've learned anything in our old age, it's to not be afraid to try.*

And so, I did. Over the remainder of the summer, I came a long way with my skill because of it. My hands, rough and calloused from working all summer with my dad, now easily found their respective places on my guitar as I played for the old women in the church. Their lips moved with the hymns, their hands with their needles and craft.

One late summer afternoon, when I finished my final song for the day, I said, "School starts up again soon, so you might not see me for a while."

"What grade are you in again, honey?" Margaret asked.

"Ninth. Freshman year."

Matilda looked up from her work, her glasses balanced on the crook of her nose. "So, they're still holding high school classes then?"

"What do you mean, '*still holding classes?*' Why wouldn't they be?" Jane asked.

Matilda pushed her glasses up and glanced around the room, a pleased smile growing as she realized no one else held the information she had. "Well, according to the scuttlebutt, that top floor is falling apart, and the administration is scared it's no longer safe. They were considering closing off the upper levels, which leaves no room for high school classes anymore. Moreover, I spoke with Miss Dunlop, and she said the school is simply understaffed. Too many folks are leaving."

"I haven't heard anything about that," I said. Could this rumor be true?

Beulah sighed. "Such a shame. Guess this town really is fading now, isn't it?"

"It's been fading for quite some time," Margaret said. "Mining is all but kaput. Sure, there's still a little happening, but it's certainly not what it was. And the war brought some much-needed hustle and bustle after the Depression left us so stagnant. But like all things, that was only temporary. Things come and go. Towns too."

I couldn't imagine the high school actually shutting down. Repairs could be made if it were that bad, couldn't they?

—

It only took a few weeks into the school year to confirm what Matilda said to be true. Principal Mathews called a formal assembly for the high school grades. We gathered inside the dust-ridden gymnasium. A swarm of rumors flew around the room. One in particular lifted the hairs on my neck, but I decided to pay it no mind. The reality would be that high school classes would no longer be offered. Our school was aging, falling apart, and the older students had been taught enough to get by. This would be the end of the road for us. Time to be turned loose into the world. The great send off. I searched the sea of bodies on the bleachers for Cliff. He sat by Maisy, their heads bent together, whispering to one another. They'd been going steady together for weeks now.

Principal Mathews whistled. The chatter died down until he announced that this school year would, in fact, be the final year in which high school classes would be offered in Goldfield.

The gym roared with life as most of my peers clapped and cheered, myself included. The eruption of excited noise muted the few worried, disappointed classmates who gasped and covered their mouths in shock at the news.

Mathews whistled again and yelled for silence. "This building has many needs that aren't able to be met, and consequently, we are forced to change what we can offer here. This year's class of 1947 will be the final graduating class from Goldfield High School. Following this school year, all high school grades will be moved to Tonopah to merge with their existing classes. Grades nine through twelve will be bused to and from Tonopah every school day for attendance there."

The sparkling, juicy rumor that had only floated into my ears minutes ago filled me with life as this glorious promise slipped from Principal Mathew's mouth. God had rolled up all my hopes and dreams and sent them flying with a slingshot straight through the universe, until everything had aligned perfectly so. Just for me.

And hopefully for Kitty too.

Tonopah.

Next year.

For the next three years.

With Kitty.

I'd spent a lot of time trying to forget her, and now that I'd finally donned a paper-thin coat of contentment, I shrugged it off in a flash, ready to chase after her again like a fool who didn't know he was a fool. I turned to Richie next to me, but his excitement failed to match mine. "What's wrong, man? This is great news!"

He whispered something, but I couldn't hear him over the jabber of our peers around us.

"Say it louder!"

He hesitated. I couldn't fathom why this news didn't fill his sails like it did mine. "You never read that newspaper, did you?" he asked.

"What are you talking about?"

"That newspaper? From earlier this summer? I told you to read it. The teenage section."

I shrugged, only vaguely remembering. It was long gone now. "Guess not. Why?"

"I'm sorry, Claude."

I didn't understand. "What did it say?"

He winced and said, "I'm paraphrasing, but basically it said, *'A goodbye party was thrown Saturday for former Goldfield local, Kitty Ralph, who recently took residence with her aunt. They are moving to New York.'*"

"You're kidding?" He had to be pulling my leg, but the pity in his voice told me this wasn't one of his jokes. "She's gone?"

"I think so, Fly."

"What else did it say?"

"That's it."

I searched for a hidden meaning, a secret message tucked privately for me somewhere within that tiny newspaper blurb as recounted to me by Richie. She left? And without so much as a goodbye? In spite of the excitement around me, the whispers and chatter of my friends, my ears muffled, and my world went black. The darkness cradled me, smothering me into a trance. I reached way down low inside myself, where the white-hot and icy-cold truths lived, and whether I liked it or not, faced reality. The fire of hope that had glowed inside of me was at once extinguished.

Without so much as a goodbye.

18

May 1947. Eight months later...

THE FINAL GRADUATING class of Goldfield High School paraded across the wooden stage in the gymnasium. Cliff held Maisy's hand throughout the whole ceremony. They wore their bliss like a celebratory banner. In their mutual adoration, they welcomed the possibilities that now unfurled before them. Within a week of graduation, Cliff proposed. Within another week, they had said their vows at the courthouse. And within yet another, Cliff informed us he'd joined the Navy.

Maisy's parents threw a big party for them at their house, where Cliff had moved in for the time being. The party was a "Congrats-on-graduation-and-getting-hitched-and-serving-our-country" mashup. There were streamers, cake, handmade signs, and meat cooked in gunny sacks underground . . . It was a proper celebration.

Richie and I ran around the yard most of the afternoon, a gaggle of young kids chasing after us, laughing so hard snot bubbles burst from their noses as they tried to catch us.

I left the crazy children outside and stepped inside the Thomas family home for refreshments. Maisy's grandmother, Ada, intercepted me, yanking me from my path to the lemonade stand and into an unexpected hug.

"Claude Fisher! How are you, honey? Oh, I'm so overjoyed!" She squeezed me against her bosom, a strand of her long, white hair somehow finding its way into my mouth. I sputtered, blowing the hair from my tongue, and waited for her to release me.

"I'm doing well, Ada. How are you?"

"We're family now." She winked at me. "Can you believe it?"

In my peripherals, I could see the big pitcher of lemonade. A pigtailed little girl, a cousin of Maisy's, flew inside and lifted the pitcher with dirty hands, her small arms shaking as she struggled to pour. The lemonade sloshed into her cup, the splashing, sugar-soaked beverage teasing me.

I tried to swallow, but my mouth was so dry I couldn't.

The girl set the pitcher down and took a long drink. She licked her lips and grinned before darting back outside to join the other kids who now had Richie pinned to the ground.

I nodded at Ada and took a step sideways, inching toward the refreshment table.

"Oh, well look at this!" Ada grabbed my arm as she noticed the local newspaper clipping featuring Cliff and Maisy that someone had taped onto the wall next to a photograph of the couple. She let go of me and fished a pair of reading glasses from her skirt pocket. "Have you read this yet, Claude? What a lovely little article. And this picture . . ." Her voice trailed away, her thin mouth remaining parted. "I remember the first time Jimmy and I had a photograph taken of us. Look at how beautiful they are . . ."

I inched another few steps closer to the lemonade.

"Now, you know what this party needs, dontcha?" she asked, turning to find I'd created considerable distance between us. She peered at me curiously, her spectacles at the end of her nose. Her face softened. "I'm holding you up. I'm sorry, dear."

"No, not at all," I assured her, chancing another glance at the lemonade. "I'm just a little thirsty."

"Well, there's lemonade right there," she said, pointing. As though I were oblivious to the very beverage that had been taunting me.

"Right," I mumbled, feeling stupid. I poured a quick cup, downed it, poured a refill, then walked back to her. "So, what is it this party is missing, Ada?"

"Music." She winked at me. "I heard someone mention something about a bonfire tonight." Ada rested her hand on my arm and lowered her voice, conspiratorially. "Jimmy always has his harmonica tucked in his pocket. He never likes to play anymore unless he's accompanying."

Ada, of course, was one of the few people on earth familiar with my music from all my time playing at their *Wilted and Quilted* meetings. It wouldn't take me long to run home and pick up my guitar. I considered it, then nodded.

Voice still low, she whispered, "And by the way, there's a plate of cookies hiding in the kitchen. Under a towel, lower cupboard. If Maisy's mama catches you, just tell her you're fetching them for old Ada." She patted my arm and moseyed away outside.

I found the cookies right where Ada told me they'd be and snatched two, shoving them whole into my mouth. Then, as the explosion of butter and coarse sugar coated my tongue, I went back outside, taking in the scene.

Cliff sat in a chair, his friends around him, the lot of them laughing and goading each other about who knew what.

Maisy fluttered around, moving from one guest to the next,

a grin plastered across her face, gracing each of them with her presence.

Mom and Dad sat at the patio table in the shade with Maisy's parents, leisurely chatting away.

Richie, still entertaining the throngs of children, hollered loudly as a child tagged him.

I smiled as I watched all of these people I cared for be swept into a wind of ease. But a hundred possibilities of how differently this day would look should Vern still be alive marched into my mind, the sadness suppressing my own happiness. *No. Not today.*

I climbed into my parents' car and drove the mile home. My guitar sat upright on a homemade stand in the corner of my bedroom like it'd been waiting for me to return. I grabbed it and paused, looking over the room.

After Vern passed, our room had changed. Cliff had moved to Vern's spot on the top bunk, and I'd taken Cliff's spot on the lower. But now something had shifted again, another round of musical chairs played as our lives were once again rearranged. Cliff had moved out and was living at the Thomas home with his new wife. He was set to leave for the Navy in a handful of days. I was the final Fisher boy in this room.

Our lives had always been one way. Now they were another, the trajectory changed entirely. Gone were the nights the three of us crowded around the radio, listening to Edgar Bergen & Charlie McCarthy or Inner Sanctum. Over were the endless rounds of cards and checkers, the brotherly fights over whose turn it was. We weren't three young boys in bib overalls, laying on our backs in the dirt, Kitty right in the middle of us, trying to find shapes in clouds and constellations in the Nevada sky. The memories curled around me like wisps of smoke, lingering and yet dissipating.

I tightened my grip on the neck of my guitar and closed the

door. And with the catch of the latch, I knew I was closing something much bigger, much heavier than this old slab of wood.

Back at Cliff and Maisy's party, when the sun tipped its hat to us, Cliff helped his new father-in-law, Robert Thomas, build the bonfire. Richie and I carried chairs and arranged them in a circle around the growing flames, while Mom and Maisy spread out a few quilts on the ground.

Our families fell into seats and soft conversation. The night hugged us all closely, the stars winking overhead. Through the smoke, I spotted Ada across from me, her husband Jimmy in the chair beside her. And sure enough, there in his front pocket was the telltale shiny glint of his harmonica.

I got up and retrieved my guitar from the front seat of the car. As I sat back down and positioned my guitar on my knee, Robert let out a whistle and someone else clapped. I felt a sudden charge of shyness, but then I realized I wouldn't be alone.

"I need a little help," I announced, nodding toward Jimmy.

Ada beamed at me through the flames and elbowed her husband's side.

Jimmy's thick mustache twitched. He reached into his pocket. He gave me a curt nod, and suddenly, by what felt like magic, my fingers knew right what to do. I hadn't played for a crowd bigger than the six ladies at the church. But playing in this moment was the easiest thing in the world. Maybe it was the intoxicating scent of the fire or the company of Jimmy's smooth harmonica . . . or maybe it was something else entirely. But I played as though I was born with my guitar in my hands.

Occasionally, I'd look up and catch someone's lips moving as they whispered lyrics to themselves. I'd see a little one being nestled safely into a lap or watch a hand reach out and interlock with another.

As I scanned the cozy circle, Cliff caught my eye. For a moment, he held my gaze. He sat on a quilt with Maisy pressed into his side, her head resting against his chest, her eyes closed. My fingers fumbled to find the next chord, but I was too scared to look away from my brother.

But he looked away first, leaning down to plant a kiss on the top of his bride's hair.

Jimmy blew on his harmonica a good long while until he tired and tucked it back into his pocket. Yawns passed around the fire, jumping from person to person. I nodded in thanks to Jimmy. He nodded back, his eyes twinkling.

I stopped strumming and extended the guitar to my father. "Alright, Dad. Show us how this thing is really supposed to be played."

"Play 'Old Chisholm Trail!'" Robert shouted.

"Yeah, that's a good one!" Jimmy agreed.

Dad chuckled and took it from me. "'Old Chisholm Trail' it is." He began to play. Pretty soon, the circle was tickled with liveliness. Jimmy brought his harmonica back out. Everyone clapped along as we sang together. Dad stretched the song on, a goofy, lopsided grin encompassing his face the entire time, and it reminded me that Vern was there with us after all.

When the song ended, Dad started in on something slower—a rendition of "Red River Valley." One by one, nearly everyone joined in to sing again. As a melancholic peace settled over us all, I had to wonder if Dad picked the song for a reason.

PART TWO

19

1949. Two years later...

SOMEHOW, DAD FINAGLED a contract to dig up abandoned railroad tracks and ties. They could be sold for good money. In between the hours I put in with him at the shop, he and I broke our backs nearly every summer morning leading up to my senior year. We woke at the crack of dawn and set out. We monotonously beat our bodies under the rising sun, uprooting the ties, tearing up the heavy tracks. Sweat seeped out of parts of me I never thought were capable of sweating.

The first few weeks were brutal. Waking up early, moving spindly muscles that weren't yet firm, the soreness that ensued. But as time wore on, it got easier and easier until it became enjoyable. I now woke before Dad and made his coffee. Eventually, I began making myself a cup too.

I whistled as I labored. My muscles hardened and grew. The best part was the time with my father, in spite of us barely speaking most days. Sometimes, I'd begun to believe, when I shut my mouth, my heart had a turn to do the talking.

And I'd never spoken a deeper conversation than those days with Dad.

—

September 1949 rolled in. One month shy of my eighteenth birthday, I stepped into a small school bus at the courthouse with Freddy Sue at the helm, ready to drive the Goldfield freshmen through senior students to Tonopah. For the past two years, two seniors had been elected to each drive a carload of us up to Tonopah every school day. But this year, the school district finally came through with their promise of a bus.

The morning wind rattled the bus the entire drive. I couldn't help but wonder if one day after I graduated this coming year, I'd live somewhere the wind didn't feel the incessant need to blow.

We finally parked at the high school on the corner of Bryan and Booker. We Goldfield kids had been attending school in Tonopah for two full years now. The change had been weird at first, but we'd integrated with the Tonopah kids quickly enough. We'd donned our roles as Muckers and Muckerettes and were now accustomed to the school's traditions, being involved in sports teams and clubs and the school band. We also concerned ourselves with the town's awaiting adventures, going all the places we had no business going. Like abandoned mines or Devil's Cave on top of T Mountain, for instance. We'd lower ourselves deep into the ground and explore underground tunnels, where we'd disturb the bats and pray our lanterns would continue to burn until we climbed back out. We rushed alongside our new friends after school, ready to explore and climb and crawl on our bellies if need be, dirtying our school clothes and racking up inevitable scoldings from our mothers.

Today was no different than any of those days, except it kicked off my final year. I unloaded from the bus with my friends and headed inside. Tall windows gave a clean look at the town and desert scrub. Dark wood underscored the interior's pomp. I ran my hand along the brass stripes in the banister as we headed up the stairs to our first class.

In the classroom, I took a seat in between Richie and Pete and watched a sea of familiar faces trickle into the room. The first day of school always carried with it an extra sparkle, a palpable buzz that hung in the air. But today felt different, more vibrant.

"Who's our teacher again?" Richie leaned over and muttered.

I gestured toward the chalkboard, where *Mr. Reynolds* was written in demanding capital letters. "Maybe this is the year you'll finally learn to read?"

He rolled his eyes and opened his mouth to retort but faltered, the breath seemingly knocked right out of his body. I followed his bewildered gaze to the doorway, and my breath was stolen away too, because, against everything that seemed feasible, Kitty May Ralph walked into the room.

She was no longer the pony-tailed girl with dirt under her fingernails and bruises on her shins. Time had closed the gap between adolescence and adulthood and had turned out a young woman. Taller, softer, swollen in places she wasn't before. The freckles on her nose were veiled with powder. Her perfectly curled, sandy hair bounced against her shoulders with each step. She didn't so much as glance my direction as she sat down in the front row next to Bethany Marshall. Richie had a perpetual crush on Bethany, a sharp-faced gal with a black bob and fire-engine red lipstick.

I glanced at Richie, then Pete, but neither could explain why this girl—a young woman now—whom we hadn't seen for four years was suddenly waltzing back onto the scene. They both looked as confused as I felt.

Kitty was close enough for me to get out of my seat, walk

two steps, and tap her on the shoulder. I considered doing so. Nerves crept up on me then. I drummed my fingers against my desk, searching for my former courage that now seemed to evade me.

But a tall man with thick, white hair and a beard to match swept into the room, his giant strides matching the big letters on the chalkboard. I wondered how often he was mistaken for a sleigh-riding, present-giving, belly-full-of-jelly fellow.

Mr. Reynolds clapped his hands. The boom reverberated through the room. Any last stragglers dropped into their seats within a second. Immediately, all of our attention focused on him.

The bell rang. At the conclusion of its shrill, he began to tap dance furiously, his feet flying across the floor, the bottom of his shoes smacking a rhythm into the tiles.

I glanced at Richie whose eyes bulged out of his head. I bit the inside of my cheeks to hold in my laughter.

Reynolds moved with a strange and mesmerizing passion. He came to a sudden stop and let out a giant, "Whoop!" His hands clapped in a commandeering way and then fell to his hips.

Not even slightly out of breath, he said, "Seniors! Welcome!" He scanned the room. "I'm Mr. Reynolds. I came aboard here as a teacher at the end of last school year. I recognize some of you, but I see a few fresh faces too. How about we get to know each other?" He pointed to the chalkboard. "Obviously, I'm a teacher, but I'll dare to assume you didn't know I'm also a champion tap dancer?" He briefly moved his feet brilliantly across the floor once again. "Most of you probably know each other. But still, let's begin today with introductions. Tell us who you are and something fun about yourself, or something you did over the summer. Who wants to go first?"

Everyone slid down in their chairs.

"Don't all jump up at once now. You'll ruin the foundation of this school too." He snickered at his own joke, told at the expense of us students from Goldfield. "No volunteers? Alright then." Mr. Reynolds pointed to a boy named Jack sitting in the front right corner. "We'll start with you, Mr. Knackey. Then work our way around the room."

Jack, and his dark comb-over, stood and moved to the front of the room, his hands shoved in his front pockets. "I'm Jack. You all know that already. Umm, I guess the most exciting thing I did this summer besides fishing was trying to make a certain girl go out with me."

I'd known Jack for a few years and thought nothing of his statement because he'd made eyes with nearly every girl in school. But then Bethany giggled and nudged Kitty. I froze. Kitty didn't move in response to her friend's goading. I stared at the back of her curls, wondering if she was wearing the same stupid, starry-eyed grin as Jack.

No one could've prepared me for this.

Introductions continued. The rest of the room flowed with ease, except for me. A jam in the road, a dam in the river. I couldn't pay attention. Kitty had sailed away from me once long ago. Now here she was again, out of the blue with no explanation. But I feared she was sailing away from me already, this time before I'd even reached the dock.

Richie tapped me with his foot and brought me back to reality. My turn was next.

I glanced at him. He raised his brows at me, imploringly. I nodded, assuring him I was okay despite not knowing if that were true or not.

Our classmate Etta finished her turn and sat down. I made my way to the front and stood directly before Kitty. The last time I was this close to her, she'd sent me on my way, making it clear that I ought to give her up for good. But that was before, right? When she thought she'd be moving away for good? Jack shifted in my peripherals. I was reminded that even now, four years later, Kitty still didn't want me. Hadn't even let me know she'd moved back to town and had apparently been here since summer.

I didn't want to introduce myself and play along with Mr. Reynolds' little game. I wanted instead to stoop down and say hello to the girl who used to be my best friend. To spark her attention enough to bring those whiskey-colored eyes away from studying something unseen on her desk and to look into mine. If she would just look at me once, I'd know. I'd see the truth, whether she wanted me to or not. But she didn't glance up. Her disregard spoke more than her eyes ever could. Too much time had passed between us, too much history set aflame; I let the final thread between us be severed and laid down my hopes for Kitty like she still clearly wanted.

"I'm Claude Fisher. I spent my summer digging up railroad ties and working on cars with my dad."

I went back to my desk. When I sat down, I noticed Kitty's head was lifted again, tilted toward Julia Garrish as Julia told us about a trip to visit her grandmother. When it came time for Kitty's turn, she flicked her hair over her shoulder and gave a cute wave. That small, quick gesture reminded me that she was a stranger now.

I knew nothing about this Kitty. My stomach flipped as I waited for her to speak, to reveal something about her life, or perhaps to confess a reciprocal love for Jack Knackey.

"I'm Kitty Ralph. Actually, I'm originally from Goldfield, but I attended here for part of my eighth-grade year before I moved away. But my aunt and I came back this July." Her eyes swept the room, briefly landing on every face, mine the last and the longest.

I stared back at her, all of our inseparable childhood years cramming into one single line that connected us from where I sat to where she stood fifteen feet from me. I could see us at five years old sitting on my porch, biting into fresh watermelon that Mom had just sliced, the juice dripping down her chin and neck. At six, when we carried an injured owl we'd found by the school all the way home and begged my dad to help us save it, only to find out it was already dead. When we were seven, gathered around my kitchen table with Cliff and Vern, playing game after game of checkers. I could see us at nine, Kitty pulled into my mother's arms, sobbing about something foul her father had said to her. I could see us at age ten when we discovered the abandoned Model-T Ford that became our secret hideout for years.

Her eyes flicked away, but mine didn't leave her face. She'd tossed me a crumb, or perhaps an apology . . . maybe a truce? I couldn't tell. But it was something. That much was unmistakable.

—

Kitty and I danced some pre-choreographed routine that prevented us from meeting, or should I say re-meeting, for a handful of days. I didn't force it. The school was small enough that I could've waltzed right up to her at any given time, had I been so bold. But then again, so could she. I aimed at being respectful, to give her space to run undetected like a quiet brook far in the distance.

Our first interaction came the second week of school. The final bell of the day rang. Our classmates filtered out of the room, but I noticed she was still scribbling away in her notebook. And so, I lingered until only she and I were left in the room.

I leaned against the desk next to hers and said, "With all that writing you're doing, you're making me second-guess my own work."

She set her pencil down and smiled. I caught a glimpse of her chipped front tooth. Age eight: she biffed it on the sidewalk chasing after Vern who'd jokingly stolen her ice cream cone.

"Claude," she whispered.

"Hi."

"Hi."

To think we used to tell all of our secrets to one another.

"So, you left. And you're back." *And you never let me know either time.*

"Yeah. It's a long story." Her forehead crinkled. "It's good to see you. How are you? How's your family?"

"We're doing well. Mom and Dad. Cliff too. He joined the Navy, got married to Maisy Thomas a couple years ago."

"Cliff and Maisy? You're kidding!" She gasped, and I drank in the twinkling of her whiskey eyes.

As much as I tried resisting the feeling, having her attention again lifted my feet off the floor. "Kind of wild, right? But they're really happy. Living in San Diego."

"Wow. Well, that's wonderful. Send them my best when you speak to them next."

"I will." I assessed her a moment, wondered how much I'd scare her away if I blurted out all my questions. The who, what, when, where, and why's.

"You look so different," she said.

"Me?" It was true I'd changed, but something about her noticing lit a fire in my core. Since she'd last seen me, I'd grown half a foot taller, had muscles that were no longer thin and ropy, but thick and tanned from my summer of working with my dad.

"Yes, you. Older, taller, bigger." Crimson dusted her cheeks. "Claude, I—"

"Fly!"

My shoulders sagged at my name. We'd been so close—on the brink, teetering on the edge.

Richie and Jack waltzed into the room. Richie tossed a basketball to me. He was lucky I didn't pelt it immediately back at his head.

"Come shoot hoops!"

Many of our friends had opted to join the football team. Since we all carpooled in one bus, the rest of us had spare time to do as we pleased for a good hour or more after school each day while they practiced, before we all met back up at Castle's Store.

Mom and Dad were sorely disappointed when year after year I decided not to play football. Particularly Mom who missed having someone to cheer for. Tossing a ball around with friends was one thing but being on a field in an actual game like Vern had been the night he died was another. Maybe if I were someone else, I'd play to honor him. But instead, I didn't play in order to preserve him.

"Alright, I'm coming," I said to them.

Richie turned to leave, but Jack lingered and strutted toward Kitty and me. I rapped my knuckles on Kitty's desk and waited a beat, but our moment was long gone. "I'm glad you're back, Kit."

I walked away as Jack reached Kitty's desk. At the doorway, I couldn't prevent myself from calling out to him, "Jack! Come on. We're wasting time."

He mumbled something to Kitty and turned back to follow me.

Kitty caught my eye. I saw a flash of something familiar, something I thought was lost forever. Blistering hope. I jogged to catch up to Richie. Even with Jack jogging beside me, my feet felt lighter than they had in years.

20

FIVE OF US—Richie, Pete, Benny, Gene, and I—were halfway to an abandoned mine shaft one day after school when the sky turned black. Richie had just finished sharing an inappropriate joke when the first rumble of thunder cracked above. Winds sprang up, blasting our faces with sand and making it impossible to see.

"I think I made God mad!" Richie yelled through the whipping gusts.

"You torqued him off with that one!" Gene hollered back.

Thunder rumbled overhead with a force that quaked the earth below our feet. But the bright flash of lightning striking the old mining hoist up ahead knocked us backward and sent us running the direction from which we'd just come.

Richie shrieked. Someone else swore. The two Tonopah kids, Benny and Gene, branched off, fleeing to their own houses. Only Richie, Pete, and I made a beeline for the refuge of the grocery store. Our pace quickened with every grumble from the slate-colored heavens. Finally, we slipped inside Castle's, free at last from the pelting rain and wicked wind.

I bent over, hands on my knees, huffing and puffing.

Richie and Pete slumped to the floor, their backs against the wall, eyes closed, chests heaving. I knew I had some loose change in my wallet, so I stood upright and assessed the store. What I really wanted, I'd find along the back wall.

I moved through the store, past shelves of beans, flour, ammunition, and coffee. At the far end of an aisle, I spied the glorious soda machine.

"—hard to get. And for some reason, I get the sense Fly's making it harder," Jack Knackey's voice said from the aisle parallel to mine. I cozied up to the soaps to get a better listen.

Another unrecognizable voice said something too low for me to hear. Whatever it was made Jack laugh and say, "Maybe it runs in her blood. She is the niece of a hooker after all."

My blood ran cold. The other voice laughed, and then they moved away from me toward the front of the store. I didn't follow them. I dug out three nickels from my wallet, proceeded to the soda machine, deposited the coins, and picked out three Cokes for me and my friends.

I walked back and slowed when I spotted Jack at the counter with a few items cradled in his arms. The mustached store owner, Bernard, helped him finish adding something to his family's tab. A guy named Ken that I recognized as a junior, but didn't really know, stood next to Jack. No Name's voice solved.

Jack signed a slip of paper and passed it back to Bernard, then he and Ken pushed through the store's door. They gave Richie and Pete a nod on their way out into the lightened rainfall.

I passed my friends each a Coke. We nursed them for a while in the shelter of the store while we waited for the bus to head back home. Bernard didn't seem to care.

When we finally made it back to Goldfield and were biking

home from the courthouse, Richie said to me, "Something's up with you. You've said jack squat all afternoon."

"Because I've been dreaming 'bout all the ways I'm going to kick the living daylights out of Jack Knackey."

Richie looked bewildered. "What are you talking about?"

The conversation marched round and round to a frantic tempo in my head. I had half a mind to hightail it back to Tonopah that very second. I gritted my teeth and snarled, "You heard me."

"Look, Fly . . ." He ran his hands through his thick tawny hair. "You gotta give me a little more to work with here. What's going on?"

I recounted to him what I'd overheard at the store.

"They were talking about Kitty like that? I can't believe you didn't start thumpin' him right then and there! But Jack? Are you sure?"

Richie and Jack had formed a decent friendship during our sophomore year when we all joined the basketball team. That was the only year I'd played, but Richie and Jack had continued on.

"I'm sure."

Richie grimaced. "I know Jack's got a bit of a reputation as a flirt, but I just can't imagine him saying something like that."

"I know what I heard and who I saw." Was Richie truly defending that weasel? "And I plan on taking care of it."

"What are you planning on doing?"

"Confronting Jack. I wish now I would've done it today, but I didn't want to make trouble for Bernard at the store. And I'm going to tell Kitty."

He sighed.

I slowed down. "What?"

He ignored me.

"Tell me."

"Nothing," he mumbled.

"Just spit it out." My patience was threadbare.

"It's just . . ." He squinted against the sun which pierced brightly now, as though it had never been shrouded by storm clouds a short while before. "Are you sure that's what you heard? Or what you *thought* you heard?"

"What's that supposed to mean?"

He held up his palm, as if to calm me down. "Look, Fly, I know you still have feelings for Kitty after all these years. And we both know Jack has been pursuing her since she got back into town."

"So?"

"So, maybe you want Jack to be a bad guy?"

"So, maybe I'm making this up? All to get the girl?" Fire flared in my core.

"All I'm saying is . . . maybe you heard things wrong, you know? You heard what you wanted to hear."

I couldn't help but laugh a deep belly-jiggling rumble; his deduction was that preposterous, not to mention insulting.

We neared his house. He slowed, but I didn't bother and continued plowing onward toward my own.

He hastened to catch back up to me. "Fly!"

"What?"

"I'm sorry. I just wanted you to consider the possibility."

"Of me being a dirty liar? Yeah, thanks, Rich."

"Of the dynamic. You and Jack and Kitty. If it's not accurate—you yourself said you only caught a fragment of their conversation—you could start a whole riff with Jack and tarnish both your reputations. And if it is true, you could risk a whole lot with Kitty if you tell her."

"What are you talking about?"

"I just don't know if coming from you would be the best way for her to hear it."

"And why not? I've known her longer than anyone else."

"She might take it the wrong way if you tell her."

"Why?"

He looked at me as though the answer were obvious. He spoke slowly, "Because you're in love with her?"

I'd done a lot of convincing myself that I wasn't still in love with Kitty. But I couldn't bring myself to argue back. "And that's why she deserves the truth."

"Do you ever think it would be easier if you just moved on?" Richie abruptly came to a halt. What he said stopped me in my tracks too.

I didn't turn to look at him, only stood there straddling my bike, letting my right leg hold up my weight. "Moved on from what?"

"Kitty."

Her name, spoken from a place slightly behind, carved itself into my back.

"Is that what you think?" I raised my voice. "I should just move on? 'Cause it's easier? Wash my hands of all things Kitty?"

"She might just think you're trying to break them up. Let it come from someone else, Fly." He crept forward to my side.

My ears burned hot. "Who's going to tell her? You?"

Richie, for once, had nothing to say.

"Yeah, didn't think so."

"You really just . . ." He sighed and rubbed his forehead. I got the sense he wanted to drop the matter.

But I was determined to do just the opposite. "I really just what?"

"Need to let her go! Get over it. Maybe it isn't your job to keep trying to save her and fix her life? You've spent so much time pining for someone who clearly doesn't want you back. Give it up and move on."

I tasted the venom that sat upon my tongue, ready to fire at him. But in a swell of emotion, it vanished. The rage, the incessant need to be understood, the desire to hold Kitty's heart.

"What a mercy it is that not everyone adopts your same attitude," I said and looked north.

He looked at me like I'd lost my mind. "What are you talking about?"

On the side of Euclid Avenue, hit by a clobbering revelation, life finally made the faintest sliver of sense. I knew I'd go against Richie's advice and tell her. And funnily enough, I knew I'd be okay if she didn't believe me, if it ruined every last chance of a future with her. Because withholding the truth and seeking cover like a coward when adversity reared its ugly head and spat right in my face was something I wouldn't do. I would lay down everything to protect Kitty.

My hopes.

My dreams.

My memories.

Whatever the cost to me. It was the only way. And if my hands remained forever empty—no hand of Kitty's to keep them warm—I knew instead they'd be full of whatever else God wanted me to carry.

—

The following day at school, I looked for an opportunity to speak with Kitty alone, but no opening presented itself. When I spotted her in a huddle with her friends at the end of the day, I decided to create my own moment.

Tapping her on her shoulder, I said, "Excuse me, Kitty. Can I have a minute with you?"

She took a step away from her friends, who collectively leaned toward us to hear.

"Sure." She looked apprehensive. Yet, a flash of something familiar—curiosity or maybe a sense of adventure—glimmered in the hall light.

"Mind going somewhere a little more private?"

She glanced at her friends, the rouge dusting her cheeks doing nothing to hide her true blush. "Okay . . . Everything alright, Claude?"

I walked down the hallway. She fell into step beside me.

"What's going on?"

"I need to talk to you about something important. Just preferably not in here with so many people around."

Kitty shot me glance after glance, trying to figure out the puzzle as we exited the school.

I guided her down a worn dirt trail that led away from any curious ears.

After a minute of walking, she stopped and gestured at the surrounding desert. "This private enough?"

The wind danced around us, subtle enough to be friendly, bold enough to carry our words in its streams and deliver them to whomever it pleased. I pretended to inspect the area, to regard the spiders and lizards that hid beneath rocks, eavesdropping.

"It ain't no Model T, but it'll do."

A smile weaseled its way across Kitty's face despite her efforts to contain it. "That was always a good spot for secrets, huh?"

I nodded. Everything seemed easier to talk about back there, back then. Her eyes sparkled for a moment, as if remembering too. I caught myself from reaching for her, for the past. This wasn't going to be easy.

"So, what's this all about?" Kitty folded her arms against her chest and squinted at me.

The words lodged themselves in my throat. For someone who'd rehearsed this meeting in his mind all day, I suddenly had no idea where to start.

"Well?"

"First of all, I need to know what's going on with you and Jack," I blurted out. What was wrong with me?

She stiffened and sharply raised a brow. "Excuse me?"

"Don't worry. I didn't bring you all the way out here to try and sweep you off your feet. I just need to know before I tell you what I have to say."

"Okay. Well, I knew him from a few years ago, you know. We were classmates here. But then Peggy and I moved away—"

"New York, right?" I told her about the newspaper blurb.

She blew a strand of hair from her mouth and laughed. "That's what Peggy wished everyone to believe. We went to Manhattan."

"Nevada?"

"No."

"And not New York?"

"Kansas."

"Kansas?" All this time I'd envisioned Kitty surrounded by skyscrapers and men who wore suits and carried briefcases everywhere they went.

"It wasn't just Kansas. We were in Knoxville for a stint. Then Roanoke."

"So, what brought you back? I thought Peggy hated the desert."

"Peggy had a hard time leaving here, actually. The place she'd met her husband, his grave, the house he'd bought for her. When she lost her job in Roanoke, she told me she hated the desert but loved him more. She decided to phone a friend here and was offered her old job back at the Miz. I think she's drifting. Trying to make sense of her life, where she fits. I'm not sure she'll ever be able to let that man go."

The map of grief. It took a person on routes that sometimes made no sense at all.

"So, you moved away and came back . . ." *And you never let me know.* I let my feelings fall along with the words I'd never say.

"And we've been living in the hotel at a discount until Peggy figures out our housing situation. They take our living costs out of her wages. She desperately wants to purchase her old home back. Wishes she'd never sold it in the first place." Kitty drew her arms tighter across her chest. "So, one day, I was sitting at a table in the Mizpah when Jack and his family came in for lunch. To be honest, when he first came over to me, I don't think he recognized me. I was kind of hoping no one would anyway. Once he really looked at me, he did. And ever since, he's been trying to make me his proper girlfriend. We've gone out a handful of times."

"So, you like him?"

"Maybe?" She shrugged and sighed. "What are you trying to get at, Claude?"

"Look, I overheard him saying some awful things to one of his friends yesterday."

"Like what?" She stood before me, stiff as a board, waiting for more.

I couldn't think of a gentle way to deliver the news. "Jack was talking about his hope to, uh, get you into bed. Something about it running in your blood, being the niece of a . . . hooker." I flinched when I spoke the last word, praying it wouldn't dig into her and fester like a splinter.

But Kitty didn't balk, didn't even move an inch, and it made me second-guess every one of my own movements.

"I'm sorry," I whispered, taking a step toward her. "I just thought you ought to know. Are you okay?"

"I'm more embarrassed than anything," she murmured. She tilted her head back, let her curls fall away and the sun wash over her face. Talking to the sky, she said, "But maybe he's not wrong."

I cocked my head, sure I'd heard her wrong.

She turned her gaze upon me. "I fought so long thinking I belonged to another family—yours. Believing I was more than my own lineage, somehow above it. But there comes a point when you can't keep hiding from what keeps seeking you out."

"Kitty." I cautioned another step closer. "What are you saying? Please don't tell me you're thinking of giving yourself up to a guy like Jack."

"If it's any of your business, I plan to wait for marriage."

That only eased my worry marginally. Her sudden coldness worried me more.

"Then I hope you won't waste your time on Jack, because he's certainly not the type to wait. Kitty, I don't want to see you hurt. I don't want you settling for someone who treats you like you're not worth a hill of beans. Why not find someone who treats you the way you deserve?"

"Maybe he is."

"Is what?"

"Treating me the way I deserve."

"Kit," I murmured, shaking my head in disbelief. "You think you deserve that? Are you delusional?"

Anger struck like lightning across her face. "I'm just trying to do my best here, the only way I know how."

"No," I argued, with a fervent need to get her to see the truth. But I had the feeling that anything I said would drive her farther away. "You don't deserve Jack or Peggy or your father or anyone else who treats you less than you are."

"Easy for you to say," she huffed.

"What do you mean?"

"I don't know, Claude." Exasperated, she lifted her hands in the air. "I've never known family in the way you have. Yours was the closest and only thing I had to it. And then, after knowing that my whole life, I was catapulted into a new life out of nowhere. My only choice is to push on and pretend like I fit in, like I'm not unwanted trash.

"My mom never wanted me. She left the first chance she could. I was just a baby. A *baby, Claude.* And she made the choice that I wasn't good enough to stick around for or to at least take me with her. And my dad? He stuck with me—a surprise he didn't plan for or desire, a human being he couldn't find the time of day for, couldn't spare some change for lest he find himself without his precious liquor—only out of obligation.

"And then there's Peggy. She never gave two hoots about me my entire life but only wants me around now because she's bored and lonely. I fill some sort of void."

Hoarseness coated Kitty's throat. She turned away, fixating on a Joshua tree in the distance rather than meeting my pressing gaze.

"And there's me," she finally croaked, still angled away. "Me, the one who's at the center of it all. I'm suffocating, strangled by it, but have no choice except to make it through. There's something carved out for me—a destiny that isn't anything you want to be a part of. I know you want to protect me, Claude. You always have. But believe me, it's in your best interest to let me go. Please. For your sake and mine. Because I'd never forgive myself if you hung your hat on me. You deserve better."

She swam before me, my eyes stinging with tears.

"You're blind," I said. "Hardened and stuck. You think your worth stems from a source that was never capable of a spring, let alone a trickle. You think a moron like Jack is going to make you happy? He's just like the rest of them. He'll never love you like you deserve, but you're too scared to actually face reality to see that. You're too comfortable. You're too satisfied with being stepped on and pushed aside. But that pushover, doormat Kitty isn't the real one. I know you—"

"You know me? Oh, really?" She flipped around, wild-eyed and cheeks beet red. She stomped toward me and looked me dead in the eye. "You think you have it all figured out!"

I swallowed and stared at her, unblinking. "Open your eyes, Kitty, and get off this dark, sad train before you crash, burn, and enjoy it."

"Are you *kidding* me? Enjoy it? You think I enjoy feeling this way? You think this feels good to me?"

"If you don't like it then why are you so insistent upon continuing down that road and putting up with it? You say you're suffocating. Maybe other people put the pillow over your face, but you're the one holding it there."

Her eyes went wide. After a handful of seconds, she whispered, "You're cruel. Mean and cruel."

"If you think that's mean, then you're not gonna like what I have to say next." I took a deep breath. "I love you. I've loved you for a long time, and it's going to take forever for me to stop loving you. But you know what I wish? I wish I didn't love you. I wish you loved yourself instead."

She looked at me like she hated me. In a way, I hated myself too for making her cry. But I think what we both hated the most was the truth. She spun and broke into a sprint, her feet kicking up dust behind her as she went. I watched her go with hopes that maybe she'd find herself along the way, wherever it was she was heading.

21

Winter 1949

THE COLD SWEPT in, stinging my wounded edges, the severed branches that once held Kitty and Richie in their places as my friends. Could I have handled things differently? Better? I still didn't have that answer, even months later.

Snow had been falling all night, and it refused to relent as we left for school one winter morning. Freddy Sue sat behind the wheel. He'd acted like a hotshot when he volunteered to drive the bus at the beginning of the school year. Then he quickly realized the position wasn't as esteemed as he first thought, considering that several freshmen and sophomore boys found it hilarious to pester him from behind during the entire drive. Boy, it had always torqued him off when they flicked his ears and shot spit wads at him every few miles. But today, he barked at them to knock it off, his white knuckles on the wheel emphasizing his obvious lackluster desire to drive on slick roads. Surprisingly, no one messed with him once. By the time we got to Tonopah, swirling flakes completely shrouded our vision, the sky dumping continually.

I flew off the bus alongside Pete. We scooped up snowballs and pelted everyone as they came off the bus. Carelessly, I slung ball after ball, all in good fun, not truly paying attention to who I was hitting. Some of the girls shrieked and complained. One or two threw a snowball back.

By complete accident, I smacked Richie right in the side of the face. He looked at me, a tight smile on his mouth. Truth be told, he probably thought I'd done it on purpose. He and I had hardly spoken since our spat about Kitty and Jack. In fact, he and Jack had only become closer friends since.

I hoped he would scoop up some snow and pelt me back. For a split second, I thought he might. But he wiped his face and turned away, heading into the school. I headed in too. Though I wasn't far behind him, it felt like we were far apart. Like I'd been left in the dust, our friendship deserted altogether.

Hour by hour, the snow hardly slowed. We monitored its accumulation from our classroom windows. After lunch, the administration made a special announcement. In order to make the most of the weather, they'd decided to let school out early. As a special treat, the fire department had closed roads and iced down KC Hill all morning.

When school was officially dismissed, everyone spilled out and raced to grab or borrow sleds.

Within the hour, I stood atop the hill, goading Pete to go next. We'd just watched our friend Miles whoosh down, flipping off his sled right at the intersection of Central Street. "I'll give you a silver dollar if you make it clear to Main."

"Nah, man. I could wind up under the wheels of a truck. I won't try that for less than two."

"You realize you've just admitted your life is only worth two dollars, right?"

197

"I don't know about you, but that's a lot of money to me!" I laughed. Some younger kid brushed past us, not hesitating as he slapped his sled down and hopped aboard, zooming away. "That young'n just showed you up."

"You know, you shouldn't be talking. I don't see you chomping at the bit for your turn."

"Alright, fine. Gimme that." I took Pete's sled and climbed on. "Give me a push, would ya?"

He sent me off alright, with the best shove he could manage. Everything whizzed past me, the cold air perma-freezing the glee on my face. With no signs of slowing down, I realized my sled was angling right for a telephone pole. I watched it grow closer and closer until I bailed off at the last minute, eating a mouthful of snow.

Sputtering, I picked myself up and waited for Pete to find another sled and zoom down. He did, right past me all the way to the old Belvada. He jogged back, pulling the sled behind him, shouting, "You owe me, Fly!"

"Heck, no! You came up short!"

He slugged me in the arm. "Oh, pay up. I could've kept going!"

"I said if you made it clear to Main, not shy of it."

Someone off to our left shouted something about hot chocolate. We looked over to see a woman standing in front of her house, passing out steaming cups to anyone who asked. Standing around a small bonfire near her house huddled a group of our classmates, among them Kitty, Bethany, Richie, and Jack. Something about the scene cinched my insides tight. It hurt to breathe. An explosion of air puffed in front of Kitty's face every time she spoke or laughed. I longed to hear that conversation, to know what tickled her ears.

Just take care of her—the same small prayer I always found myself muttering whenever it came to Kitty these days.

Pete and I trudged back up the hill for another slide down. Though this time when we reached the bottom, Kitty, Richie, Jack, and the rest of them were gone. In fact, Richie stayed gone. He wasn't on the bus to go home. I figured he stayed behind to hang out with Jack.

Freddy drove us back to Goldfield. We pulled up to the courthouse having only slid on the roads twice. I rose to get off the bus, my thoughts on warming up by the fire and Mom's cooking. Franco held out an arm to stop both me and Pete before we hopped off.

"Wait a minute," Franco muttered.

We let everyone younger than us filter off the bus, let all the girls our age go ahead too. Once they'd gone, Freddy jumped from behind the wheel and slid a wooden box from beneath the driver's seat, revealing a stash of beer.

"Wanna join us?"

Pete and I exchanged glances. We both knew better than to ask where they'd gotten it.

"Yes!" Pete said.

Five of us drove out into the cold winter night and climbed into an abandoned boxcar. Pete, Freddy, Franco, Mickey, and me. We brushed aside snow and sat on the wooden floor, our legs dangling off the sides. Freddy handed each of us a bottle. There was one left over, which undoubtedly would've gone to Richie should he have been with us.

I didn't know quite how to make sense of the way things were turning out. I'd been replaced by the same person when it came to the two best friends I'd ever had. I took a swig of my beer, the first of my life, and my innards twisted at its unpleasantness. I tried again, taking another pull. I stared up at the stars, looking for a bend in the Milky Way, a falter in the constellations. Any sign to tell me that God was up there looking down on me, ready to give me the answers. All I saw was a sea of blinking dust, collapsing on itself and making me feel lonelier than I already was.

Pete nudged me, waking me from my thoughts and clinking his bottle against mine. Cheers were passed around the five of us. I took another swig, but all the thrill of this contraband only tasted bitter. I thought of Jeb Ralph. I hopped down from the boxcar and walked around its backside, my boots crunching prints into the fresh snow as I went. I poured out the remainder of my beer, watched as it hissed into the snow, and then rejoined my friends.

No one said a whole lot. Because of the cold, we couldn't do much besides sip beer and hug our coats around us. But that was okay. In the silence, I tasted something I hadn't in a long time—the inkling of a new beginning.

22

Spring 1950. A few months later . . .

THE BALMY CALIFORNIA air prickled my skin. I wondered how long it had taken Cliff, a boy with high desert heat in his veins, to get used to this unrelenting hug of humidity that rolled in from the coast. We chugged along in the night, windows down, Dad at the wheel, our destination only miles away. Mom and Dad bickered about directions; she swore Cliff had said to turn right, while Dad held steady that Cliff had said left.

Tuning them out, I closed my eyes and sprawled across the backseat, exhausted from the hours on the road. My parents had squeezed out every drop worth of driving from me the past two days.

The motion of the car nearly lulled me to sleep, but then we finally arrived at Cliff's rental home. We gathered our bags from the car and approached the small, shoddy house with its grimy shutters and cracking exterior walls. A dim light switched on inside. A small commotion followed. A dog barked. Cliff opened the door to greet us with bags under his eyes and a sleepy smile.

"Mama," he said and scooped our mother into a warm embrace.

A small shadow skittered around him. Suddenly, I felt the paws of a dog jumping at my calves, its wet nose pressing into my skin.

"Ike!" Cliff called to him. "Down!"

Ike promptly sat down beside Cliff, his body wiggling with excitement the longer he tried to contain himself. From the faint light streaming through the open door, I saw he was a beagle. I squatted down and extended my hand. Ike bounded toward me in an instant and ducked under my touch. I scratched him, and he collapsed against me, going belly-up.

Cliff let Mom go and held his hand out to Dad. "Pops," he said.

But Dad smacked his outstretched hand away and pulled him into a hug.

When Dad released him, Cliff turned to me. To Ike's disappointment, I stood. "Fly!" He didn't bother this time with the attempted handshake, but went straight for a hug, bridging the three-year gap since we'd last embraced.

He let me go and led us into his home. A dank smell protruded from behind the walls. Ike rushed past us all and leapt onto a sunken couch, claiming his throne.

Maisy emerged from a room at the back of the little home. We certainly didn't expect her to look like she'd swallowed one or two of the beach balls we'd seen blowing around on the beach as we drove in.

She burst into tears the minute she saw us, as did Mom. But Cliff—I'd never forget the look on his face—wore a grin bigger than any I'd ever seen.

They had phoned months ago to tell us they were

expecting. We knew she was roughly seven months along now, but I hadn't expected her belly to be quite so swollen.

"I know! I know!" Maisy sobbed, though a smile was visible through the curtain of tears. "I'm huge!"

"You're beautiful," Dad said and gave her a hug.

"And I'm so, so sorry about the house." She sniffled and looked around. "I wanted to make it more presentable, but it's just been so hard to do chores these days. And they've been working Cliff to the bone, so he's hardly been home, and . . . and . . ."

"Honey, take a breath." Mom held her by the shoulders until she calmed down. "Just breathe. It's okay."

Maisy wiped her eyes, her breathing ragged. All she could muster was a thankful smile.

Cliff crossed the room and wrapped an arm around her. When her breathing slowed, she said, "I just feel so overwhelmed. And I saw a midwife last week who told me, based on my size, she wouldn't be surprised if there were two in there."

"You sure there aren't three?" I quipped.

That, apparently, was the wrong thing to say. Maisy began crying again.

Mom whipped around, shooting daggers at me as Dad flicked my ear. I held up my hands. "I'm sorry. Just trying to lighten the mood."

"Stop it," Cliff said to Maisy. "You're brimming with life, that's all."

"Maisy, honey, you should sit down." Mom directed her to a chair.

Maisy sat, leaned back, and rested her hands on her stomach, over the life that rested beneath. "How am I going to stretch any more than I already have over the next two months? I just keep half expecting a naval ship to show up, haul me off, and dump me into the ocean along with all the other whales."

Cliff brushed a hair from her face tenderly. "Sweetheart, stop saying those things."

She shrugged and muttered, "It's just how I feel."

Mom dragged a chair over and sat down next to Maisy. She grabbed her hand. Together they dove headfirst into pregnancy talk.

I took a seat on the couch, as far away from their conversation as possible, and tried blinking away the dampness that permeated the air. Ike wiggled over and laid his head in my lap, his energy waning. "Still can't believe I'm going to be an uncle."

"Try coming to terms with fatherhood." Cliff laughed and ran a hand over his buzzed hair. "So, as you can see, we don't exactly have a lot of space." Cliff gestured around him and pointed to the mattress in the middle of the room. "I got a mattress set up here for Mom and Dad. Claude, you can take the couch. It even comes with a dog to keep you warm. I'm sorry it's so crowded. Maybe we should've set you guys up in a hotel."

"We'll make do," Dad said. "Unless it feels too cramped to everyone else, in which case we can send Claude to sleep outside."

"I don't care where I sleep at this point." I stroked behind Ike's ears. He cracked an eyelid, winking at me in approval. I stretched out and rolled over with Ike snuggled into my torso, the two of us drifting off to sleep on the couch.

—

I woke to the sounds of my mother humming and bacon grease popping. I got up from the couch and was amazed as I looked around the home. Curtains back and windows thrown open, the space was flooded with daylight and fresh, salty air. The whole place shone, scrubbed and clean.

"How long have you been up?" I asked my mom.

She fluttered around the kitchen, in search of something. "Oh," she said as she blew a strand of hair out of her face and smiled. "A while."

I sniffed the air. "I see bacon and biscuits, but why do I smell lemons?"

"There's a lemon tree outside," Mom whispered in a hushed tone. "Not sure who it belongs to, but I picked a few anyway. For cleaning the house."

"California's turned you into a downright criminal," I muttered. "It looks wonderful in here."

"Thank you," she said. "Now let's get this gravy done. I can't imagine the two lovebirds will sleep much longer."

Cliff and Maisy eventually emerged from the bedroom. Maisy's eyes welled as she saw all that my mother had done.

We all ate breakfast together, crowding around their tiny two-person table, our plates clanking together. Ike paced around under our feet, looking for crumbs to rain down for him. I slipped him a slice of bacon.

Later, we went to the beach. Cliff and I stood, hands shoved into our pockets, laughing while we watched Mom and Dad squeal like a couple of kids as the tide swept in and over their feet. Never before had my parents or I seen anything like the great expanse of the ocean. Over the last few years, Cliff and Maisy had sent us postcards, many with photographs of the beach dazzling the front of them. Now, I felt like I was living inside of one. Stuck in time. In paradise. A moment too good to be true.

Out of nowhere, Cliff scooped me up, catching me off guard. He ran straight into the water and deposited me into a breaking wave. I surfaced, my clothes clinging to me. I shook my hair and sent water droplets flying. "You're a dead man!" I took off out of the water to chase him down.

Maisy sat in a chair on the beach, her swollen feet soaking in a small pool of water that Cliff had dug for her, and laughed at the flock of us. Mom and Dad frolicking together like young lovers. Cliff and I wrestling like only brothers could.

"Before you leave, I'm takin' you to ride the coaster," Cliff said, brushing sand from his shorts. "That rickety beast is the most fun you'll ever have for twenty-five cents." He held out his hand to me and helped me off the ground.

"That's a lofty promise. Let's go tonight?" The sand clung to my wet clothes, and my incessant brushing did nothing to get rid of it. I peeled off my shirt and headed for the water to rinse it out. Cliff followed, but I sensed what he was up to. I waded in up to my knees, bent over to soak my shirt, and watched his every subtle move.

When he thought I wasn't paying attention, he jumped on my back to push me in the water. I crouched down at that moment, and he soared over top of me face-first into the waves. By the time he gathered his legs beneath him, I was standing on the shoreline, smiling. "Whatcha doing over there?"

He spat sand from his mouth and belly laughed. "Well played. You're quicker than I remember. Maybe a little smarter too."

"And better looking. Don't forget that one."

He trudged out of the water and slapped me on the shoulder. "I will say I like the bit of stubble you got coming in. I'm a little jealous you're allowed to grow a beard, no matter how measly. Now that I'm finally able to, it's against regulations."

I stroked my jawline. "You think I should let it grow? Mom says I ought to be clean-shaven. Guess she wants me baby-faced like you."

If I hadn't run, he would've tossed me back into the water.

That night, Cliff took me to Belmont Park. I stood, arms

crossed, watching a series of carts barrel along a rickety wooden track, the people inside shrieking with either fear or delight. Bright lights beat down upon us, illuminating the ride. Somewhere nearby, a bell rang out. Within a minute, the coaster glided to a halt in front of us. Its passengers scrambled out with grins on their faces. Except for one young kid, whose pants were darkened with a pool of urine.

"If you piss yourself, I'll make you pay me back," Cliff whispered. "Come on!"

He took off sprinting and dodged around people who were trying to exit in order to claim the front cart for ourselves. He dove in and looked back for me. My stomach flopped.

"Not so much afraid of peeing myself as I am re-tasting my lunch."

"It's not that bad, ya pansy," he said.

And he was right on two counts. It really was the most fun I'd ever had for twenty-five cents. And it wasn't that bad. We rode it a second time, then walked around the grounds awhile, where we bought ice cream and watched throngs of people meander about.

"How are things back home?" he asked.

"They're alright. You miss it at all?"

He scoffed, looking at me like I'd lost my mind. "Definitely not. If I ever feel a little homesick, I stare into the dirt for a minute, and that solves that."

I knew it was a joke, but for some reason, it stung. "Always were hell-bent on getting out of there," I muttered.

He flung his arms open wide and spun in a circle. "You can't tell me this is worse than that wretched desert?"

"That wretched desert? Really? Man, you're dramatic." I looked away from him and noticed a group of teenage girls gathered beside a carnival booth. One girl with voluminous, auburn waves and the color of deep wine on her lips caught my eye and smiled before shyly turning away.

"So, what then?" Cliff asked, continuing to walk on. "You can't stay in Goldfield forever. What are you going to do in a few months when you graduate?"

"I haven't really thought of it."

"Maybe it's time you start."

Maybe. But the truth was I had no idea where to begin, though I couldn't admit this to Cliff. Already I could hear his response. *Join the military like me,* he'd say. *Whatever you do, just get out of Nevada.*

"Come on! First toss free! How about it, boys?" A carnival worker, clad in a red and white pin-striped suit, hollered to us from his booth. He leaned against one of the poles that held up his canvas tent. "Alright, alright. Two tosses . . . free! Let's see what yer made of!"

"These games are rigged," Cliff leaned in toward me and muttered. Then to the worker, he shouted, "How about you show us how it's done first, huh? You toss one of those rings around one of the bottles, then we'll play."

The worker pointed a finger at him. "Now, come on! That'd be bad for business."

Cliff shook his head and laughed. We rounded the ring toss tent, and at the booth in front of us stood the same girl I'd seen minutes before. Her friends stood idly by, watching as a carnival worker, dressed the same as the ring-toss guy, insisted she take a ball and throw it at a stack of milk jugs. She shook her head but, in a moment, relented and took the ball. Her aim was atrocious. At her failure, the man came out of his booth and sidled up behind the girl, pressed the front of his body into her back, and grabbed her wrist.

"The trick is, ya gotta throw like this," he said, moving her body through the motion.

I caught a glimpse of her face, her features scrunched up in disgust. I exchanged a quick glance with Cliff and bounded over to them. Clearing my throat for emphasis, I said, "Excuse me." I grabbed the man's shoulder and pulled him off her, not as gently as I could have. "Don't touch her like that."

He scowled and straightened out his rumpled sleeve. "What are you, her boyfriend or sumpthin?"

I opened my mouth, but the girl interjected before I could answer. "Yes! He is!" She glared at the man, fire in her eyes.

"Here," I said, holding out my palm. She placed the ball in my hand. The man winced like I was about to hurl it at him. But I scanned the stack of milk jugs and let it fly, sending them scattering to the floor. The girl screeched beside me.

"I believe you owe the miss that stuffed dog right up there," I said to the man, pointing at a black Scotty dog on the shelf.

He grumbled under his breath, pulled out a step stool, and reached for the dog. He reluctantly handed it over to the girl. I nodded in approval and turned back to Cliff.

I'd only made it a handful of steps when she called out to me. "Wait!"

A small hand rested on my arm, urging me to turn around, so I did.

She looked up at me, her lipstick-smeared mouth grinning. "Thank you. That was . . ." She shrugged and hugged her new Scotty. "What's your name?"

"Claude Fisher. Yours?"

"Marla. Marla Coffeeman."

"Well, Miss Marla Coffeeman, the honor was mine. I hope you have a nice rest of your evening."

She looked bewildered. "That's it? You swoop in, rescue me, then bid me farewell? Some pretend boyfriend you are!"

I glanced at my brother, who slapped my shoulder. "I'll let you handle this one on your own," he murmured. "I wanna get home to Maisy soon. Meet you at the entrance in a few?" Cliff walked away, weaving in and out of the crowd. I watched until he turned a corner and disappeared from my sight altogether.

Alone, I looked back at Marla. "That son of a gun just ditched me."

"Brother or friend?"

I looked for Cliff in the crowd one more time before answering. "Both."

Without even realizing what was happening, I wandered through the park side by side with Marla, her black dog tucked under her arm.

"Where're you from?" she asked.

"Goldfield, Nevada."

"Goldfield, huh? Never heard of it. Are there really fields of gold?"

I snorted. "Not that I've ever seen. Hills of dirt, fields of sagebrush and cacti? Sure. Gold, nope. That's been all but gone a long time. What about you? Where're you from?"

"Here. Well, I was born in Long Beach, but my daddy's job moved us down here when I was a baby."

"What's he do?"

"Architect."

"Impressive."

"I don't know how impressive it is. We don't really see him enough to know," she said, adding an empty-hearted laugh at the end. "So, what are you doing in San Diego?"

"Visiting my brother and his wife. He's stationed down here, and they're expecting their first child soon. Maybe three."

"Triplets?"

"No, that's just a bad joke." I laughed. "You give him a name yet?"

"Who?"

"That dog of yours."

"Oh." She giggled and held him up in the fading sky. "I

don't know. Perhaps Pablo?"

"Pablo?" I grimaced.

She stuck her tongue out at me. "Don't make fun. Pablo's a perfectly good name."

"For a Spanish breed! That dog is Scottish."

She covered the stuffed dog's ears and shushed me. "He's *American*."

"I should get a say in this. I mean, I did win him for you."

"You do have a point there." She thrust Pablo into my hands. "What do you think then?"

I scratched Pablo behind the ears and stroked his back. "Oh? What's that, buddy?" I held the dog to my ear and nodded, knitting my brows together. "Mmm. I see. Alright, alright. I'll tell her." Looking at Marla, I delivered the news. "He wants you to know that Pablo is an acceptable first name, though he requests Jacques for his middle name."

"Jacques? That's neither Spanish nor Scottish!"

"Does it matter? I thought he was *American*."

"Fine. Pablo Jacques Coffeeman it is." She took back the dog. "What a name."

"It was nice meeting you and Pablo, but I really need to catch up to my brother before he decides to ditch me altogether."

The way she angled her body told me she didn't want me to leave. "How long are you in town?"

"We leave day after tomorrow."

"Well, my friends and I are having a bonfire at the beach tomorrow night," she said, her voice lifting with the stirrings of hope. "Seven o'clock. South of Crystal Pier. If you're interested?"

Her forwardness struck me. I didn't know how to feel about it. I reached out to pet Pablo Jacques' faux fur. "Uh, maybe?"

"So, I'll see you there then." She grinned and flipped

around, bounding back to her friends before I could argue, the black stuffed dog tucked carefully under her arm.

When I caught up with Cliff and told him about my short time with Marla on our way home, he urged me to see her again. "Do you like her?"

"I don't know her. But maybe? I don't really know." And I didn't. I wasn't sure how to allow myself to feel something for someone who wasn't Kitty.

"Well, she's cute, right? Seems nice? Fun? Obviously is interested in you."

I was willing to wager a bet that my whole family would encourage me to pursue even the faintest glimmer of someone who wasn't Kitty. "I don't live here, so I'm not sure I see the point."

"I'm not telling you to marry the girl, sheesh. You always think too far ahead. Go to the bonfire, Claude. You never know where life will lead you."

—

I wrestled with my decision throughout the next day until six o'clock. Down to the wire. Cliff enlisted Maisy into convincing me to go. I finally made up my mind and left, if anything, to get away from their prodding. They let me borrow their car, and I drove to the pier.

A decent-sized gathering had formed down on the beach. Guys and girls sitting around a fire, tossing balls back and forth, running down into the water. Marla, in a polka dot swimsuit, frolicked out of the water to me, skipping and singing when she saw me approach. "You came! You came!"

"I'm only here to see Pablo."

She frowned and folded her arms. "Pablo's at home, I'm afraid."

"Rats." I clucked my tongue, feigning disappointment. "I guess you'll have to suffice."

She grinned, big and toothy. I couldn't deny how easy it was to banter with her, or how pretty she truly was. "Come on," she said. "I'll introduce you to my friends."

She led me by the hand. I felt something like a celebrity as she brought me around to everyone, telling them about me swooping in and saving her from a creep at the milk-jug stand. When the thrill of the story tired out, she slipped a loose dress over her head and led me away for a walk.

A certain buzz of whimsy hung in the air, and I felt myself loosen. I took off my shoes and rolled up the cuffs of my pants. As we walked, our bare feet pressed into the sand. The edge of the water yearned to tickle our toes. The tide worked to give it its wish.

Words came easily to her. She prattled on about anything and everything, genuinely entertaining me with her charm. The breeze coming off the water whipped through her hair and carried whiffs of perfume to my nose. The blend of the sea and hydrangea sent a spike of intoxication through my body. Marla staring up at me with her bright, curious eyes didn't help either. I wanted so badly to forget everything to do with Kitty, to be a different person in a different life. Maybe here, I could be? Perhaps, this was how I started over? The idea of moving here to live near Cliff or joining the military suddenly didn't seem quite as preposterous as before.

We stopped to watch the sun droop lower. Its yolk bled into the horizon.

"Thank you again for yesterday. I truly mean that. You are a true gentleman," she said. Reaching on her tiptoes, in true forward-Marla fashion, she suddenly pecked her lips to mine.

The rush of cold water over my ankles was second to the warm flood of emotion inside me. The wet sand squished beneath my feet as I stepped closer to her. As my limbs and lips operated by some separate order, my mind scrambled to make sense of this turn of events.

You can't tell me this is worse than that wretched desert? Cliff's voice echoed through my mind. No, I couldn't quite say this was worse. Maybe he was right all along? I couldn't count all the times he'd preached a bigger, better world to me outside of our central Nevada desert. All the times I'd rejected the notion and scoffed at him. What if something—or someone—out here had been waiting for me this whole time, ready to pass me by on account of my stubbornness?

Yet, something didn't feel quite right. Where, in the midst of this excitement, was the love? The years of friendship that surpassed in magnitude a single sunset walk? Where was the understanding of a soul? The knowing? The true intimacy?

I pulled back. This wasn't the kind of man I wanted to be. It frightened me how easily I'd fallen off course from that.

Marla looked at me, spell-bound, her skin dewy. I knew a complex spider web of events had transpired in order for her to be here on this beach with me. But suddenly, the shimmery glint of romance looked like nothing but dust.

"Sorry," I whispered. "I'm no gentleman at all."

"What? Yes, you are." She searched my face.

"What's the difference between me and that guy at the milk jug stand?"

"For starters, I'm agreeing to this," she said cautiously. "Not to mention liking it."

My pride temporarily flared. But I shook my head. "A gentleman wouldn't be kissing a girl he'd just met." This much was evident to me: I didn't want to spend a lifetime getting to know Marla, as pretty and soft and droll as she may be. I knew deep down that it wasn't fair to waste any more of her time polluting her with the notion that I did. Not with my words and certainly not with my lips.

Marla chewed on the inside of her cheek. Was she waiting

for me to come around?

I couldn't do it. I wanted no part in taking something that didn't belong to me. A kiss, one could argue, was a trivial thing, innocent enough. And how could I be taking something that was clearly being offered to me?

She kicked at the water. "I'm beginning to feel quite stupid," she muttered.

But suddenly nothing seemed trivial anymore, the magnitude of life's every minute detail overtook me. I'd failed her. Failed myself. And even worse, I came to the sinking realization that I wasn't only comparable to the slimy carnival guy, but to Jack Knackey himself, who was the king of taking things that didn't belong to him. The only difference between my actions with Marla and his intentions with Kitty was a few articles of clothing and a little self-control. But the desire and the temptation were there. Wasn't that close enough to the same?

The beach suddenly felt too empty, too dark. We'd drifted far from her friends. "We should head back." I took a few steps, but I realized she wasn't following, so I stopped.

"I don't understand." The tide nearly drowned out her voice.

Walking back to her, I said, "I'm sorry, Marla. I'm leaving tomorrow. We shouldn't be getting tangled up in anything."

She came out of the water now, hugging herself as she shivered. "My friends and I went by the fortune-telling booth earlier. Want to know what he told me?"

I shrugged. "Sure?"

"He told me I'd fall in love tonight."

I bit my lip to keep from laughing. A quick scan of her face let me know that she'd taken the man seriously. "I think you met a con artist, not a fortune teller," I said as gently as I could.

She bowed her head, looking stung. We began walking

again toward the distant glow of the fire. She let the silence ride for a while, let the light fade before asking the question that undoubtedly had been pressing into her mind for minutes on end. "Is there something wrong with me?"

My gut twisted. "No. You seem wonderful, Marla." I felt sorry for her and enraged at myself for my part in eliciting any sense of doubt within another human being.

"Then do you have something against relationships?"

"No." I sensed she still clung to the hope of us. Something about the way she'd seemed so ready to dive headfirst into a romance with someone she hardly knew worried me.

"How about long-distance relationships?"

"I couldn't even make it work with a girl who moved twenty-six miles away."

"Oh," she murmured, peering up at me. "Did you like her a lot?"

The last thing I wanted was to be talking about old wounds. Even so, I couldn't deny the truth. "I loved her."

"Marla! There you are!" One of her friends stood near the fire, squinting into the darkness, waving her hands over her head as we slowly approached.

Marla sighed, slowing her steps, all of her disappointment rushing out.

"I'm sorry," I said, overwhelmed with the urge to protect her. "Marla, listen to me a minute. I don't know you, but you seem like a real swell girl. And that's precisely why you should be careful. Not going around kissing guys you barely know. Guard what you have."

She looked at me blankly.

"I should go. We're leaving in the morning."

She shivered and said, "I've learned too many times that when things seem too good to be true, they usually are."

My heart broke for her, but my convictions held fast,

unable to be swayed.

"Can I write you?"

I hesitated. Again, what seemed so harmless and trivial, I knew wasn't. "I don't think that'd be wise. I'm not trying to hurt you, Marla, but I don't feel right creating hope where it ought not to be."

She nodded as though she understood, but deep down, I doubted she did. "Well, Claude from Goldfield where fields aren't made of gold, I guess this is goodbye."

"Stay safe, Marla." I let my words hang in the air, hoping the weight of them would seep into her being. "Have a good night."

I shoved my hands into my pockets and walked away.

From behind, she blurted out, "You were wrong, by the way. About the fortune teller. What he said came true. He just left out the part where it wouldn't be reciprocated."

217

23

"WHY DON'T I stay?" Mom said, more to herself than to anyone else, not even ten minutes before we planned to leave for home. "Len and Claude can live without me a couple months. Can't you, boys?" She raised a brow at us, with an expression that felt like a challenge to disagree with her. Then she looked to Maisy. "I'll be here to help with the rest of your pregnancy and then whenever the baby comes. I hate to say it, but it's not getting easier."

With one quickly exchanged glance with Cliff, Maisy agreed. The next thing I knew, I was unloading Mom's bag from the car and hugging her goodbye too.

Dad and I, and the mountain of peanut butter sandwiches Mom had made for the drive, glided onto the open road. Save for the fuzzy AM radio scratching through the speakers, quiet settled between us. That was the thing about my dad. He could hold a lively conversation as comfortably as he could sit next to someone in silence for nine hours straight.

I drove for the first few hours until my eyelids grew heavy. Then we switched. In the passenger seat, the road lulled me into a nap. When I woke, the radio was off, no signal to be found. No palm trees or concrete or water or high-rise buildings. Just the old familiar desert and the never-ending road ahead of us.

"How long was I out?"

"A while. Hungry?" Dad asked and reached into the bag beside him, handing me the last of the sandwiches.

I was sick of those stinking sandwiches. But I took it and ate, quickly realizing how hungry I actually was. "You gonna miss Mom?" My mouth smacked with the thick peanut butter.

"Of course, I will. But she's right where she needs to be. Just don't expect anything fancier than sandwiches from me while she's away."

"Please." I groaned, shoving the final bite into my mouth. "Anything but more sandwiches."

"Spam and apples, then. Maybe a pork chop if you're lucky."

"Fine by me. Hey, won't Mom be missing work? Is she allowed to just not show up tomorrow?"

He pushed his sliding sunglasses up the bridge of his nose. "She was quitting anyway."

"Since when? Why?"

"She told her boss last week. She said as much as she enjoys being helpful, it felt pointless to shuffle papers around all day. You and I both know that's not Mom's purpose."

I chewed on that a moment. Of course shuffling papers wasn't Mom's purpose. Anyone could see that. Her purpose was taking care of others like she was doing now with Maisy.

I thought of Cliff and Dad. Both of their purposes seemed to align perfectly with what they were each currently doing—jobs they were proud of, providing for a wife and family.

What about Vern? The notion that his purpose had been cut short—or worse, that it had been fulfilled—pained me. But I could write an endless list of things my brother had taught me, whether he'd meant to or not.

Going down the list of each of my family members, I realized I was the only one left. But as I considered my life, I could find no definitive purpose. At least, it wasn't inherently obvious to me. I did have one, didn't I?

"Cliff and Maisy seem happy, don't they?" Dad said, interrupting my thoughts.

"They do. I can't believe they're having a baby. How's it feel to know you're almost a grandparent?"

"It makes me feel old. But wonderful. It's wonderful. Hey, by the way," Dad said, a slight hesitation in his voice. "Not that it's much of my business, but Cliff mentioned something about a girl? Is that why you disappeared last night?"

My face flushed, a twinge of guilt in my chest. *Marla*. Not keen on Dad seeing my reaction, I turned my gaze out the window and searched for jackrabbits. "Yep," I said, hoping he'd leave it alone at that.

After a moment, a deep chuckle rumbled from his throat. "Okay, then. I guess that's all I need to know."

I wondered what Marla was doing. Did she still have her trusty Pablo tucked beneath her arm? Or had she already tossed it out as a sad reminder of me? I cranked the window for fresh air and wished I'd never met her, wished she'd never met me. What had been the point? Our brief encounter was enough to confuse her, to give my clumsy feet something to stumble over and into.

A pang of worry gripped me. The desperation for love that simmered in her heart could lead her places only God could foresee. I hoped with all my might it would be to a place full of His light and love. I knew I couldn't be the man protecting and loving her, but I prayed that some man someday would. Maybe this weekend hadn't been in vain? Maybe God would use it to steer her toward that future?

Vern entered my mind again. If he were still alive, would Cliff and Maisy have a baby on the way? Maybe Vern would be the one about to become a father right now. Maybe, though, things wouldn't have worked out between him and Maisy anyhow. Maybe she'd have ended up with Cliff regardless, that tiny life inside of her always bound to be knit together no matter what.

Was this all an orchestration of fate? Is that how it worked? Would God pull strings, shifting the world however it was meant to be, delivering us to His divine will? Would the things meant to be elbow their way through whatever they had to in order to get to us?

A rabbit jumped into the road right in front of our car. Dad didn't seem to see it. We drove over the small animal. I looked in the side-view mirror, and there it was, standing erect in the road, looking around as though a moving vehicle hadn't just rumbled directly over its head.

Fate? I couldn't help but think it was.

24

THE BABIES CAME in early May.

There really were twins in there after all. Two boys. Henry Vernon Fisher and Randall Robert Fisher. Small, but robust. Healthy.

When Mom decided to stay with Cliff and Maisy, she hadn't considered the timing—the fact that she might miss me marching across the graduation stage, moving my tassel to the left, and tossing my hat into the air. But I graduated with my eighteen classmates, Dad my only family in the audience. The rest of them were snuggling my weeks-old twin nephews almost five hundred miles away.

That night, long after refreshments and games in the gym had ended and Dad had driven himself home, I sat around a bonfire in the middle of the desert with my freshly-graduated class. I'd fancy to assume every policeman and local in town knew what we were up to out here, but not one of them tried to stop us. Where my classmates had smuggled so much alcohol from was a mystery to me, but they paraded around the fire that somehow smelled both of new horizons and the comforts of home. They passed around bottle after bottle, can after can, singing, "Tonopah! Tonopah! Beer and shine! Liquor us up and we'll be just fine!"

I waved the bottle away every time one was thrust in my direction. It had been years, but all I could hear alongside the sloshing liquor was Jeb Ralph's warning burning in my ears. *Don't ever set your lips to this, kid.*

Richie, Jack, and two other guys came up with the bright idea of seeing who could leap over the fire. All the girls either squealed or scolded them, Kitty included. She sat pinched between Bethany and Julia, a steel can of beer clutched tightly in her grip as she dutifully watched the flame jumpers try not to catch fire.

Pete tapped my shoulder and motioned me away from the group. Mickey was unloading a couple of shotguns from his truck. The three of us snuck away in search of jackrabbits in the moonlight. I spotted one and then another but didn't take aim, didn't whisper a word to my friends. I pictured that witless rabbit, standing clueless in the highway somewhere between here and California, and decided to let them go. Something about the mercy whisked away some of the pensiveness that hung like a humid oceanfront night in this bone-dry air.

Mickey nabbed one unlucky bunny. I had no idea how his aim was so sharp in the dark and with alcohol running through his veins. Must've been his strong military genes, I presumed.

Pete took at least three shots and missed them all. We trekked back to the party after a while, the shenanigans still going strong. Mickey soon said he was ready to call it a night. Since he'd had too many beers to drive, I volunteered to take anyone from Goldfield home in Mickey's truck, but we were the only two.

I started the engine and began pulling away when I felt the bump of a body dive into the bed. I hit the brakes. I turned to look out the back window and saw Pete's face smashed against it, pig-nosed and grinning like an idiot.

"Get in here!" I shouted through the glass.

He hopped out and climbed in next to Mickey. "Changed my mind. Thanks for stopping."

The whole way home, we talked about being foolhardy kids, lowering each other down mine shafts, throwing blasting caps at one another in the name of fun, trying to make our own fireworks out of dynamite. Only by the grace of God had we all survived to graduation. Not to mention the town, too, considering how many close calls we'd had in nearly starting a devastating blaze.

Kitty had always refused to join us on these excursions. She never did feel safe. She had more sense than the rest of us. The image of her through the flames, sitting opposite me in front of tonight's bonfire, burned in my chest. If I could, I decided I'd dump the boxes full of memories with her straight into the thirsty, licking flames. I was ready to start over and welcome the next phase of life, though I had no idea what that might be.

Mickey, next to me, prattled on about joining the army. And Pete had decided to attend college in Arizona. They asked me my plans. But I had nothing tangible to give them, because I still hadn't figured it out.

We got back to Mickey's house. The three of us crashed there, stretching out in sleeping bags in his screened-in front porch and trading stories until the early morning hours.

In the midst of my friends' snoring, I realized I had done something Vern would never do—graduate. Frozen in time, forever seventeen. I'd passed my eldest brother. I wondered where he'd be tonight, should he be alive. Would he have been there next to my dad to hear my name be called? Or would he be someplace else, his hands too full of his own life to hold part of mine? I wondered what he'd think of me now, what he'd tell me to do next.

The night stretched. The stars winked. And as I stared through the screen at the same sky that Vern had lived under— the same sky Kitty was under some twenty-six miles away, the same sky that Jesus himself had taken rest beneath every night, the very sky God created—I breathed a liberating, full-to-bursting breath deeper than I had in some time.

I would be okay.

We all would.

25

DAD AND I took a fishing trip up to Rye Patch a week after graduation. As we passed through Fallon on our way, a shiny Sheridan Blue Ford pickup for sale caught Dad's eye. And two days later, as we passed back through on our way home, he stopped in for a test drive.

The truck was ours within the hour. He told me, "As long as you mind yourself and continue working with me this summer, you can drive it all you want. So long as I don't need it myself. Consider it half mine, half yours."

I soon figured out that Dad needed it far more often than he ever seemed to need any of our other vehicles. But one Saturday afternoon while Dad napped, I decided to take it for a little joyride, bumbling around town with no rhyme or reason but fun. I stopped by Pete's house to show off and take him for a spin, but he wasn't home. Nor was Mickey.

When I drove past Richie's, I slowed, our splintered friendship gnawing at me. I still didn't understand how relationships ebbed and flowed or sometimes ended all together.

But as luck would have it, he stepped out of his house, so I pulled over and got out.

He whistled as he approached. "Nice ride! This yours?"

"My dad's." We faced off for an awkward moment. I finally jerked my head toward the truck and said, "Come on. Wanna go for a ride?"

Richie wasted no time and got into the cab. I hadn't fully realized how much I'd missed him until he was next to me, hatching more of his hare-brained plans—everything from riding wild burros to testing the truck out on Dynamite Road. In the middle of one of his stewing ideas, he stopped and looked over at me, grimacing.

"I owe you an apology, Fly."

"It's alright," I said, taken off guard.

"No, it's really not. I've been the worst friend. You were right about a lot of things. I should've supported you. I'm sorry."

I wanted to know what he meant. Right about what? I wanted to ask about Jack. Were they still friends? Were we? But I simply said, "Let's let bygones be bygones."

Something was humming below the surface. I sensed his deliberation. But whatever it was, he let it go. We continued our jaunt around town as though no time had passed between us at all. He asked about my life, all the things he'd missed since our spat, how my family was getting along, and about my trip to see Cliff. I purposely left out everything to do with Marla, even though Richie would've loved to hear it. He told me how his failing grade in history had almost prevented him from graduating, about a brawl the basketball team had gotten into at an away game, and how his crush on Bethany, Kitty's best friend, had all but faded.

Eventually, we stopped at the drugstore where we found Pete and his five-year-old sister, Jessie. We joined them for a

Coke and then crammed all four of us into the truck. We paraded around town until Jessie wanted to go home. We dropped her off. Then the three of us boys stirred up dust and wild ideas for a final summer project. We decided to catch and tame a wild horse until everyone went their separate ways at the end of summer.

—

Richie talked Leland Gray, a withered old man who lived just out of town, into letting us use his long-empty corral. Outside of our jobs, Richie, Pete, and I worked on our plan. We secured the dilapidated corral and rebuilt part of it, so that the large gate now opened to the south, away from Leland's home and away from town. Then we bought a mineral lick from a shop in Bishop and set it a considerable distance away from Leland's property, near the place wild horses had been spotted numerous times as they grazed or passed through. After the horses had discovered the lick, we moved it closer each day and replaced it as needed, sometimes adding whatever medley of food we could get our hands on. Hay, turnips, apples. Little by little, our luring bait brought the horses clear up to the corral, where the gate had been indefinitely propped open. We bought a fresh lick for inside the enclosure and hauled in water and a trough of hay.

Our patience grew thin as we waited for the right opportunity. On a morning following a campout, it finally came. With three horses in the corral, Richie sprang from our hideout beside Leland's old barn and into action. Two of the horses bolted at his sudden movement, barreling out of the pen and to their freedom. Richie was able to slam the gate shut before the final horse could escape.

The one we caught was angry. The way it thrashed and bucked and snorted furious huffs of fear messed with my head a little. But in the excitement of my friends and the prospect of one day hopping on its able back, I ignored the horse's fussing.

We didn't have long to gawk at the strong, golden bronc, or else we'd all be late for work. Dad and I were back in our groove, working in the morning to dig up ties and then finishing out the day at the auto shop. Richie was still working for Phil Fickland at the drugstore. Pete was washing dishes at the diner in Tonopah.

So, we secured the gate that morning and knocked on Leland Gray's door to tell him there was a surprise in the corral. We went on our way, hoping it would still be there when we returned.

And it was.

Day after torturous day, the wild horse remained in the confines of the corral. We brought it food and tried our best to coax it near us. But that horse was bent on staying wild, on putting us into our rightful places if we dared get too close.

Richie leapt onto its back from the fence once. The horse bucked him right off and back to the fence, slicing his arm open.

One late morning, two days after the Fourth of July, Dad and I rumbled down our road in our Sheridan Blue Ford following a few strenuous hours of digging and hauling heavy ties. Stomach growling and muscles aching, I had my sights set on a meal and a few minutes of rest before we headed to the shop.

"Are you expecting company today?" Dad asked, squinting into the distance. "Who is that?"

I squinted too, trying to make out who was sitting on our porch. I didn't recognize the pale blue dress, but the girl wearing it I certainly did. "Someone I never thought would be sitting there again for a million years."

Dad parked and climbed out of the truck first, hollering, "Do my eyes deceive me, or are you really Kitty Ralph?"

I hopped out too and watched Kitty's face slowly melt into a smile, shy and soft, as she and my father hugged. What brought her here, of all places, in the middle of the day?

"Hey, Kitty," I said rather lamely, suddenly becoming aware that I stank to high heaven. "What's going on?"

"New truck?" She dodged the question and pointed. "It's nice."

"Thanks." I glanced at my dad, who opened the front door.

"Come on in," he said. "Have you eaten lunch?"

"No," Kitty said.

"Would you like to join us? If you let me get cleaned up, I'll whip something up before we head to the garage." He slipped through the door, leaving us standing outside. I still didn't understand how he had the endurance to break his back working all morning and then head off to the shop to break his back some more. Even in my youth, I never outworked him.

"Hope you like spam and apples," I muttered to her. "That's about all he's good at cooking."

Her face twisted. "Oh. So, where's your mom? Is she not around?"

"No," I said. "Is that . . . Did you come here for her?" I felt like an idiot, aware of how foolish it was to assume anything about this girl. We hadn't talked for months.

"Uh, yes actually. I was hoping to speak with Ginny about something. Will she be home soon?"

It wasn't as much a blow to my pride as it was my own frustration with myself for allowing one tiny ounce of hope to slither into my chest, for allowing myself to think she'd come seeking me. What could she possibly need my mother for?

"If soon means a few weeks or maybe a month, then yeah."

She looked at me curiously, no doubt hearing the glibness in my tone. "Where is she?"

"In San Diego, helping Cliff and Maisy with the babies."

"Whoa, whoa, whoa. Stop right there. *Babies?*"

In spite of myself, I smiled. Any mention of my two new nephews always did that to me. "Yep. Twins."

She gasped.

"Two little boys. I guess Cliff fainted when he first saw them."

"Twins." She swallowed hard, her eyes wide. "Those male genes run strong in your family, huh? Wow."

"Poor Mom's always been outnumbered."

"Well, it's a good thing you all are alright." She smiled, tossing me what seemed like a feeble attempt at a truce.

"Just alright? That almost sounds like an insult."

"No offense, Claude, but you're covered in dirt. Let's just say I've smelled better," she teased and pinched her nose.

I looked down at myself. My work shirt, which had started out white, had now turned a dingy brown with dirt and sweat. I laughed. "Maybe 'alright' is a compliment after all, huh?"

She nodded and watched me carefully.

"How about I go clean up, and then you can tell me what you're doing here."

"I already told you."

"Well, then you can tell me how you've been. How about that?"

She shrugged one of her bare shoulders. Only then did I notice how drawn her face looked. "I'll tell ya when I can't smell ya," she said.

I gestured toward the door. "Alright, come on."

When I finished washing up and changing into clean clothes, I found Kitty and my father at the kitchen table, eating pickle loaf sandwiches. I sat down, too, and began eating mine.

Dad popped the final bite of his into his mouth and rose, dusting his hands of the crumbs. "I've gotta get to the garage."

"Let me just eat real quick, Dad." Kitty's surprise visit had made me forget all about the brake job we had lined up for the afternoon.

He waved me off. "Take the day."

"You sure?"

"Sure." His eyes flicked between Kitty and me. "You two alright here?"

I locked eyes with him, hoping to reassure him of my commitment to never put another woman in the position that I'd led Marla into. "We're good."

He held my gaze a moment longer and punctuated his sentiment with a prolonged cautionary stare. "Good. Kitty, I wish I didn't have to run off so quickly, but it's mighty good to see you."

She stood and threw her arms around him like she hadn't gone years without doing so. "It's good to see you too. I saw you at graduation. I wish I'd come to say hi. Wait? I didn't see Ginny at graduation."

"No, Ginny's been gone a long time. It's too hard to leave those grandbabies," Dad said. "We're looking forward to her return soon, though. Take care, Kitty. Don't be a stranger." He stood and left.

Kitty and I sat at the table in silence for a long moment.

"So . . ." I raised my brows.

She quickly looked away from me and down at her fingers she was drumming upon the table.

"How have you been?" I asked, then laughed.

"What's so funny?"

"It's just that, I've seen you five days a week for months on end, and we've only been out of school for what, six weeks? Yet I couldn't answer anything about you if I tried."

"We haven't exactly spoken much, have we?"

I narrowed my eyes.

"Or at all," she said softly.

I couldn't shake the sense that she was pleading with me. But for what?

"I've been okay. Peggy and I finally moved out of the hotel into a little house on Florence," she finally said. "And yourself?"

"Been good. Busy. Can't think of much to complain about. Other than the spam and apples, of course."

She smiled. "When does your mom return?"

"I believe in a week or two." I watched her a moment. "Why do you need to talk to her? Is it, you know, girl stuff?"

"Claude!" She gasped and leveled me with a glare. "I just do, okay?"

"Okay, okay." I tried one more time. "If it's something I can help with . . ."

"No, definitely not," she murmured, all traces of light now snuffed out.

I knew the look, and I didn't like it. I'd pry her out from beneath its clutches if I could.

"Kitty, if you're scared—"

"I'm not scared," she snapped, defenses up. Her shoulders sagged. "Well, maybe I'm always a little scared." She tried underlining her statement with a laugh. If it were meant to convince me what she'd said was a joke, it didn't work.

"You're always scared? Of what?"

"Scaring people away." She spoke gingerly.

I resisted the urge to reach over and place my hand on top of hers. "Kitty, you realize we've known each other forever, and you haven't scared me away after all this time. Not even when you lost both of your front teeth and squirted water on every unsuspecting victim who passed by, which most often was me."

She buried her face into her hands and laughed. "Oh, I forgot about that!"

"I thought it was hilarious. Kinda cute. Also, kinda terrifying."

She dropped her hands and gazed at me. "It's always been easy with us, hasn't it?"

For whatever reason, that made me look away. My eyes burned through the window, through the heat simmering in the air. "Hey," I said, getting up. "Come on."

She followed me outside to her old home. "Wait. No one lives here?"

I turned the doorknob. The old door creaked open. "Been empty since you left. Your dad signed it over to us. We just haven't done anything with it."

"Oh." Her eyes widened. "He did?"

"Sorry. I figured you knew."

Shielding her face from the sun, and quite possibly from me, she surveyed the unruly property. "I suppose it's just as well, right?" The corners of her mouth pulled into a stiff smile, as though a puppet master tugged on just the right strings. "Shall we?"

I gestured, allowing her inside before me. The baking stuffiness inside the house consumed us. I set to opening all the windows for fresh air.

Kitty milled about, her footsteps light and tentative as she went from room to room.

"Is it hard to be here?"

She didn't answer right away. That in itself was answer enough. She moved into the kitchen. I watched her drag a finger along the counter. She held it up, a thick hill of dust heaped on the tip.

Something occurred to me suddenly.

"Stay here. I'll be right back." I bounded out the door and into my own home. Standing in my kitchen, I gazed through my own window, seeing Kitty standing there in hers, just like old times. She was oblivious at first, but after a moment, she spotted me waving at her like a buffoon. She gave me the first real smile I'd seen all day. We attempted sign language a minute until we both burst out laughing. We were a patch of dirt and two windowpanes apart, yet we were more connected than we'd been in ages. Kitty bent halfway over in stitches. I could've watched her laughing like that forever.

She finally righted herself and motioned to her wrist, asking the time. I glanced at my watch and held up one finger, then two, then made a zero. She nodded and disappeared. We met on my porch.

"I'll be leaving soon," she said and dabbed sweat from her hairline. "My ride said they'd be back sometime between one and two."

"Your ride?"

"Adam and Phyllis Hadlow. I babysit for them occasionally. They have friends here they visit every few weeks—you know, the Parnell family?"

"Oh." I turned my head and eyed the pickup still parked in our drive. Dad had taken the LaFayette instead. I smiled. "I could drive you? If you want."

Tick, tick. I felt the seconds pass.

"I understand if you don't want to. You know, with Jack and all."

Kitty shook her head, visibly frustrated at the mention of his name. Moving into the shade, she mumbled, "No, that's not a concern." She sighed.

I suppressed the urge to ask for more.

"You sure you don't mind?" she asked.

"Not in the least. But do you need to leave right away?"

She eyed me. "No. Might I use your phone to call over to the Parnell's and let them know?"

"You know where it is."

Kitty nodded and headed inside.

I leaned against the wall in a thin sliver of shade and

waited. My mind flickered with questions I knew I'd never get the answers to.

"So, you got anywhere to be today?" she asked as she emerged from the house.

I thought a moment. Did I? I'd told Margaret I'd come by their *Wilted & Quilted* meeting tonight. It had been a while. "Sort of. Not until later though."

"Oh, what're you up to?"

"Just a little thing at the church." I wasn't sure what stopped me from telling her the full truth.

She eyed me suspiciously. "The mysterious, pious type now, huh?"

I laughed. "Want to check out something cool?"

"What?"

"Come on." I held onto my air of mystery and ducked inside to grab the keys.

Kitty was already waiting in the pickup when I came back out, looking ready for one of my surprise adventures like we were thirteen again. But we weren't. Whatever future had once been in store for Kitty and me was long ago ruined. And now we only had this haphazardly sewn-up one. Whatever that was.

I got in and drove down Columbia.

"Bob Dunn still got that stupid chicken he loved so much?" she asked as we passed his house.

"Nope." I spied his new coop as we bumbled by, painted red and filled with a few birds. "Replaced her with a new flock."

"What was her name again? Wilma? Wanita?"

"Something like that." The name eluded me. I made a turn, and then another, and took us south, fully aware that Kitty would have no idea where we were going. "So, Rich, Pete, and I might've done something a little dumb."

She gazed out the open window. The wind tickled stray

hairs around her face, coaxing them from carefully placed bobby pins.

I gave her a chance to respond, but she didn't.

"Kitty?"

The sound of her name jostled her from her thoughts. "Hmm?"

"Did you hear what I said?" I pulled down the road leading to Leland Gray's property.

"I'm sorry. I don't think I did."

"I said Richie, Pete, and I might've done something dumb."

"I can't say that statement surprises me. What have you boys done?" Her brow furrowed as I drove up to Leland's two-story house. She stared at the home's chipped, white paint and the way it seemed to lean to one side. "Where on earth are we?"

"Come find out."

She followed me around the backside of the home, and the corral came into view.

At the sound of us, the palomino horse came to life and trotted around its pen, snorting in disgust at the sight of me.

"Whose horse is this?"

"We call him Gold Nugget," I said proudly. "Caught him ourselves. You should've seen Richie try to hop on him."

Her face contorted. "You guys caught a wild horse and decided it would be a good idea to ride it? Boy, you really are dumb."

"I specifically told you we were." I laughed and leaned against a post to watch Gold Nugget. "But it's kind of cool, right?"

"More cruel than cool," she said, her eyes locked on the spooked animal.

"I know it seems that way. But how do you think any horse was ever tamed? They were first caught. Gold Nugget's still young. We plan to train him."

Her eyes never left the animal. "Let it go."

I laughed, but after looking at the pools forming in her eyes, felt bad for doing so. "What do you mean, let it go? Do you know how long it took for us to catch this thing?"

"Look at it, Claude. It wasn't born to be in this pen. You know that as well as I do."

I opened my mouth to protest. The horse whinnied and paced the far side of the corral, its anguish and misery on full display.

Kitty grimaced and turned away, trudging back to the pickup.

I started to chase after her but halted, the horse keeping my attention now. It stopped pacing and held its head in the air, whinnying again. No longer free, its fate rested in my hands. Who was I to take what didn't belong to me? My heart sank.

"Kitty! Wait!" I shielded my eyes against the sun, searching for her.

She stopped short of turning the corner around Leland's house.

"Wanna help me?" I hollered.

"Help you what?"

"Let it go! You're right. More cruel than cool."

She walked back to me. "What about all the time it took to catch it? All your plans to tame it?"

"Not mine to tame."

I watched her soften. The storm clouds in her eyes parted.

"Tell me what to do," she said. "Let's free this beauty."

We stood at the gate on the far side of the corral, and I instructed her to stick beside me. Slowly and quietly, I unlatched the gate. We gripped the thick wooden boards. "On the count of three, walk backward to open it up all the way. We should be safely wedged behind the gate. Be ready to scramble over in case Gold Nugget gets angry and tries to kick or charge us on his way out. You know how mean these horses can get sometimes."

She nodded, her breath unsteady, a smile on her face. "Got it."

I counted to three, and we swung open the gate, its rusty hinges alerting the horse of its release. Its hooves beat against the ground as it galloped right past us and took its chance at freedom. We watched plumes of dust explode in its wake. Wild and fierce, it slowed a moment, taking stock of its surroundings, then bolted again until it was out of sight.

We pushed the gate shut, and I said, "Feel better now?"

She threw her arms around my waist. The sudden touch was enough to both melt and freeze a man at once.

"Thank you," she murmured against my chest.

I patted the space between her shoulder blades uneasily, too afraid to truly hug her in return.

But a second later, her soft body stiffened. She took a step back. "I shouldn't have asked you to do that. That was between you and your friends."

"It was the right thing to do." I looked toward the hills the horse had galloped off to.

"So, you and Richie? You're friends again, then?" She tilted her head, waiting, and something in the small pinch of her mouth made me wonder if she had something else to say, to ask.

"Yeah, we made up shortly after graduation."

Her brows shot up. "Really?"

I regarded her cautiously. "You seem so shocked."

"Well, I think I hung out with Richie more than you did this past year."

She looked down and away, the movement tinged in . . . something. Was it sadness? Fear? Did she know that the fissure in my friendship with Richie—the one that had stretched into a gaping ravine—began with a conversation about her?

"Richie and I worked it out," I said and walked away from the corral. Her steps were nimble and light beside me. "So, if I drive you home, will your aunt go bananas on me?"

"Frankly, I don't think she'd recognize you."

I glanced at her.

"You must not realize how much you've changed since she last saw you. I mean, don't get me wrong, you're the same old Claude in a lot of ways, but you look older and . . ." She stretched her arms, first tall, then wide.

"You callin' me chubby?"

That made her giggle. "Not fat, you bozo. Buff."

I turned all the way around and raised one eyebrow, throwing in a quick flex of my bicep. "Oh, really?"

"Stop that!" Her cheeks lit up pink, but her eyes never left me.

"Alright, so if I see ol' Peggy, I'll just introduce myself as Clyde. Clyde Trout."

"Is that your alias nowadays? Clyde Trout?"

"Sure." I opened the door of the Ford for her. "Unless you can think of something better?"

"Clyde Trout's clever enough." She laughed as I closed her in, the door letting out a short-lived squeal just before it latched.

Once we were on our way, she said, "I think I heard you went down to see Cliff and Maisy over Easter vacation, right?"

"Yes'm."

"How was your trip?"

"Good. It's sure beautiful down there. Wait until you see the ocean one day, assuming you haven't already?"

"No. What was it like?"

As innocuous a question as it was, a prick of guilt still troubled me when I thought about the ocean.

Kitty smiled at me, waiting expectantly.

"It's hard to describe. Not like anything we've ever seen while trapped here in these desert plains. But it's breathtaking," I said.

"Careful now. You sound an awful lot like your brother, pining for someplace else. You think you'll follow in Cliff's footsteps? Join the military?"

"Hard tellin' where I'll be come this time next year."

"Is it something you'd like to do?"

"Am I un-American if I admit it's not?"

"You're a true disgrace to the stars and stripes, Claude Fisher." She clucked her tongue and shook her head. "Why not, though? It's a noble thing, wouldn't you say?"

"Nobility set aside, it's just not something I feel led to do, let alone choose on my own volition. I have other dreams."

She shifted, turning sideways in her seat, and propped her elbow against the headrest. "Dreams? Do tell."

I smirked and shook my head, but she continued prodding me. I didn't give in right away, solely for the fact that she was so darn adorable in her desperation to pry this secret out of me.

"You really want to know?"

She nodded eagerly.

I relented. "Alright, fine. When I visited Cliff, I was amazed by this little life he and Maisy were building. Getting to live in a beautiful city, a small place for themselves, starting a family. But Cliff's gone a lot, and Maisy is lonely and overwhelmed. And then there's this threat of moving on a whim to wherever the military sees fit hovering over them. Or worse, Cliff being deployed, leaving Maisy and his kids behind for months on end. It's sacrificial and noble, sure. But I don't want that."

"Okay . . . so then what do you want?"

"A simple life." I shrugged. "I know when we were kids, I listened to Cliff's dreaming and formed my own visions of getting out of this place too. But the truth? I want a routine, a home, a wife, a family to come back to every day. Doesn't really matter to me if that's in the desert or on a tropical island."

"Anything else?"

I laughed. "I'm spilling my heart. Is this not sufficient enough for you?"

"It sounds like you want a life like your parents."

"I do."

She whispered something inaudible. I tightened my grip on the wheel, resisting the urge to reach over and squeeze her knee reassuringly. I could read her mind before she even had the chance to tell me what was going on in there.

"Kitty—"

"It's funny how some people have parents they strive to be like, while others, well . . ." She punctuated her sadness with a laugh and a shrug. "If my life turned out anything like your parents, I'd say that would be a pretty darn good life. The best."

I would've given anything to wrap my mother in a hug at that moment, to say thank you. The same to my dad. The greatest gift they ever gave me, perhaps even Kitty too, was loving each other and us.

"How stupid an idea would it be to try to find my mom?"

I failed to disguise the shock and disgust on my face.

"Oh, come on now! You look like I've just asked if I should grow an extra foot."

"You might as well have," I muttered. "Sounds more interesting if you ask me."

"Claude." My name fell from her lips, wistful. "You really think it's foolish, don't you?"

"You want my honest opinion?" I glanced at her, my gaze lingering on her trembling lower lip. The truck bumped over something in the road, and my eyes flickered to the rear-view mirror. "Whoops."

"What was it?" She looked over her shoulder.

"Don't know, but it's roadkill now."

Her lip trembled more. She started to cry and looked away from me. "I just wonder about her. Is that so wrong?"

"What are you wondering about?"

"Mostly if she's wondering about me too."

If there were a decent place to pull off, I would have. I envisioned myself throwing the truck into park and marching around to her door, pulling her out into a hug that would melt away all of her doubts, her insecurities, and the thoughts that lured her into darkness. But I kept my eyes fixed on the road ahead, knowing we were only a few miles from Tonopah and not knowing if she'd even want to be in my arms. I cleared my throat. "Do you really think about her a lot?"

She tucked a strand of hair into a bobby pin, swiping covertly at a tear as she did. "Not a lot, no. Just sometimes. With Peggy, try as she might, she's no mother. And sometimes I just wish I had a mama to run to when I need one."

"You know you always have mine."

She flung me a look of despair.

"Oh. Right." My mother was hundreds of miles away. "You could try phoning Cliff and Maisy's home? If you really need to talk to her that bad."

With a hand, she waved my idea away. "It's fine."

"Sorry, Kit." I didn't know what else to say.

She straightened and took a deep breath, her soft features hardening. "Did you know my dad's getting out of prison? Yep, this month. A little earlier than expected. He called me a few weeks ago."

"Wow," I said, at a loss for words.

"He has some work lined up already when he gets out. In Reno."

The air went out of my lungs. "Are you moving?"

"No. Well, I don't know what I'm doing. Bethany keeps trying to convince me to apply at UNR. But my dad didn't invite me there with him, didn't make any mention of living near each other for the sake of family. It would've been nice to feel . . . wanted, especially after four-and-a-half years of not seeing me."

I gritted my teeth. How could anyone disregard a girl like Kitty? She was an absolute dream.

A fit of laughter shook from her suddenly. The joyous noise filled the cab.

"What is it?"

"We don't talk for a year, and then you capture me alone for a few hours, and I'm already spilling some of my saddest secrets."

Years of rust and crust fell away, a dormant trust rousing from slumber. It warmed, stirring back to life like muscle memory. This time, I laughed too, though not for the same reason as she. *Forget it,* I thought, *I'm not taking her home.*

As soon as I parked outside the Butler Theatre, I hopped out and flew around the pickup to open her door before she had a chance to realize my plan.

"What's going on?" She stepped out. I shut the door behind her.

"Almost five years ago, we had a movie date that never happened. And I think it's high time we make that right. What do you say?" I extended my hand to her.

The corners of her eyes crinkled with her wide smile. She took my proffered hand. "And what if the movie isn't set to start for another hour?"

Our fingers intertwined, each of them finding their place like the position was our fondest memory. "That much more time to tell you how badly I've longed to do this." I winked and tugged her toward the ticket counter.

26

"JUST COME IN!" I yelled to Kitty from inside the lake. "You'll get used to it after a minute!"

But Kitty, ankle-deep in frigid lake water, wasn't having any of it. "I haven't swum since we were ten! I don't remember how!"

"Look." I lifted my hands out of the chest height water and held still. "I can touch the bottom. You'll be fine."

Her feet danced as she worked up the courage to plunge in, but with one step and splash against her thigh, she retreated again and folded her arms across her blue-and-white-checkered bathing suit. A gust of wind blew her hat off her head. Her hair looked like a drawn curtain across her face. She ran after her hat as it skimmed across the beach.

Within the two weeks following our overdue, yet impromptu, movie date, my otherwise unsuspecting and muted life suddenly teemed with color. We saw each other every chance that time and money allowed, her catching rides down to Goldfield or me driving up to her. It tasted like old times before everything fell apart, only sweeter. The blend of old familiarity and the budding promise of something new was intoxicating to us.

I watched her pick up her hat and apologize to a man whose beer she knocked over. Kitty scanned the horizon, and I maneuvered to do the same, wondering which of the dark specks far off in the bright blue water was my dad's rented fishing boat. Was he actually catching anything out there or were the snow-dusted peaks of the Sierra's too mesmerizing? Only two days before, the three of us had been sitting inside my house playing gin rummy, when Dad threw down his cards and announced that he wanted to go to Tahoe.

He and Big John used to flip a coin and take a trip to Tahoe every July, just the two of them. Heads, they'd cast their lines in the Truckee River, Dad's favorite spot. Tails, they'd try their luck right in the middle of the lake, Big John's favorite spot. Big John had canceled their trip in '45 for reasons Dad didn't understand at the time. They were made evident within months when Big John divulged his cancer diagnosis.

I turned my attention back to Kitty. She walked along the water line, her hand firmly holding her hat in place. A sea of pines blurred behind her. I hoped Dad's view out in the middle of the lake was nearly half as good as mine right now. I waved Kitty in again, but she plopped down in the sand and shook her head.

The past two weeks had been a whirlwind. It felt like Kitty and I were making up for lost time. But there was something wrong that I couldn't quite put my finger on. In the midst of our swift bliss, entangled within this Technicolor dream, were patches of black and white, moments where Kitty pulled away, and I didn't understand why. It had only happened a handful of times where she grew quiet, distant, and unreadable, like she'd been troubled by an unexpected blow of bad news. I could only attribute her sudden introspection to the space of time in which we'd been absent from each other's lives. There were things I no longer knew about Kitty. Things I still had yet to learn. But the prospect of discovery only thrilled me all the more.

I ducked underwater and burst back into summer's heavy breath to join Kitty on the beach. She held out a towel for me. I dried off, then spread it out to sit. Our hands found their way together, and I gave hers a squeeze.

"Everything okay?" I asked.

She smiled wide and nodded. For some reason, I didn't believe her.

—

Two days after returning from Tahoe, I drove along the highway. I was Tonopah bound, half hanging out the driver's window, desperate for the rush of air through my hair. Never mind the harsh sun that beat down on my head; this was at least better than inside the baking cab. When I parked outside of Peggy Littleton's home, I took a long swig of water from my canteen and got out.

The front door to the house flung wide open. Peggy marched across the lawn, a cigarette hanging from her lips. She fumbled with her lighter, trying to ignite the end, though her furious steps made it difficult. She looked up at the sound of my closing door, and her face clouded with wrath, her path changing to head straight for me.

Shoving a finger in my chest, she sputtered, "Are you the wise guy who just cost her her future?"

My eyes flicked to the house, the open front door. "Huh? What are you—"

"Oh, save it! If I wasn't already so late for work, I'd stay here and beat the tar out of you right now." Suddenly she reached for my face, her thumb pressing into one cheek, her other fingers wrapping around and pressing into my other cheek. "You trashy little desert rat. You got her into this mess. Now you get her out. Take care of it." Her brows lifted fiercely as though she'd just passed me a secret message, but I had no fathomable idea what was going on. She let go of my face abruptly, adjusted the waist of her skirt, and stalked away to her car.

My feet couldn't bring me into the house fast enough. There, on the floor of the cramped living room, was Kitty. Her knees were to her chest, and her hands covered her eyes.

"Kitty?"

She peeked from behind her fingers, took one look at me, and crumbled.

"What's going on?"

An incessant flow of tears streamed from her eyes. She wiped her nose, red as a cherry tomato, and let her face fall into her palms. Gingerly, I tried prying her hands away. But she ripped herself away from me, curling into an untouchable ball. The cagey distance that had randomly clouded her over the past two weeks nagged in my mind, and it turned into a violent storm before my very eyes.

"Kitty." My voice broke. "Come on. You're scaring me."

She continued to weep. I grew in my helplessness, the unknown unraveling me to the point of desperation. I begged and pleaded with her to tell me what was wrong. But she refused. My mind raced to one made-up catastrophe to the next, until it finally settled on my innermost fear—she'd decided she wasn't in love with me after all.

But I thought of what Peggy had said to me outside. What mess had I gotten Kitty into? Peggy's disdain for me and my family had always been overly evident. The very idea of Kitty having a romantic relationship with me must have sent her over the edge. She thought she'd gotten rid of me years ago, that Kitty had moved on from me. And now she wanted to sever the fibers that had only recently been stitched back together.

I began crying now too. I waited, hoping with each passing minute that Kitty might let me near her, but she only howled with each attempt. We sweltered with emotions and summer heat, boxed inside Peggy's home. Out of frustration, I yanked repeatedly on the ceiling fan, willing it to turn on, but I snapped the chain off by accident instead. So, I scooped Kitty up from her place on the floor. Her rust-colored dress was damp against my skin, and I couldn't tell her tears from sweat. I carried her to the screened-in back patio, but there were no chairs. Gently, I set her down on the floor, and she leaned against the wall. I left her there to fetch a cup of water.

Upon returning, I knelt down and held the cup to her lips, instructing her to drink. I poured a splash in my hand and swiped it across her forehead, her neck. "Just tell me if you're okay," I pleaded.

Her gaunt face sent a shiver of fear through my belly. "No," she whispered.

When she offered nothing else, I fought through the dread and asked, "Are . . . are we okay?"

Her downcast eyes brought me to the ground. I dropped down next to her. "You can't leave me in the dark like this, Kitty. It's not fair. Tell me what's going on."

"Claude, I'm so sorry. I . . . Oh . . . I don't know how to tell you this." Her voice, though weak and small, was sharp like a whip. I braced myself against the house, the weight of the world crashing over me. "I can't."

"Put me out of my misery, Kit." A tear rolled down my cheek. "Just tell me."

She drew in breath after breath, steadying herself until she was calm enough to speak. "I came back to Goldfield searching for Ginny. I didn't intend on seeing you. Never would've thought in a million years that . . . that you would sweep me off my feet that day."

I couldn't look at her. "And let me guess; you've realized that was a mistake?"

"No." She pressed her eyes together. "It wasn't, Claude. But I need you to know I wasn't intending for this to happen. I needed your Mom—"

"Why'd you need to see my mother?"

"Last year, you told me Jack wasn't a good guy."

The mention of his name sent a wave of something sour up my throat.

"You tried to warn me of things I wouldn't listen to at the time," Kitty said. She wrapped her arms around herself and sniffled. "You told me things about myself I never could've admitted, let alone realized, on my own. I didn't want you to be right. Not about him. Not about me."

"Kitty?"

She shushed me, shook her head. "I need to finish this while I can. Please."

A deep ache gnawed behind my ribs. I conceded.

"Graduation night," she began. She wiped her eyes, though the effort was futile. "Jack offered to drive me home. We'd both been drinking. And in his car, he came onto me. I was so tired. I didn't know what to do but let it happen. My voice was gone. All my strength too. I thought maybe this was how it happened, at least for a girl like me. But the whole time, as much as I could formulate a thought, I hated myself. A small, stupid girl who couldn't stand up for herself, even in the face of my innocence being snatched away."

I reached for her, my entire chest splintering with the sting of her truth.

Her chest heaved with deep, ragged sobs. As much as I didn't want to hear anymore, I held her close to catch her next words.

"The whole rest of the night was hell, Claude. And all I

could think about was how you were right. I didn't sleep a wink. The next day I walked straight to his house. I was so upset. I wanted to understand what happened and why. But he acted like he didn't remember a thing. He didn't even answer his own door. Richie did. I pleaded with Jack, tried talking to him, but he didn't care. After I'd left, Richie came after me to make sure I was okay. He walked me home."

Fire flared in me. Richie and I had only recently regained our friendship, but he'd never uttered one word about any of this. "Have you reported this? Please tell me you told the police."

She shook her head.

"Why not?"

"Because what am I supposed to say? I was drunk and slept with my sort-of boyfriend? Everyone around here knows Jack and I were seeing each other this past year. He made that very clear to anyone he could."

"He can't be allowed to just get away with this."

Her brow furrowed. "No, Claude. Jack made a bad choice, and I did too."

"Kitty, come on—"

"You've told me my entire life to stand up for myself. I should have done that then, and it's what I'm trying to do now."

I leaned back and closed my eyes, unable to stop myself from envisioning her entangled with Jack in the back of his car, more unwilling than unable to fight him off. Better to tiptoe around the broken glass and clean it up unasked than demand it never happened in the first place. I shook my head. Was this her finally learning to fight for herself, for her dignity and respect?

She gripped my arm. "Claude . . . There's more you need to know."

"What?"

Her stillness unsettled me. Pieces slowly clicked into place. I lowered my voice, afraid to even ask. "Kitty, what does all this have to do with why you came to see my mother?"

She rested her head back, let it roll to the side so she could gaze at me.

I stared into her eyes, pleading with her not to shatter all my hope, not to re-break my heart.

"I'm afraid I'm pregnant."

Her words took the wind from my lungs. If she said anything else, I didn't hear it, couldn't over the screaming inside my mind. I squeezed my eyes shut, willing this reality away. But all I saw in my head were inky, agonizing images of the two of them together. Those thoughts could only be swept away if replaced with me imagining all the ways I'd bust up Jack Knackey's face should I ever see him again. And then came the most crushing, most confusing, and most overwhelming thought of them all. A baby, the only entirely innocent party in all of this, was nestled inside Kitty's womb.

"So that's what Peggy was blowing up at me about," I murmured.

"I didn't want to tell her. I wanted to talk to your mom. Ginny's the only person I could think to run to, but she hasn't been home. And this morning, I felt a little sick when I woke. Peggy made a joke when I refused breakfast. She said, 'Don't tell me you're knocked up.' And I just started crying."

The ache behind my ribs spread throughout the rest of my body like a dangerous mold. It hurt to speak. "Does Jack know?"

"That morning I went to Jack's house, I said to him, 'What if I'm pregnant?' And you know what he said to me? 'It won't be mine. But if you are, your aunt will know what to do.'"

"No." Angry tears spilled down my cheeks.

"Yeah." Kitty closed her eyes and covered her stomach with protective hands. "I've never in my life wanted to hurt you, Claude. I'm so sorry. I didn't expect anything to spark between us when I came to see your mom that day. It knocked me plumb off my feet, and I tucked all the worry away, praying constantly it wasn't true. That it was only rooted in fear, not reality."

"Maybe it is."

"Maybe," she mumbled. For a moment, she looked longingly at me, her eyes welling up with tears. "I know this changes everything between us. I tried to tell you a long time ago to stay away from me. You deserve better than this."

"Kitty, it wasn't your fault!"

"Or was it? I put myself in that situation. I paid no heed to your warnings. At any rate, you simply don't understand. This is who I am."

I cupped her face in my hands. "No, it's not. How many times do I have to try and convince you that it's not?"

"I should have never allowed these last few weeks to happen."

"You regret these weeks with us?" I was sure I would vomit any second.

Her mouth fell open, aghast. "Never! I've never regretted any time with you. Oh gracious. No. Please don't think that for a second! But Claude, you deserve more than me. We both know it. So, I want you to go. Go find a future that doesn't involve me weighing you down and messing up your life too."

I watched her heart crumble before my eyes. Neither of us could pick up the words that had tumbled from her mouth and put them back. We sat there stunned, the dry desert air soaking up our sweat, our hopes for the future shrinking. Words evaded me as Kitty wept. The only thing I could think to do was slip my arm around her and hold her while our worlds collapsed.

When she'd cried her eyes dry, we stood and moved back inside.

"I need you to do me a favor," Kitty said. "I need you to leave."

I didn't say anything. Couldn't. I wanted to hold onto her forever, to hug away all her pain. I fought the urge to fall to my knees right then and there.

"I'm serious, Claude. I feel so embarrassed. I don't want to be seen right now."

"I don't want to leave you," I whispered and cupped her chin, my thumb brushing the thin, faded scar of an adventure long ago. "Come with me."

But she didn't budge.

"My mom will be home this weekend or next."

"Good," she murmured. "She's the only one I trust with this."

"Kitty." I wove my fingers through her hair and pressed my lips to her forehead. "You really want me to go?"

"Yes," she said, though her eyes told a different story.

"Well, can I get you anything first?"

"No."

"You sure?"

She nodded, attempting to remain stoic, unmoved by my departure.

"Okay," I whispered. "Call me if you need me. I'll be here at the drop of a hat." I untangled my fingers from her hair and walked out the door.

With every step that led me away from her, I questioned if I should turn around, if I was wrong for listening to her, for leaving her standing there scared, possibly pregnant. Alone. But I didn't know what else to do. Against every shaking cell in my body, I drove away. My mind didn't have the capacity to generate more than angry strings of words as I beat the steering wheel and snaked through the streets like a madman, carefully scouting every house, yard, and business for any sign of Jack Knackey.

I couldn't find him, but it was for the best. I couldn't have guaranteed my ability to stop once I got my hands around his neck. Suddenly, Jeb Ralph's face flashed in my mind, bloody and pulverized, his glazed eyes showing a momentary spark of recognition as he stared at me before his lights went out.

I pulled over right then, leaned out the window, and puked my guts out on top of a sagebrush.

When I finally made it home, Dad took one look at me and asked, "What's wrong, Claude?"

"Everything," I whispered. I ached to tell him. If there ever was someone who would know what to do, it would be him. But I saw time stretching out before me, pain stitched into every possible future. And as much as I wanted his advice, I said, "I can't talk about it right now. It's not my story to tell."

He studied me, which gave me a chance to change my mind. I didn't budge. "Okay," he said, disappointed. He puttered back to the sink to rinse the dishes. After a minute, he said, "Here if you need me, son."

"When does Mom come home?"

"I talked to her this morning. She decided to stay another week. Her train is 'spose to get into Vegas next Friday evening. You thinking about driving with me? I figured you might have plans with Kitty?"

Something about the way he said it made me think he was fishing, trying to figure out if trouble was brewing between her and me. I decided I didn't want to give anything away, so I said, "Oh, yeah. Probably so."

"It'll be late. There's a chance your mom and I might find a motel and come back Saturday." He reached for a towel and eyed me sideways, looking for my reaction as he dried a cup.

"You'll be wise if we stay overnight, I expect?"

"Of course, Dad."

His satisfied nod signified his trust in me. "Oh, I almost forgot to tell you. Margaret and Ada stopped by earlier looking for you. Said her and the ladies were a little worried since they haven't seen you for a while. Said they'd been missing their musical mascot. I think her exact words were, 'Knittin' ain't the same without his finger pickin'.'"

I'd failed to make an appearance at any *Wilted and Quilted* meetings for months, and not even ten minutes ago I'd passed the church, noting the familiar cars. Guilt punched me in the stomach. I knew how fond they'd all grown of me. And I of them. They'd become like a herd of grandmothers.

"Claude?"

I glanced at my dad.

"You look sicker than a dog. You sure you don't want to tell me what's wrong?"

"I just need to lay down." I moved past my worried father to my room and lay in bed. The world spun. And in spite of the roaring silence around me, Kitty's giggle resounded between my ears. That easy laughter that softened all my hardened parts, that brought the world to a standstill. All I wanted was to hear that laugh again, to replace her heartache and fear, to watch her eyes twinkle and glow, to ignite fireworks inside of her. I wanted her to be okay, free from the shackles of the lies that wrongfully defined her. I wanted *her*. That's all I wanted.

Her.

Whatever that meant.

I glanced at my wristwatch. Seeing the time, I sprang out of bed and fetched my guitar. I sped through the house, passing my confused Dad.

"I'm going to the church," I blurted and dashed out the door to the pickup.

Margaret about fell out of her chair when I walked in. "Now, what a pleasant surprise! We were just talkin' about you!"

Matilda set down her fistful of cloth and took off her cat-eyed glasses, pretending to wipe them clean with her shirt. "Am I seeing this right? I think I need new glasses . . ."

"I don't think I recognize you, sir. How may we help you?" Ada winked, her thin mouth drawn into a pleased line.

I'd come to enjoy their teasing over time. "I was told there was a group of old women who needed serenading in here, but all I see are young ladies. I must have the wrong building." Several of them tittered. I leaned my guitar against the wall and took a seat next to Ada.

She reached over and squeezed my hand. "I'm so jealous your mama's been cuddling those babies these last couple of months. You know Maisy's mama is on her way out there right now, and she didn't even bother to invite this old bird." Ada laughed and then sighed, her sadness billowing out. "No one thinks this bag-of-bones grandma should be traveling that far. I'm just hopin' Maisy and Cliff can come visit before the twins are too old. Or before I kick the bucket."

"I haven't met them yet either. Maybe you and I can hop on a train one of these days and make it happen."

Her eyes glistened at the possibility. "Now that's the kind of spirit we've missed around here." She smiled at me, but drew back, letting go of my hand as she carefully scoured my face. "Jane," she muttered, elbowing the woman next to her. "I might be out of touch with this type of thing, but does Claude look lovesick to you?"

They'd found the chink in my armor. All gumption faded quickly from me.

Jane leaned over. My cheeks burned. Before I knew it, I was surrounded. The weight of their shared concern nearly cracked me open.

"Lovesick as I've ever seen," Jane assessed, clucking her tongue. The other ladies murmured in agreement around me.

"What's wrong?" Margaret asked. "Honey, don't tell us you went and got your heart broken?"

"Oh, I think he's just in love," another said.

"Who is it, Claude?"

"Shh! Let's hear what he's got to say!"

Ada, who'd started this whole circus, waved everyone back. "Alright, stop badgerin' the boy. Give him some space."

They moved an inch. I sensed they weren't going to drop the matter easily.

"I said, give the boy some space!" Ada snapped, receiving a few glares. But the ladies retreated, going back to their own seats. But my relief was short-lived. "Now then," she said, folding her hands together. "Tell us what's going on, honey."

"I can't do that, Ada." I almost felt sorry for letting her down. She looked at her hands, and her wedding ring caught my eye. "But may I ask you all a question?"

"Go ahead. We're open books. Maybe some of us too open," Margaret roared, eagerly welcoming my request. "I know I could learn a lesson from you about keeping my business to myself!"

To Margaret's left, Edna chuckled under her breath, nodding in silent agreement.

"How old were each of you when you got married?"

"Well now, there's a darn good question. Lemme see, here." Matilda tapped her fingernails against the table. "You'd think I would remember this type of thing. Old Bill and I were young'ns. 'Bout fourteen, I do believe. The both of us."

"I was fourteen too. One day shy from fifteen, actually," Jane chimed in. "But we didn't do things in order. I was plump and pregnant on my wedding day."

Margaret pointed a knitting needle my direction. "I was married twice. My first husband didn't last too long."

"Did you run him off with that loud mouth of yours?" Edna chirped, sending Matilda into a giggling fit.

Margaret didn't let the banter faze her. She put the end of her knitting needle into her mouth, appearing deep in thought. "Huh. They told me it was a mining accident, but you know, your theory might make more sense. Ha! Well, at any rate, his death brought me my Orin. We married when I was eighteen. He was twenty. Never did have any kids. Just wasn't in the cards for us, I guess." She turned to her left, pointing her needle again. "How 'bout you, Edna?"

"Oh, I wasn't near as young as the rest of you. I was twenty-two. Walt, twenty-six."

The ladies exploded into chatter around me. I sat in the midst, overwhelmed yet trying to soak in all the tiny tidbits of advice they doled out to me like my mother's hotcakes. The fact that so many of them married even younger than me at eighteen struck a chord in my heart.

"What about you, Ada? How old were you and Jimmy when you got married?" Edna asked.

"Eighteen and nineteen, but I would've married him sooner had my daddy let me. Babies started coming a year later."

"You don't have to tell us all your business, Claude. But maybe you can spare us a crumb or two?" Margaret asked. "You got marriage on your mind?"

All eyes once again zoned in on me. I tugged at my collar, unprepared to answer. "I think maybe it's time for some hymns?"

"Lovesick as all get-out," Ada muttered, a sly smile on her face. She leaned in close. Her breath prickled the skin on my neck. In a low voice, she said, "Nod once if it's the little Ralph girl."

I swallowed hard and nodded curtly; that was all I was willing to give away.

She patted my leg and straightened herself. All these women around me were once Kitty's age; already started, starting, or soon to begin their lives of matrimony and motherhood. It went without saying that Kitty's situation wasn't ideal. The shame that had marked her face haunted me now as I thought of it. If I could, I would strip that shame from her in a second, wad it up, and throw it in the trash. Set fire to it if I had to. And then I'd hug her far into forever, assuring her that she was okay as many times as needed until she finally believed it too.

But right now, she was another town away, alone with no one to confide in or seek comfort from. And here I was in a roomful of women willing to give their ears and opinions all night. With a father waiting at home who would help me at the drop of a hat should I just say the word. The thought made my heart pound like an angry fist against my chest. The tiny ember of hope, of Kitty being wrong about her pregnancy, glowed on the outskirts of my mind. But for some reason, I couldn't bring myself to believe it, not even for a second. It all felt too concrete, sealed. Everything about her future, my future—our future—was already changed. More life-altering decisions were in store.

Even though I hadn't played a single song, I grabbed my guitar and bid farewell to *Wilted and Quilted*. When I got home, Dad was already in bed. The house was quiet. I made a long-distance call to Cliff. He answered, though neither of us could hear much above the wailing infant he held in his arms.

Mom took my nephew from him, and Cliff gave me his attention. But suddenly it felt wrong, seeking his advice without giving Kitty the chance to tell her story first. So, I asked, "How's life as a new dad?"

He blew into the receiver. "It's, well, harder than the military." He busted up laughing. "Mom's been a lifesaver, I'll say that much. But, you know, they're smiling and laughing like crazy now. I find myself grinning for so long with them that my cheeks hurt. They're pretty precious, Fly. I wish you could meet them."

A dreaminess laced around his gravelly voice, and I pictured him cradling his sons, enamored with the newness of life. But another long wail pierced through the phone, either Henry or Randall, I didn't know which.

Cliff said, "Gotta go." And that was that.

I phoned Kitty after, but no one answered at the Littleton residence. Not the first, second, or third time. I paced the kitchen, tried convincing myself that sleep might help give me the answers I sought. But I wound up leaving the house and heading to the school gymnasium instead. Vern had once taught me about a secret way in. I scurried up the ladder to the roof and snuck in through the manhole. Once inside, it took a few minutes of feeling around blindly in the dark to find the lights. A lone basketball rested against the far wall. My footsteps echoed as I made my way across the court. I'd never been here by myself before, having only broken in with my brothers or my friends.

Shooting hoops, it turned out, wasn't as fun alone with no one to scrimmage against, no one nearby to fetch the ball when a shot went rogue. But the monotonous routine—dribble, shoot, fetch, repeat—put me into a stupor. An empty, echoing, pacifying stupor.

27

THE HOT BREEZE wafting through the kitchen window sent dust scampering across the top of the telephone. I pressed the receiver into my ear, trying to catch Kitty's every word. "I'm okay, Claude. I just wanted to give you time, that's all."

Time to worry more? I resisted firing back. The past week had inched by slowly with no answer from Kitty any of the dozen times I'd phoned. Between the heat, her aunt, and her maybe-baby, worry had tunneled itself deep into me like it was the shaft and I the mine.

"Okay. My dad is picking my mom up tonight. They'll be here in the morning. How are you feeling?"

She didn't answer right away, the first slip-up in her façade of confidence. "Scared," she whispered. "Just really scared."

I grumbled, resting my forehead against the wall. "You're not alone, okay? I'm here for you. And my mom will help you first thing tomorrow."

"I feel guilty. I mean, she's just getting home from being away so long. The last thing she'll want to do is deal with my mess instead of enjoying being with you and your dad again."

Would Kitty ever cease seeing herself as an outsider in our family? She'd been one of us for nearly fourteen years. Yet, she still berated herself as a burden, a bother, a guest, a stranger. "Don't put this off any longer, Kitty. My mom would love nothing more than to help you. I know it, and I think you do too."

She drew in a ragged breath. After a moment, she whispered, "Okay. You're right."

"When I get done helping Dad at the garage today, would it be okay if I came and picked you up?"

"To do what?"

I swallowed. "Take you on a date. Whatever you want to do. Actually, I saw a poster in the gym the other day. They're projecting a movie in there tonight."

In her silent deliberation, I imagined the fear she wrestled with—that she was a burden not worthy of my attention. That I was only being nice to her out of pity. That further romantic involvement with me would be unwise should she truly be pregnant.

As I opened my mouth to comfort her, she blurted out, "I'll be ready whenever you get here."

Hope festered within me. I knew precisely what I planned to do.

—

Dad only felt like working a few hours. He wanted to be on the road in a timely manner should Mom's train arrive in Las Vegas earlier than expected. Standing on the porch, I watched him go. He asked me to tidy up, so I wiped the dust and swept the floors before cleaning up myself. Mom was sure to have a fit when she saw how much I'd let my hair grow out since she'd left. Not to mention that I'd perfected the art of slicking back the sides and tousling the front with pomade Cliff had left behind when he moved out.

I finished getting ready, a nervous snake looping around my belly. I called Kitty to let her know I was heading out.

Peggy's car was absent when I arrived. I breathed a sigh of relief. The last thing I wanted was a run-in with her. For whatever reason, I couldn't strike up the courage to get out of the truck though. That pesky snake continued its path, 'round and 'round, tying itself into a knot around my innards. Why was I so nervous? On today of all days? I took a swig of water and told myself to get a grip.

Kitty didn't answer the door right away, which made me sweat even more. I gave it a minute and knocked again. This time I heard her call out, "Just a minute!" I paced and gave my arms and legs a good shake out, flinging all the excess energy off me like a stupid wiggling worm.

Then I heard Kitty's giggle, the one I'd been aching to hear for days. She stood in the doorway watching me, a light cotton dress flowing loosely around her body, her hair curled and pinned back in the front, a light dusting of makeup across her face. She stopped me dead in my tracks.

"Have you learned a new dance, or shall I call the priest?"

"No need." I straightened up. "Just full of beans."

She stepped out and shut the door behind her, catching my gaze. "Full of beans, huh?"

Taking my eyes from her would have been impossible. "Kit, you look . . ." I didn't have the words. The right ones simply weren't invented yet. I swallowed hard. "How are you doing?"

"I'm really glad to see you."

Closing the gap between us, I held out my hand to her.

Her eyes flickered away from mine to my hand and back again as if she expected me to retract it. As though I'd made a mistake in offering it at all.

I didn't waver, and she slid hers into mine.

We ate omelets and soup at the drugstore in Tonopah. Then

I fueled up and headed back to Goldfield. But a mile or two outside of town, I pulled off the road and untied an old bandanna I'd looped around the rearview mirror earlier in the day. I motioned for Kitty to scoot closer to me.

"Put this on, please."

"What? Why?"

"I can't tell you. It's a surprise."

"Is this really necessary? Can't I just close my eyes?" Kitty asked as I wrapped the bandanna around her head, securing it with a tight knot. "I promise I won't peek!"

"Won't peek? Yeah, sure. I don't believe that for a second."

She poked her bottom lip out in an exaggerated pout. "You never blindfolded me when you took me on surprise adventures as kids."

"Well, we aren't kids anymore, are we?"

She pinched her forehead and fidgeted as she tried coming up with a clever retort.

I waved my hand in front of her. "You promise you can't see anything?"

She shook her head. I began driving again, cutting down familiar roads, the great depleted mountains welcoming us like they were still stuffed with gold. The road turned rough and jostled us around in the cab. When I came to a stop, the dust billowing in our wake caught up to us, encapsulating my pretty blue pickup in a puff of brown.

"Are we here?" Kitty murmured, reaching for the bandanna. "Can I take this thing off yet?"

I playfully swatted her hands away from her face. "Not yet. Wait right there." I got out and rounded the hood to her door and helped her out.

She smoothed her cotton dress and huffed.

I took her hand. We walked together. "Almost there."

The groaning whine of the old Model T's door gave the

whole charade away. Kitty whipped off her blindfold in a flash. A statue, she stood a moment and simply gazed.

"Our secret spot," she murmured. A hot gust of wind tousled her hair and made the end of her dress flap against her knees.

"Come on. You won't be able to smell the rat piss from standing out here."

Her steady gaze crumbled into a grin. "What're we doing here, anyhow?" she asked, not even flinching as we climbed inside and sank into the dirty, worn-out seats. "This smells worse than I remember."

"Reminiscing or something of the sort."

Her eyes narrowed. "I feel like you have something up your sleeve. Then again, you always have, haven't you? Really is like old times."

I chuckled and watched a jackrabbit bounce nearby, its body disappearing behind a cactus, its shadow still visible. "Remember when I gave you that essay I wrote about you here?"

"The one Mrs. Newton forced us all to write because she was peeved at you?"

"Punished for making a pretty girl laugh. I still can't believe the injustice."

She wagged a finger at me. "Tsk, tsk, tsk! I hope you learned your lesson."

"Unfortunately, I don't think I did. Do you remember what my essay said?"

"Not really." Her lips poked out as she thought. "I wish I did, though. That was one of the last times I ever felt sure of anything in life," she admitted.

"I need to tell you my intentions, Kitty."

"Oh?" Her eyes widened. She lifted her chin, stoic and somber. Slowly, her hands drifted over her stomach. "Okay."

I shifted in the seat and dug from my pocket two neatly folded pieces of paper. No going back now. "This might jog your memory," I said, smoothing out the papers. I began to read.

When I finished, I cleared my throat, not yet ready to look at Kitty's face, afraid of what I'd see there and afraid she'd see the tears swirling in my own eyes. "We aren't thirteen anymore, Kitty, but everything I wrote back then still stands now. I didn't exactly imagine this being where we'd find ourselves five years later, but welcoming this unexpected gift not with closed hands or crossed arms, but an open embrace? That's my intention. Loving you until you see yourself as I do? That's my intention. Never leaving you? That's my intention."

I listened to her breathe.

"Claude. This is different. Things are . . ." She blew out a breath and asked point blank, "What exactly are you trying to say here?"

I gave her the papers. They shook in her hands. "I meant what I wrote. I'm ready to face this with you, to walk by you every step of the way, to have a life together, to raise that baby together, should you truly be pregnant. And before you give me a thousand reasons why I shouldn't, why I deserve something different, let me give you one reason that tells you why you're wrong: I love you. There's not much more to say except for that. I love you. I'll say it again and again if I have to. I love you. I love you. Do you get it yet? I love you." I'd never been surer of anything in my life.

Her chest heaved, a violent swelling and falling. She turned my essay over in her hands.

"I can't believe you kept this," she whispered, closing her eyes. "I'm so sorry for everything. You know I'm not asking you to save me, Claude. I just want you to forgive me. Because I should have listened to you. I could have stopped it. I should have—"

I placed my hand on her knee.

She took a breath and said, "I just feel like it's too much for you to carry."

"That's the beauty of it. You and I, we don't have to carry it. Lay it down, Kitty. Let's move forward, together."

She looked at me. "Even if it's not your own baby? You're really okay with that?"

"It's not the baby's fault, is it?"

Tears fell onto her lap. "No."

"Those are my intentions, Kitty. Now you know." I wiped her cheeks with my thumb. "Take as much time as you need to think about everything I've said. I won't change my mind though. Unless you truly believe we aren't meant to be together."

Her forehead wrinkled. "That's the thing. I really think we are. I just feel so terri—"

"Stop it." I cupped her hand in mine. "Is there any part of you that wants to be with me forever?"

"Yes."

"And setting aside all your shame and worry and fear, is there any part of you that doesn't?"

She relaxed into me as she admitted, "No."

All the world slowed to a crawl. Lord willing, I would make this beautiful soul my wife.

"You know, when I first read you my essay here years ago, I wanted to kiss you."

"Did you really?" She looked at me with surprise.

I nodded, my eyes darting briefly to her lips, nearly admitting that's what I wanted to do right then and there.

"There's always a chance to right your wrongs," she said with a giggle.

I felt my cheeks redden, being put on the spot. In a brief

moment of hesitation, I gazed at her, looking for further permission. Her eyes sparkled as her lips curled into a smile. I moved closer, and the next thing I knew, my lips were pressing into hers. Right there in that rat-piss junker, all of my dreams came true.

—

We barely caught the showing of *Frankenstein Meets the Wolf Man* in the gymnasium. As we walked in, the lights were already off and the wall was lit up with the opening credits of the film. A whisper of voices came from a cluster of people sitting on the far side of the wooden bleachers. I couldn't be sure, but I thought I heard Richie say my name.

Kitty and I, fingers intertwined, slid into an empty spot on the back row, opposite where the murmuring crew sat. Still reeling from the day, I couldn't concentrate on anything other than Kitty's body curled in close to mine. I slipped my arm around her and squeezed her tight.

If anyone had asked me afterward what the movie was about, I couldn't have given an answer. But we slithered out as soon as it ended, and no one did. Darkness swept us into a hug as we exited the gymnasium. Now that the sun had given up its post for the day, the drop in temperature was refreshing. We climbed into the pickup.

"Guess we should get you back home?" I said, even though the last thing I wanted was for her to be alone. "Why don't you just stay in Goldfield tonight? By the time we get back to Peggy's, it'll be late. My mom will be home in the morning. Might as well already be here when she arrives."

"And where will I stay?"

"My house?" The look on her face made me realize how my half-brained idea might be taken. "You can sleep in my room. I'll sleep on the couch. No funny business, I promise. Or one of us could sleep next door at your old place? Or maybe, Julia's house?"

Kitty curled her feet beneath her. "I really don't want to be around Peggy if I can help it. She's been so cruel since she found out. And Julia would have a lot of questions if I just showed up on her doorstep in the black of night. Not to mention if she heard me retching in the early morning."

I let her think about the offer, aware now of the people trickling out of the gym. I didn't feel like socializing, so I started the engine. We left, aimlessly weaving around town as she deliberated.

"You really think that'd be alright?" she finally asked.

"I don't see why not."

"Okay, then. Thank you, Claude."

—

I was careful not to so much as hug her in my own home. I set her up in my bedroom, attempting to make her as comfortable as I could. I gave her a set of my mother's clothes to change into, should she wish. We said goodnight, and I closed my bedroom door, going to the couch where I tossed and turned in discomfort. Yet, I found great peace in knowing that Kitty was on the other side of the wall.

Sometime well into the night, I woke to a whisper. "Claude, are you awake? I just can't sleep."

I cracked an eyelid. The room was dark, my brain foggy. It took me a moment to register where I was and who was speaking to me. "Kit?"

I felt her sit down on the end of the couch, barely missing my foot. "I'm sorry to wake you. I'm just driving myself crazy in there."

"It's okay. Just . . . give me a minute." I rubbed my eyes and turned on the lamp.

Kitty scooted in, taking my blanket for herself. Her eyes, dancing in the dim light, searched mine. Instantly, I knew that it was doubt that kept her awake.

"Tell me what's going on in your head."

She snuggled deeper under the blanket. "Regret."

I knew she would change her past actions if she could. I would even change them if it were in my power. The thought of her being overpowered by Jack brought me to my knees with heartache. The subsequent fallout made me queasy if I thought too hard about it. "What's done is done."

"I should have listened to you."

"Maybe I should've tried harder to make you listen."

"Don't you dare blame yourself," she said, her hand flying out from beneath the blanket to grab mine. "I just keep having these thoughts that this is all so unfair to you. You're a noble guy, Claude. The fact that you're willing to set aside a different future all for me? It's kind of overwhelming. What if you realize one year into this that it's just too much, too hard? What if you change your mind?"

"Can I ask you something?"

She nodded.

"If I were to ask you to marry me, would you say yes?"

Her eyes widened, and she slowly answered. "Yes."

"Why would you say yes?"

"Because I love you. I trust you," she whispered. "Because you love me."

"And a year from now, are you going to change your mind? Do you think we're just being rash right now, rushing into this?"

She subtly shrunk away from me, as though my question was a suggestion. "What do you think?"

Letting go of her hand, I stood and removed an old photograph of my parents from the wall. "You see this? This is what I want. I want us on a wall, photographed and framed. I want our grandchildren, even our great-grandchildren to take our photo in their hands one day and ask their parents, '*Who is this? They look so in love.*' And I want for their parents to be able to tell them, with complete honesty, how truly in love we were. You, Kitty, are what I want. Plain and simple, from now 'til forever. It's always been the two of us. And that's the way it's supposed to be. No changes of mind or heart. I'm committed."

"You really love me." Her voice cut through the night, a sparkling wonder to it. The full realization of my love seeped in, filling all the spaces, the minute and invisible cracks.

"I do." I sat back down beside her.

She touched my cheek and brought her forehead to mine. Her lips parted. But just then, the front door jiggled open.

Dad stood in the doorway. He cleared his throat and let Mom's baggage fall to the floor with a thunk. "Claude?" His voice was low and angry. "What's going on here?"

Mom took two steps into the room, her eyes stuck on Kitty. "Hi . . . kids?" She tried to maintain the buoyancy in her voice, but her disappointment couldn't be masked. "Late night, huh?"

Sheepishly, I clamored to my feet. "I thought you guys were staying the night."

Mom raised her brows. I realized that my remark sounded worse than I intended. "Checked the mattress at the hotel. Bed bugs. So, we decided to come home, although neither of us expected to be interrupting such a romantic evening."

"It's not—" I looked back and forth between my parents, my pulse pounding in my ears knowing how poorly this reflected on Kitty and me. "Don't worry. This isn't what it looks like."

They both narrowed their eyes at me.

"I'm serious. We were just talking. Look, it was my idea for Kitty to stay the night, because she wanted to see you tomorrow, Mom. She . . . she needs to talk. I figured it would be better if she just stayed, because we saw *Frankenstein*, and it was late. And that way she wouldn't need another ride tomorrow once you got back into town. But don't worry, we weren't, you know . . . She was staying in my room. I was on the couch, but she couldn't sleep, so we were up just talking—"

Dad held up a hand to stop my rambling. Mom dropped into the armchair. With trembling hands, she withdrew bobby pin after bobby pin from her hair. She stuck them between her teeth as she went until they were all out, and then she tucked them into a pocket. She leaned forward, crossing and uncrossing her legs, leaning back and then forward again. Finally, she sighed and dropped her face into her hand a moment. She took a deep breath before righting herself and giving us her attention. Exhaustion marked every line on her face. "What's so pressing a conversation that Kitty had to stay the night?"

"It can wait until the morning, can't it?" I looked forlornly at Kitty and my parents, asking their permission to sidestep this land mine for a few more hours.

"Kitty?" Dad ignored me and locked eyes with her. "Can it wait until morning?"

Mom reached for Kitty and sleepily said, "Oh honey, it's good to see you again. Are you okay?"

Kitty tried to smile. "Yes. Let's talk about it in the morning. I'm sorry to disturb this whole night. You must be so tired from all your travels."

"Alright," Dad grumbled, flashing me a look of concern and warning. He picked up Mom's bag and disappeared to their bedroom.

Mom, too tired and stunned, sat in the chair, gazing blankly at us. I went to her, bent down, and hugged her. "Welcome home, Mama."

"Claude, your hair!" She gasped and reached for my locks. "You couldn't have taken yourself to the barber while I was away? Kitty, is it not embarrassing to be seen with a mop-head in public?"

"Alright, maybe it's about time for a trim," I said.

"A trim, a buzz, tomato, tom-ah-to." She rubbed her temples. "I can't stay up any longer, kids. Kitty, you're sleeping in Claude's room, is that right?"

"Yes."

Mom's expectant silence brought Kitty to her feet. She sped down the hall and into my bedroom by herself. Once she was out of sight, Mom stared at me. "Claude Fisher, you will stay on that couch all night, do you hear me?"

"Yes, ma'am. Mom, it's really not what you're thinking."

If only she knew the actual truth.

Mom waved her hand, brushing me off. "We'll talk in the morning when I can think straight. Goodnight, honey."

Surprisingly, I passed out quickly, my body making up for lost time. I heard my father rustling about in the kitchen, percolating the coffee. I opened my eyes, realizing morning was already half over. He greeted me with a grim nod, giving me the notion that he'd either slept poorly or had lost trust in me.

Time moved thick and slow all morning. Like God was stretching it out uncomfortably thin. After a while, the four of us were seated at the dining table, a makeshift breakfast of whatever could be found in our cupboards in front of us.

"Well, it's the morning," Mom said, taking a sip of her coffee. "It seems we had a pressing matter that needed to be discussed?"

Kitty pursed her lips and stared at her plate. I leaned over, whispering in her ear, "Do you want me and my dad to leave? Or would you like me to stay?"

She turned her face to me now, the pain evident, and whispered, "Stay."

My parents waited patiently, intently watching our

exchange.

"You or me?" I whispered.

She pointed to me.

"Right. Okay." I nodded and exhaled, then looked at my parents. "So . . ." I suddenly scrambled for the right words, for the right delivery to soften the news. "There's a chance that Kitty might be pregnant."

Not a soul dared to take a breath. Mom hung her head. Dad pushed his chair away from the table. He looked at me in disbelief. "How could you?"

I held up my hands in innocence. "No, no, Dad. Don't worry. It's not mine!" As if that statement made it any the better. I shook my head, trying to reel in my words. I grasped Kitty's hand in solidarity, saying to her, "I really butchered that, didn't I?"

"I've seen more graceful houseflies," she muttered, flashing a quick, forgiving smile that made me want to wrap her in my arms.

Mom and Dad whispered together on their own. When I met Dad's eyes, he jerked his head toward the door. "Come on. You and I are having a talk."

We probably should have just stuck to the original plan, Kitty talking to my mother alone from the get-go. But truthfully, I didn't mind having the news out in the open. I squeezed Kitty's hand and kissed her on the cheek. "It'll be okay. I'll be back soon."

Dad and I drove in dead silence to the drugstore and ordered a soda from Phil, opting to sit in the back corner booth for as much privacy as we could get.

"Go ahead," he finally said. "Give it to me straight."

I told him everything.

Dad scrubbed his face with his hands. "How sure is Kitty that she's pregnant?"

"I mean, she hasn't seen a nurse or doctor or anything. She's been hoping to talk to Mom. But a lot of the signs are there, you know? She seems certain."

"I'm sure Ginny will help her figure it out. We'll give them a lot of time today." Dad took a moment to collect his thoughts. "I don't think you're thinking this through clearly, Claude. It's not going to be easy. It's hard enough when you've planned for it. Maybe you ought to take a visit to your brother and see just how much work it is."

I thought of my phone call with Cliff, thought of my screaming nephew in the background. "I know it won't be simple. But listen—"

"Claude—"

"No, please. Just hear me out, Dad. You may think I'm jumping into things, but I've actually given it a lot of thought. I love Kitty. We've been best friends our entire lives. I've been wild about her for years. And you know I'm a hard worker. I've been saving up most everything I've earned so far. I can work full-time and make enough to provide for us. And if you'll let me, I'd like to buy the Ralph's old house from you. I know Jeb turned it back over to you. Of course, I'd want to fix it up a bit, try to make it not remind Kitty of her father. But then we'd be right next door to you and Mom for help if we need."

"So, you two will just move in together? You're going to raise another man's baby?"

"Just move in together? 'Course not. I'm going to marry her first. I'm going to raise a family."

He stilled.

I capitalized on his silence. "Do you really want me to clap my hands together, shake off the mess, and send Kitty on her way? She'll go back to Tonopah, raising a baby under the roof of a bitter woman. Alone. No support. No father. I know you love Kitty like a daughter. Is that something you're okay with?

Because I'm not. Or would you rather know she and that baby are safe next door with your son who'll love them both for the rest of their lives?"

He seemed to consider this. "I want you to be honest with me. Are you doing this because you feel obligated?"

"I'm doing this because I love her. Before I even knew about the baby, I was dreaming about marrying her."

Dad chuckled and grabbed his bottle. He tipped it back, taking one long sip, smiling all the while.

"What's so funny?" His sudden change in demeanor made the hair on my neck stand on edge.

He set his bottle down and leaned toward me. "I'm not laughing at you, Claude. If anything, I'm proud. You've never been a man to hide your feelings or to shy away from doing what's right."

"And who do you think I learned that from?"

"Your mother."

I snorted. He wasn't wrong, Mom had taught me that too. But he also knew I was talking about him. "How old were you and Mom when you got married?"

"She was eighteen. I was twenty."

"How about when you had Vern?"

"Nineteen and twenty-one."

"Kitty and I aren't that far off from you guys."

Dad bobbed his head. "Before you make any rash decisions, can I suggest you wait for confirmation on whether Kitty's really with child or not?"

"Sure. But if she is or isn't, I need you to understand these are my intentions."

"Your mind's made up then?"

I nodded with confidence. "Do I have your blessing?"

Dad ran a hand through his hair. He blew out a breath that turned into a whistle. "If that's the case, then yes, son. You do."

Unexplainable tears gathered in my eyes. I blinked them away.

"Let me ask you something," Dad said. "Will it bother you what other people might think?"

"Not really."

"How come?"

"I guess I don't care if they know the truth or if they judge me for what they think they know. This town isn't an audience I need approval from. The ones who really matter know the full truth."

"Couldn't have said it any better myself. You're a good guy, Claude." Dad finished off his soda and shook his head. "Life can sure change in the blink of an eye, can't it?"

If the last few years had taught me anything, I'd learned that God's will always overpowered our own.

28

Three weeks later . . .

CHICKADEES SANG BEYOND the window, cheering along the rising sun, giving their praise for another morning of life. In the growing light, I turned the ring over in my hand. Mom had pressed it into my palm the night before, assuring me of her support in my decision. The ring, a simple band, was encrusted in tiny diamonds set in such a way that they reminded me of stars. It had been her mother's, and Mom had kept it safely tucked away all these years. But now she passed it on to me, saying it would do more good on Kitty's finger than it would collecting dust in her drawer. A lot of things didn't make sense to me, but near the top of my list was the capacity my parents had to embrace the chaos, to field the unending changes life kept dishing our way.

In the span of a few weeks—once we'd received confirmation from the doctor that Kitty was truly with child— life had drastically changed. We moved Kitty out of Peggy's house the same day as her appointment, bringing her home to Goldfield. I gave Kitty my bedroom and moved in next door for the time being. I rose early every morning to work on restoring Kitty's old home. I wanted to transform it into a refuge, warm and safe, to welcome my bride and the small bud that sprouted within her.

I thought about these changes as I got out of bed, set the ring on the table, and got to work. My stomach growled, but I ignored it. After an hour or two of working on the house, I planned to head over and snag something to eat from my mother's kitchen. Then I'd go to the shop to start my shift with Dad.

I brushed aside endless cobwebs and wiped away thick dust that held past memories hostage. Time to change and replace those memories. The house needed to be cleansed of the poignant memories contained within the walls. With paper and pencil in hand, I inspected each room, making note of which floorboards still needed replacing, which pipes needed fixing, which window locks were loose.

A small knock on the door interrupted my cleaning. I opened it to find Kitty on the other side. Her hair fell in a frazzled braid behind her back. She wiped the crust from the corners of her eyes as she came in. "Good morning. You sure?" she said.

I laughed. What started as a sincere question, spoken every morning since she moved in with my parents weeks ago, had quickly turned into a running joke. She asked the same thing every morning, providing me the opportunity to change my mind, quietly fearing deep down that I actually might.

But I answered the same way every time. "I'm Claude."

She always laughed, the repetition tickling and assuring us both. We knew this was all unconventional, that we were being catapulted into the fast lane with our relationship, our marriage, our future. But there was no way of slowing down. So, we took a page out of my parents' playbook and embraced what we could the best we could.

This morning I changed up the routine, however. I guided her to an old dining chair where she squirmed and waited for me to say my part of the gag. *I'm Claude.* But instead, I slid my grandmother's old ring from the counter and got down on one knee in front of her.

"Does this answer your question?" I held up the ring. "I'm sure, Kitty. As sure as I'll ever be about anything."

Her lips parted, releasing a sound as soft as a bubble. She leaned in for a closer look at the ring. A band of light from the window struck across her features. Her whiskey-colored eyes dripped with honey. She clamped them shut, closing off tears, and I took her hand.

"Kitty, will you look at me?"

Her eyes fluttered open.

"You don't ever have to doubt me. I don't care how many times a day you need to ask me if I'm sure. I don't care how many walls I have to tear down over the next eighty years. I'll answer every time. I'll dismantle every wall. I'm yours forever if you'll have me. Will you? Will you marry me, Kitty May Ralph?"

She nodded vigorously, tears pouring freely now. "Yes," she finally choked out.

I slid the ring on her trembling finger and laced our hands together. She cried on my shoulder. With each passing minute, she relaxed a little more and pressed harder into me, surrendering to the reality that now surrounded her. She said goodbye to the past and stepped into the future with me.

Kitty pulled away, wiped her eyes, held her hand out in front of her, and allowed the diamonds to twinkle in the streaming light. "So . . ." she said.

"So . . . ?"

"So, when's the big day?"

"I'd sign this deal today if I could."

She threw her head back and laughed. "You don't want to wait?"

"Do you?"

"No. I'd marry you today too."

I sat in a chair next to her. "Well, I suppose we have to figure out some details, right? Like what kind of wedding you want? We can make it simple. Go to the courthouse and sign a paper like Cliff and Maisy did? Or we can do something a little more proper. Your wish is my command."

She looked down, then back up at me through her lashes.

"Tell me," I said.

"I've always wanted to wear a wedding dress," she admitted, her voice small. "I don't want a lot of people, don't need a big party, don't really care about those things. But I want a dress."

An idea came to mind. "I can make that happen. But I have a few telephone calls to make."

———

After my shift at Dad's shop, Kitty and I walked into the church. Six beaming women greeted us. Each had boxes full of fabric and lace and delicate beads on the tables before them.

"Kitty," I said. "These are the lovely ladies of *Wilted and Quilted* whom I play music for now and again."

"Boy, you must all be something special. He hasn't even played music for me!" she quipped.

"Yet!" I proclaimed as they all laughed and introduced themselves. Only a matter of minutes had passed before Margaret declared they had a lot of work to do. They set to holding up sheets of silk and lace of white, sprawling all of the materials out on the tables before Kitty. I hung back and watched my fiancée peruse her options. She took every fabric and ran it through her hands. Ada held out a combination of silk and tulle, suggesting they would blend well together. Edna rolled her eyes, elbowing her way in to explain why they wouldn't. The ladies spouted their opinions. But Kitty, who'd been clutching the same bundle of fabric and lace for a while, finally spoke.

"I'd like this," she said.

At once, the chatter stopped. Margaret turned to me. "You heard your bride. It's time for us to get our measurements and get to work. Go on. Shoo now! Someone will bring her home when we're done."

Kitty's eyes widened. "You're leaving?" she mouthed.

I had to admit, I was bewildered too. But as my dear friends surrounded her, pins and scissors and sewing machines at the ready, I knew she was in good hands. I went home.

—

"I can't believe how quickly this is happening. By next weekend, really?" Mom mused as we sat in the living room while she tailored one of Vern's old suits for me. I'd sorely outgrown my own. She smoothed a pant leg over the table. "Have you thought to telephone your brother yet?"

"No, I know he's so busy."

"He may be busy, but this is certainly news he'd make time for."

"I'll call him tonight," I said. "I can't believe Dad and I still haven't met Henry and Randall."

"It's killing your father that he hasn't met his grandsons yet. You know, it wasn't that long ago that grandchildren were a faraway thought. Now, it's like they're coming out of the woodwork."

If she cared that the child Kitty carried wasn't blood-related, she did a great job of hiding it. Dad too. Sometimes I wondered if they'd forgotten I wasn't the real father after all. Did they see Kitty, and everything attached to her, as I did? *Mine.*

Mom suddenly looked up from her stitching, as though the

full weight of everything had washed over her for the first time. "My baby boy is getting married," she murmured, mystified as she stared at me.

I put a hand on her shoulder. "Not if my mother doesn't finish sewing my suit."

She smacked my hand away. "Watch it, mister. I'm not so sentimental that I won't poke you with one of these needles."

Within the hour, Ada brought Kitty home. "She's going to look heavenly," Ada announced. I knew *Wilted and Quilted* would get the job done. Kitty thanked Ada profusely, making what offerings she could to repay them for their charity. But Ada dismissed every one of them. "It is our honor, Kitty. Don't you worry about anything, okay? We'll have the dress finished up by the end of the week."

Kitty looked exhausted. "Okay," she relented. "Thank you."

Mom and Ada fell into chatter about the twins. Mom gave Ada play-by-plays of every tiny movement she'd witness over the months she was in California. I walked with Kitty to my old bedroom—hers for the time being. She curled up on the bed. I lay down next to her.

"You look spent. They didn't yank you around too much, did they?

She laughed. "No, they were so endearing and helpful. I'm just so tired from being out all day. I think a little nap will help. Thank you for this today, Claude." She touched my cheek, her warmth a welcomed rush. "Are we really getting married?"

I picked up her hand and checked for the ring. "Phew. Good. It's still there. Yep, looks like we are. Kind of surreal, isn't it?"

"It truly is," she whispered. "The dress is going to be perfect."

Her worries, fears, and grief were faraway in this moment. I hoped they stayed away, absolving forever.

"So, it went well?"

"It went magically," she murmured.

"So, you're happy?"

She wriggled closer to me, her eyes now closed, a sleepy smile on her lips. "I'm Kitty."

29

THE THING ABOUT living in a small town in the middle of nowhere was that so little a fuss could be made about the extravagant and so extravagant a fuss could be made about so little. The other thing about a small town was that word traveled faster than the speed of light. The whole town often became involved in business that didn't rightfully concern it. But every once in a while, something would shift, and the scales would balance out just right to permit plans to unfurl exactly.

Neither Kitty nor I wanted a frenzy; all we cared about was getting married. We desired something quiet and private. But once the community found out, they swooped in like the helping hand of a mother, providing to us whatever they could in order for our dream to succeed. They offered their assistance or their absence, whichever would bless us most. To our knowledge, no one knew that Kitty had another life growing within her. Though what with our shotgun wedding and all, many probably assumed as much.

"So, you're really getting hitched in a matter of days, Fly?" Richie scratched his head as we walked into the hardware store in Tonopah. "I still can't believe it. Can I bring a date?"

"No. I told you it's just something small." I looked over the list of supplies I needed in order to finish a few projects before Kitty and I officially moved into her old home. "Who do you want to bring anyway?"

"Bethany."

I rolled my eyes. "She's invited."

"Now you tell me." He picked up a hatchet and gave it a swing.

"Watch it, Rich. You're gonna slice my face off right before my wedding."

He set it back and rummaged through a bin of screws. "So, who's all invited?"

"My parents, you, Pete, Bethany, and Julia."

I moved through the store with an extra bounce in my step as I scanned over the available paint colors and looked at lumber. Ideas formulated in my mind as I envisioned the homemade crib I wanted to build in the future. I would surprise Kitty one day with the perfect nursery. Something soft and inviting. Something that would make her eyes glisten. But I couldn't buy any of those materials now, couldn't divulge those thoughts to Richie.

Once we'd gathered my supplies, we stopped in at Henry's Sweets so I could buy Kitty her favorite treats. I tossed a few lemon candies into the mix, thinking of Big John, wondering if they might help Kitty's nausea like they had his. Though Mom insisted that it would lift from her soon.

I paid my tab and turned for the door. Richie bristled beside me, and then I, too, saw who had just entered the store. One of the two men who had hurt Kitty the most.

Jack headed straight for us. I swallowed the sudden flare of fire in my chest, tamping down the flames.

"Fly!" His dark eyes were the blackest I'd ever seen them. "I heard some news about you. Congratulations."

Nothing good would come from engaging with him. I nodded and headed past him, but he pressed a hand against my chest to stop me.

"I do find the timing kind of funny though. You don't just up and marry someone out of the blue."

I didn't acknowledge this vague accusation. Jack kept his hand firm on my chest.

"Tell me something, and be honest, Fisher. Were the two of you fooling around while I was dating her all last year?"

"Jack." Richie's voice came as an icy warning.

"Is that all you care about?" I asked. "Whether you were wronged by me or not?"

"What do you think you're doing with my girl?" he spat.

I nearly laughed in his face. *My girl?* She was the farthest from being his. I looked at him flatly and said, "Everything you couldn't."

He recoiled. "What's that supposed to mean?"

I shook my head and removed his hand from my chest. "If you'd move out of my way, I'd like to bring my fiancée her candies now." I jiggled the paper bag in the air.

"What'd you do? Knock her up and now you're stuck?"

Richie's hand flew to Jack's collar. He yanked him face-to-face.

"What's the deal, Rich?" Jack sputtered.

"Claude's not the kind of guy who would do that," Richie said.

Jack looked pliable in Richie's hands, like putty or clay. It further cemented the fact that he was no man at all, but still only a boy, selfish and juvenile and unable to provide the respect for others he so clearly lacked for himself. For a guy with such an arrogant air, Jack lacked the peace that I'd learned only came from a freedom that couldn't be found within maintaining control but in relinquishing it. I knew Kitty's freedom was something he could never steal, could never tarnish. And I wasn't about to let him mar mine either.

I nudged Richie. "Let's go. Come on."

Richie hesitated, stealing a confused glance at me. He let the wad of T-shirt slip from his hand.

Outside, Richie paced the parking lot, his hands behind his head. I yelled to him to get into the pickup.

"How are you not more upset right now?" He slid into the passenger seat.

Through the window, I could see Jack grumbling to someone at the counter inside Henry's. "I don't think I have the room for anger anymore."

Richie fidgeted next to me. "He's got a lot of nerve; I'll give him that. I can't believe . . ." He blew out a breath and looked at me.

"That he'd accuse me of the very thing he did?" I finished the sentence for him. Richie's brows shot up. I decided to tell him everything. "Kitty's pregnant, Richie."

"You're kidding." His face fell. "With . . . ?"

"Jack's."

Richie shook his head. Another cloud of anger rolled over his face. "There was a day—the morning after graduation— when Kitty came pounding on Jack's door, sobbing. I answered it. Jack came to the door eventually but basically spat in her face. I gave them their space, but I got the sense that something bad had happened. But I didn't realize . . ." Richie bristled. "And you just passed up the opportunity to beat the living snot out of the guy who did that to her?"

"I guess so." I pulled out of the parking lot, mercy and justice beating in my mind like a drum the whole drive home. Everything that had for so long been foggy suddenly became clear.

—

Richie helped me out for a few hours once we got back home, but he left by early evening. Paying no mind to the heat or my hunger or the eventual setting of the sun, I worked tirelessly the rest the day in the soon-to-be home of Mr. and Mrs. Claude Fisher.

At nightfall, Kitty let herself in and took a look around. "Oh, Claude! It's really coming along in here. You need a hand with anything?"

"Well . . ." I pulled myself to my feet and tossed my dirty work gloves to the floor. "I fixed some areas with wood rot this morning. And I think I fixed a pipe alright. It's nice and clean in here, wouldn't you say? There're only a few things left on my list. But I'll make sure it's ready in time."

"No matter what, it's going to be perfect, Claude. I'm so thankful. By the way, the final adjustments were made to my dress today," she said.

I scooped her up and carried her to the old couch that I planned on replacing as soon as I could. "Tell me about it."

"No! It would ruin the surprise," she protested and buried her face into my neck. "How was your day? I feel like I hardly saw you."

I thought about Jack. The run-in would be something I kept to myself. "It was good. Got a lot done in here. How are you feeling?"

"I've had a lot on my mind, actually."

My stomach flopped. "Everything okay?"

She got silent. "It's probably stupid, but today I stood in Ada Thomas' living room, trying on the most beautiful dress I've worn in my life, and I realized that neither of my parents will be here to see me get married. It's not like my mom was around for anything. My dad wasn't exactly present for much either, but . . ." Her voice got lost. She shrugged. "It still makes me sad."

I closed my eyes. "Would you want him here?"

"No," she whispered. "I wouldn't want to do that to you or your parents. It's just an odd thought, you know? To be honest, I wonder sometimes about what life would be like if my dad never made the decision to drive that night."

I snuggled her into me and kissed the top of her head. "I wonder that too. Some questions will never be answered, as hard as that might be."

"Do you think he'd have eventually figured things out? Put the liquor away? Found a steady job? Would he be anticipating handing me off to you a few days from now? Watching his little girl grow up?" She frowned. "Do you think he wishes he could get back all the moments he stole from himself over the years? You know he's out of prison now, onto some new life in Reno? Doesn't even know I'm gonna be a wife, a mother. Unless Peggy told him. I wonder what he'd say if he found out. Would he be happy for us?"

"He's the only one who can answer that for you. I know you always wanted him to change. I'm sorry he never did."

"I always had your parents. I don't know what I would've done without you and your family. Still don't." She tilted her head up. I pecked her on the lips.

"Want to know what's been on my mind?" I asked.

"Please."

"I've been thinking about your dad too."

"You have?"

I nodded, pulling her closer. "About all the things I hope he's learned. And that, despite everything, I forgive him."

She eyed me curiously and with caution. "You do?"

"I do."

—

Two days later, I stood in my parent's living room, the smolder of dusk curtaining the house, the furniture inside rearranged to make space for the ceremony. My mother and closest friends sat on the couch and in chairs lined up against the wall. Pastor James quietly stood beside me.

I shook out my pant leg and fussed with my tie, feeling the jitters and the promise of our future, as I waited for Kitty to make her grand entrance from the bedroom.

Richie made a few wisecracks to clear the air, but even as I laughed, I listened for any indication she was on her way down the hallway. *To me.*

But what I heard instead was the slamming of a car door, the squeal of an infant, the creaking of our porch. My brother came through the front door with one of my nephews fast asleep in his arms. He was followed by Maisy, my other nephew in hers.

"We're not late, are we?" he quipped.

My knees threatened to buckle. I couldn't cross the room and throw my arm around him like I wanted to, but he came straight for me.

"What are you doing here?" I blinked away my tears.

"Are you kidding me? I wouldn't have missed this for the world." Grinning, he clapped me on the shoulder and looked past me. "Looks like the show's about to begin. Better find my seat."

I turned around in time to see Kitty emerge from my old bedroom. My dad escorted her down the hallway on his arm. I felt like my legs had been obliterated all together, and only by the grace of God did I remain upright.

Kitty gazed at me, her eyes already moist, her dress flowing around her like a perfect, silken hug.

This wasn't what I'd spent years on end praying for. No. It was more. This was more than any amount of riches extracted from the mines, more than any record high or bone-chilling low.

Dad brought her to me. She left his arm to join hands with me.

Pastor James spoke, but I was too mesmerized by my bride, too lost in the mighty grace of God to fully hear the words he said. Kitty's eyes curled into a smile, the freckles on her nose winking at me. For a flash she looked like she was twelve again. It reminded me how far we'd come, the heartache and hard times we'd endured to get to this very moment.

In our forsaken desert wrought with rusted dreams and abandoned hills, where the shimmer of possibilities had all but lost its shine, we had suffered many a fiery trial. In spite of it all, we now embraced as husband and wife, ready to come forth as gold.

30

TWO MONTHS LATER, we sat in our living room. I rested my hand on Kitty's protruding belly. It seemed to swell more each day, slowly and surely, though so did my love for her.

"Whenever you're ready," I whispered.

But she shook her head and handed over the letter for me to read.

> *Kitty, I received a newspaper clipping in the mail from Peggy. A photo of you and Claude together on your wedding day. You were always a beautiful girl, but now you're a beautiful woman. I always did have a hunch you'd wind up with Claude, and for what it's worth, I'm relieved that came true. Congratulations to you both. Peggy also informed me you're expecting a child. I know that baby will be well loved and cared for.*
>
> *I've been sober a long time now. And I've been working on a road maintenance crew here in Reno these past few months. I don't write to you*

for accolades, nor do I write to interfere with your life. I've had so much I've wanted to say for a while now, but I've been afraid of causing problems where I'm not welcomed. But yet here I am, writing to you anyway. I guess the thing I want you to know is this: If I could go back and do it differently, I would. You have the chance to do a heck of a lot better than me, and you will. I know Claude will too.

Wishing you both nothing but the best.
Your dad.

I searched for the right words, but nothing seemed to fit. Jebediah Ralph wasn't too far gone after all. Maybe my mother had been right in her hope for him all along. I handed the letter back to my wife. "How are you feeling, sweetheart?" I asked.

She thought about it a moment. "Bewildered. Thankful. Sad."

"Why sad?"

She rubbed her stomach. "Thinking about the past, trying to understand. I think I'm mostly sad because I'm already so attached to this little baby, whoever he or she may be. I can't imagine the thought of leaving this baby behind. It makes me not understand my own mother even more. Sometimes I've wondered if I'll be like her. If the baby will come, and I'll have the urge to up and leave. Or if I'll be like my dad, absent in most ways except the physical. But I won't. I know I won't. I'm always going to choose to stay. I'm always going to choose my baby."

"You are *not* your parents—neither of them. Not their mistakes, their shortcomings, or their sins. You are Kitty. Soft and warm and kind and funny and strong and faithful. You're you. And you're going to be the greatest mother in the world."

"Thank you. It really helps to hear that," she whispered. She reached for the letter and gave it a shake. "Why couldn't he have figured this out long ago? Why did it take so much for him to finally learn?"

"I guess the important part is that he finally did, right?"

Kitty didn't respond. She was lost deep in thought, her brows knit together, her lips pinched. Finally, she said, "I'd like to see him. Will you take me?"

I rested my hand on top of hers. I couldn't give a hoot if I ever saw Jeb's face again. But if this was important to Kitty, it was important to me. "Do you want to see him? Or do you want to see if he's really changed?"

"I need to know if this is true or not."

"Okay, then. Arrange it and let me know when we leave."

—

Kitty fidgeted, restless and grumbling, nearly the entire drive to Reno three weeks later. We checked into our hotel and headed to the restaurant for dinner where she withdrew all the more.

"You don't have to do this if you don't want to."

She looked at me from over the top of her menu. "I do though."

"How come?"

"I need to see it for myself, all those things he said in his letter."

"And have you considered what it will do to you if he lets you down?"

"I've been let down by him enough times that I think it'll feel nostalgic." She winked at me, folded the menu, and set it aside.

"I'm serious, Kitty."

She grumbled under her breath, a lifetime of sadness rearing its ugly head. She finally regarded me fully. "I think this one would hurt the most, but at least I'd know and wouldn't waste any more time wondering. Then I could move forward without anything tying me to the past."

I worried for my wife. Was it my place to step in, to protect her from the potential oncoming blow from her father? Jeb Ralph had already taken so much. Was it wrong of me to allow him the opportunity to take more? I considered scooping her up and taking her home. But deep down, I didn't want to be the one to blot out the hope of healing. That wasn't my place. Didn't we all deserve the chance to redeem ourselves? Didn't we all have things we needed to forgive and things we needed forgiveness from? I only hoped Jeb was truly as different as his letter seemed to indicate.

Kitty's bouncing foot jiggled the table. She blew a hair out of her face as she glanced around and mumbled about the slow service.

"If he lets you down, I hope you know it doesn't change anything. You know that, right? You and me, our baby, our happiness."

She only nodded, her brow furrowing further.

The waitress came and took our order. We sat in silence until she returned with our food. I attempted in vain to lure Kitty into conversation.

I suggested we visit the casino afterward, but Kitty wanted to go straight to bed. She changed into her nightgown and slid between the sheets, where she tossed and turned clear until morning's light. We ordered breakfast to our room, but she was too nervous to eat. She dressed and redressed twice.

Finally, I took her by the shoulders and directed her to the edge of the bed.

I squatted down in front of her and rested my hands on her knees. "Whether or not your dad has changed is not your burden to bear. Him being different is no reflection of how wonderful and worthy you are, Kitty." I sat down beside her, the mattress dipping with my weight.

She leaned into me. "What if I see him and just can't do it?"

"What?"

"Forgive him."

Jeb Ralph. So much of my life had been spent despising the guy. If anything, he'd taught me the type of man and father that I never wanted to be. My own dad came to mind, and I hoped beyond all hope that I could end up being half as good as him.

"I want to tell you something," I said, still thinking of my father. "My dad once told me that if I wanted to know anything about freedom or peace, I needed to look to the cross. I'll admit the advice felt empty at the time. It took me a long time to grasp what it means, and I'm still learning."

Kitty sighed. "I never did go to church much. You know that, Claude," she said softly. "Your parents read us Scripture when we were young, but it's not like I remember much about it or the cross. Except that Jesus died."

"Do you know who He died for?"

She stilled and looked for me to lead her.

"You. Me. Your dad. Your mom." I squeezed her thigh.

Her eyes searched mine expectantly as she waited for more. I deliberated on telling her things she didn't yet know. "I wanted him dead," I admitted.

"Who?"

"Your dad. I never told you this, but I beat your dad badly the night Vern was killed. If it weren't for someone pulling me off him, I might never have stopped. And for so many days following, I wished I could have kept going until he died too."

She recoiled. "Why are you telling me this?"

"Because for a long, long time I had a lot of hate in my heart, Kitty. But God had other plans. He took all the darkness in me and transformed it into something else entirely. I was never as alone or helpless as I thought I was. God was with me every step of the way. I don't have to live in that darkness anymore. We none do. Shame, guilt, sin, sadness, anger . . . none of it. He gives us a way out. Makes us new.

"And this is something I hope you can understand: God is with you too. Always has been. Through every detail, every tear, every word. We're His. And He loves us. No one can take that away. All He asks is that we rest in His love and trust Him. Do you think you can trust Him? I mean, look at what He's done for us." I cupped her face in my hands. "Look at what He's brought together in spite of everything."

She brought her hands to mine and held my gaze. After a moment, her mouth curled into a smile, and she murmured, "The baby's kicking."

I slid my hands to her belly. Sure enough, the confirmation of God's goodness nudged my palm. "I love you."

"Which one of us are you talking to?"

"Both," I whispered and leaned in to kiss her lips. "What time did you tell your dad to meet us?"

"Ten o'clock. Are we late?"

I looked at my watch. "If we don't leave soon, we will be. Are you sure you still want to do this, sweetheart? It's okay if you don't."

She shook her head and smiled. "I'm ready."

On Jeb's suggestion, we met him at a local park. Kitty requested that I give her time alone with her father before I joined them. So, I sat in the pickup and watched Kitty cross the grass to the bench where her father sat waiting. Her back to me, I couldn't see the expression on her face. But I could see Jeb's, and his tearful smile created new fields of grace and mercy and hope to bridge the ground between us. I suddenly found myself rooting more than I'd ever expected for Jeb and his relationship with Kitty. For his future. For his redemption.

I watched as he stood, lifted his arms for an embrace, then

awkwardly dropped them to his side only to lift them again. Kitty danced the same awkward jig. In the end, they both just sat down.

I could see that Kitty stayed mostly quiet at first while Jeb did the talking. I wondered what he said as his hand gripped his chest. Was he grasping for the untouchable, for the guilt and shame that had taken residence inside? Had he been freed of those things? I watched him talk and swipe at falling tears, saw the tremble in his hand as he gestured while he spoke. I watched Kitty's face cloud with anger more than once, sat amazed as the anger passed and was replaced with joy.

I didn't know what might come of today's exchange. Would it open a door to a future? Or close the door on the past? Either way, I knew that every word Jeb and Kitty spoke was stitching them together in the way God meant for them to be. He would work this out for good, that much I knew.

A full hour passed. Kitty finally waved me over. As I got out of the truck, a hundred thoughts rushed into my mind at once. But the loudest of them all, the one I couldn't have imagined myself saying to God five years earlier, I uttered out loud as I closed the space between us. "Thank you."

Epilogue

Present day. Seventy-two years later . . .
I STARE AT the ceiling, trying to remember the day we got Kitty's lung cancer diagnosis, but I can't. I know I should, but as I lay here, I don't. I've blocked it out, I suppose, and thinking back seven years ago now, my mind will only bring me back to a few weeks after we found out, when we got into a fight.

I'd gotten off work early only to come home to find Kitty on the back porch, her back to me, unaware of my presence, the telephone wedged between her shoulder and her ear. I hadn't interrupted her or let my presence be made known right away. I had stood back and admired my girl, thankful for our years together and for whatever time we had left. That was when I noticed the wisp of smoke rising before her, curling around itself in a seductive victory dance. Thinking back, I wish my mind would block out that moment too. Because I'd lost it, ripping open the sliding glass door and storming over to her.

"What are you doing?" I had roared.

Kitty's eyes had widened at the sight of me. She stammered goodbye into the phone and hung up, tears sparking instantly behind the hazy veil in front of her as she blew out more smoke.

"Do you *want* to die?" I'd plucked the cigarette from her grasp and crushed it beneath my boot. I sputtered a string of nonsense in my fury. We both knew her life was at stake. "You're selfish," I accused her. "The doctor told you to quit."

"I *am* quitting."

"Yeah, looks like it to me."

"One cigarette isn't going to kill me, Claude."

"It's not going to help keep you alive, either." I paced in front of her. "Where'd you get it?"

She sat in silence.

I persisted. "Where'd you get it? I thought we threw them all away."

"I had an extra. Just in case."

"In case you want to die sooner?" I stopped pacing; my eyes fixated on the breast pocket of her shirt. "You had an extra cigarette or an extra pack?"

Her face hardened.

I held out my hand, and after a moment of standoff, she reached into her pocket and handed over the pack. Something had told me not to do it, that maybe I didn't want to know the truth. But I opened the pack anyway. It contained only one cigarette. "Did you smoke all of these today?"

She wouldn't look at me. I knew I had my answer.

We had skirted around each other that whole night, engaging not in the joy of spending time together, but in the misery of our own storms, which were destined to collide. There's an old saying, *Never go to bed angry*. But Kitty had retreated to our room early without so much as a goodnight.

I'd plopped myself in my chair without going after her and watched episode after episode of *McHale's Navy* until I couldn't help but laugh. When I laughed, I'd realized I never wanted to laugh by myself. And I got angry again at Kitty for smoking when she shouldn't have been. And I got angry that she had ever smoked at all.

My mother's warnings flitted around my mind too quickly for me to truly remember exactly what she'd said, but the message was still there: *Smoking is bad. It can kill you.* I'd given the habit a try once, years into my job at the car dealership when I was offered a cigarette at work. But every second that thing had been pressed to my lips, I could hear the pain in my mother's voice. I could hear her broken heart when she'd caught Cliff smoking all those years before. I put it out, never to pick one up again.

But when Kitty had gotten into the habit, thanks to her girlfriends in her bowling club, it simply became part of who she was. Nearly every candid photograph of her included that little white stick cradled gingerly between two of her fingers. I didn't think too much of it, honestly. I had my view on the matter, but never pushed it onto her. *It wouldn't kill her. She wasn't going to get cancer.* We both believed that kind of thing simply wouldn't happen. It only happened to people you didn't know, to strangers. Not to the only woman you'd ever loved in your entire life.

Halfway into another rerun of *McHale's Navy*, it had occurred to me that it wasn't only my world being flipped upside down, but quite literally Kitty's. It was her body that was failing. Her decades-long habit that she had to kick. Her impending death that she had to face. *How addicting must it be,* I wondered, *that she couldn't so easily walk away from it, even now?* Part of me wanted to go smoke that last cigarette, had I not already flushed it down the toilet. Just to see if I experienced a hankering for another one afterward. I practically felt my mother slapping me from her grave at the thought.

We had made up after that awful night. The days became

weeks. The weeks, months. Kitty deteriorated quicker than I ever expected. Suddenly, she was on hospice, set up in a special bed in our living room, palliative care only. We could both taste the nearness of death. But in an unspoken agreement, we'd decided to stave off the reality of what was to come in exchange for what joy we still had. It feels wrong to call it joy, because Kitty's suffering, particularly on her hard days, still haunts me when I think of the pain that overshadowed all traces of happiness that had been etched into her face over the years. Each laugh line had transformed into wrinkles of sheer agony.

On her final night of life, our kids had already gone home for the night, tucking their own children into bed.

"We'll stay," all four of them had said. "Mom's not good. We're scared to leave."

But she'd told them to go tend to their little ones. That she'd see them in the morning. So, they obeyed their mother one last time and left.

Later, in between coughing fits, she whispered to me, "You're the only man I've ever loved, Claude. The only man who's ever truly loved me."

I stared at her a moment, noting the sincerity in her eyes, in her weak voice, in this sentiment she clearly wanted to express to me. I'd felt the tension in my own forehead, in the wrinkling of my brow, all the stress of the last several years pooling together there between my eyes. "Now that's not true," I'd said.

"It's not?"

"No." I shook my head. "You'll soon be walking into the arms of another man who loves you even more."

With what strength she had left, she smiled and closed her eyes against the tears. "What's it going to be like?"

Her fingers, losing their warmth, twitched under my hand. I wrapped them in mine and gave the lightest squeeze. I gasped for breath as I considered what it would be like to meet our Savior who awaited her on the other side. And yet there was my sweetheart, teetering on the edge of where this life ends and the next begins.

"Claude?" she'd whispered, still awaiting my response.

"Perfect," I answered. "It will be perfect."

She smiled her best smile and closed her eyes again, exhausted from even this short exchange. Soon, she drifted to sleep. I moved to my recliner chair, my place of watch. I closed my eyes, listening to the ragged sound of her chest rising and falling. At some point that night I'd dozed off. I later woke to the deafening sound of complete silence.

It's not silent around me now, seven years after Kitty's death, as I rest in my own special hospice bed. Two of my daughters sit beside me. Lorraine, the eldest. And Hazel, the youngest. A gaggle of grandchildren sprint through the house, loud and rambunctious, just the way I like them. Lorraine attempts to settle them down, but I tell her to let them be. I want to memorize their sounds. It brings me back to childhood. To running with Kitty. My brothers. Vern has been gone seventy-seven years. Cliff, fifty-eight. Vietnam claimed his life after seventeen years in the service.

My parents had grayed and withered. When their time came—within a year of each other—it had been devastating, but it felt natural. They were both ready. But losing Cliff in his mid-thirties had been quite the blow.

I think back now to the night we got the news about his death and remember how deeply it had hurt to breathe. I'd told Kitty, "The darkness—this world our children are inheriting with the violence, the wars—I can't handle it."

Kitty had laced her fingers with mine, rested her head against my chest, our old bed creaking as she snuggled in close. "I don't understand it either, Claude. But tell me, what's the opposite of darkness?"

"Light."

"And what is light to the darkness?"

"I don't know."

"Hope. It's hope, Claude. We've never been promised a life without darkness, but we have been given hope that one day all darkness will be replaced with light. Hold onto that hope, that light. Okay?"

I hold onto that light now as my heart drums in my chest for Kitty. I've lost so many people I love, endured so much loss. Yet, I am not broken. And I know that is because there's something holding me together—Christ.

Maisy's still keeping on, living down the road. She's about to turn ninety-two this year. She and Kitty formed such a deep bond, becoming best friends over the years. After Cliff's untimely death, Maisy moved to Colorado to be near us. We'd settled here when our second daughter, Gloria, was born. I can hear my nephew Henry in the kitchen now, chatting with my only son, Al. Their wives are surely flanked by their sides.

"Where is Gloria?" I ask.

"She had to work late," Hazel says. "She'll be here any minute."

"Oh, good."

The doctors have told me my time is short; my cancer is spreading at an alarming rate, wreaking havoc uninhibited in my body. There's nothing more they can do except wait for the Lord to do with me what He will. It's my kids I feel most sorry for, having to go through this all over again. First with their mother. Now with me. But I trust they'll be alright, that they'll hold fast to the light.

Gloria, the carbon copy of Kitty, finally arrives and leans in to kiss my cheek. "Dad, you're crying!" she says and brushes my cheek with a finger. "Why?"

I weep a little longer, feeling the pain deep in my bones, feeling the yearning for what's to come. I don't tell her these things. I don't tell her I see her mother. I don't tell her I see Jesus. I don't tell her that it's almost time to close my eyes and greet them both on the other side.

I reach out for my children, my family, for everything I'm leaving behind. I whisper into the air for a final time, "Thank you."

Author's Note & Acknowledgments

Most people have never heard of Goldfield, Nevada, and if they have, it's usually due to the nearly abandoned town's "ghost hunting" adventures that have been featured on popular television programs. My granddad was born in Goldfield in the '30s, where he was raised with his five siblings. His special childhood is what inspired me to write a story set in this unique town. While the storyline and characters of *Come Forth As Gold* are fictional, there are certain aspects of my novel that were inspired by real-life events. For example, my granddad's younger brother was struck and killed while riding his bike as a teenager. Unfortunately, my granddad and the rest of his siblings have long passed on, so I couldn't explore the realities of this situation with them. As I was contemplating this event one day, I began to wonder about the fallout from this horrible tragedy. What must it have been like for my great-grandparents to lose their youngest son? For my granddad and his siblings to lose their baby brother?

While I do not hold these intimate details regarding my great-uncle's death, I began exploring this grief through the fictional lens of Claude mourning a similar death of his brother, Vern.

I grew up hearing tidbits of stories about my granddad's childhood, and the tiny town of Goldfield was always tucked into the back of my mind. As I grew and writing became a central part of my life, I knew I would one day write a story set in this small town. My granddad passed away from cancer when I was young, and my beloved grandma only a few years later. From small pieces of stories I can recollect from childhood and stories passed down from my own dad, I began constructing this manuscript. In my research of the town's history, I decided to reach out to the Central Nevada Museum and spoke with a kind man named Allen, who, come to find out, knew my granddad's family and went to school with my great-uncle who was killed in the bicycle accident. He put me in contact with a former schoolmate/childhood friend of my granddad's, and she put me in touch with others. To Allen, Fran, Don, and Peter, thank you for your invaluable insight into your childhoods in Goldfield and Tonopah. Thank you for answering my questions, sharing your memories with me, and for all of your conversation and shared photographs of my granddad. I will cherish you all forever.

While my story is a work of fiction, I attempted to do justice to the settings of Goldfield and Tonopah by incorporating real-life activities the residents participated in and by incorporating historical facts about the area and time. For example, The Goldfield School did in fact cease holding high school classes after the graduating class of 1947. Upperclassmen were thereafter bussed every day (at the time via personal vehicles driven by senior students and eventually in an actual school bus, still driven by senior students) to attend classes in Tonopah. Keeping in mind my imagination and the creative liberties I took for the sake of the storyline, I can only hope I've still done justice to these two towns.

During my writing of this novel, my sounding board, my biggest cheerleader, my fellow writer, and the woman I was blessed to call both grandma and friend passed away less than two months prior to the completion of my manuscript. She offered all of her love, encouragement, and ideas to me up until she fell ill, and I'm not sure I would have had the heart to finish after her death had it not been for an encouraging voicemail I discovered I'd saved from her on my phone. Gram, this novel wouldn't have seen the light of day if not for you. To all of my grandparents, I love better because of you. I cannot wait until the day we are all reunited again. Granddad, what I would give to be small and bouncing on your knee again, pretending to ride one of the horses on the old Westerns you loved to watch when you got home from work. I wish you were here to tell me your stories and for me to present this book to. We all miss you so much.

This novel was incredibly special to write as I had a space to explore grief, trauma, and faith. My faith in Jesus Christ is the most important thing about me; in fact, it is the one thing that defines me. My hope is to glorify God through this story of love, redemption, and forgiveness. To my Lord and Savior, it is because of You that I live, and it is for You that I live. Your perfect love has set me free.

Mom, Dad, Corey, Carey, and all my family. Thank you for supporting me and believing in my lifelong dream of being an author. You are all so special and dear to me. I love you so much. Thank you to my editor, Jeanne Leach, for whipping my manuscript into shape and encouraging me along the way. To my dear friend, cover designer, critique partner, and marketing manager, Brittany Howard, thank you for your amazing help in making this book become a physical reality. To my friends and writing community, you all played a part in getting me here too. Thank you. To my readers, thank you for your support. It means the world to me. I hope you are touched by this story.

Patrick, my husband and best friend, your unwavering patience and your steady, unconditional love to me and the kids are the greatest blessings. This couldn't have happened without your help. Leo and Nora Boo, for being such young ages you sure teach me big lessons every day. Mommy loves you all the way to God and Jesus, as you both like to say.

Printed in Great Britain
by Amazon

28716705R00178